HEART ON ICE

BOOK 2 - MANHATTAN MAVERICKS

JA LOW

Cover Design by Simply Defined Art

Model: Enrico

Photographer: Wander BookClub

Editor: Lisa Edwards

❀ Formatted with Vellum

1

PIERRE

K itty is driving me crazy with her fucking texts about the god damn wedding. I'm at a fucking wake. I don't give a shit what color the linen napkins are or that the color roses she ordered don't match her bridesmaid's dresses perfectly. I head upstairs to deal with her insane number of texts alone. I thought she was busy at a photoshoot, I mean, it was one of the reasons she couldn't be here today. I let out a sigh as I step into my childhood bedroom, instantly consumed by the memories, mostly good, some bad.

Issy and I shared a bathroom which was sandwiched between our rooms. I remember the first time we ever met. I'd flown in from Quebec after saying goodbye to my family. I was scared, excited, and apprehensive about my new life in New York. I jumped in the shower to wash off the plane stank and get ready to meet Mr. Alessi's daughters for dinner. I thought I was alone until the bathroom door burst open and in walked the most beautiful girl I had ever seen, long dark brown hair that was dead straight, the darkest chestnut-colored eyes, and the prettiest pink lips.

"*WHO THE HELL ARE YOU?*" *she shrieks as she stares at my naked form before her.*

I've started to fill out and I know that I'm nothing but muscle right now, so I hope she is appreciating the view. I grab the towel from the rail and throw it in front of my now semi hard dick as I turn the water off and step out, securing the towel around my hips.

"Hey, you must be my new roomie, Isabelle. I'm Pierre," I say, introducing myself to her, trying to forget the awkwardness of her seeing me naked.

"Roomie?" she asks with fire in her eyes.

"Yeah, I'm in the room next door, your father said it would be cool," I tell her.

"Dad," she screams as she runs out of the bathroom.

THE MEMORY MAKES me laugh as I continue walking through my old room. Not much has changed since I lived here, which is a trip. I head back through the bathroom and into Issy's room, what a blast from the past as I stare at all her things still left there as if she were still sixteen. Suddenly, her bedroom door bursts open and a distressed Issy barrels into the room, those chocolate eyes filled with tears, unaware she's not alone. I couldn't keep my eyes off her today, watching her stand there stoically for her sisters, hugging them tightly as they struggled throughout the day.

"What the hell are you doing in here?" she yells, noticing me standing there.

It's been what feels like a lifetime since I've seen her. She was living in London for nearly a decade after we broke up, but she came home when her dad had his first heart attack a couple of years ago. We ran into each other in the hospital, and after that time, she made sure it never happened again. I've run into her on the odd occasion since we broke up, but not as frequently as I thought, nor hoped I would.

"I needed a moment. Looks like you did, too?"

Those chocolate eyes narrow on me, and the tears that were ready to fall seem to vanish as her anger takes over. "Yes, in my room."

"It's been a long time since I've been in your room," I say, cracking a joke, trying to make things less awkward.

"You're not welcome here."

I thought after all this time and after today that maybe ... guess I was wrong. "Issy ..." I say.

"No," she answers as I notice the tears starting to fall across her cheeks. I go to take a step forward to comfort her, but she stops me. "No."

"I just want to help," I tell her. Seeing her so broken is my undoing.

"I don't want your help," she says stubbornly as she wipes her cheeks angrily.

We glare at each other.

Fuck it.

She needs me. "Well, you're going to get it anyway. You've always been so stubborn. I've watched you be strong all day for your sisters. You held them, comforted them, but no one comforted you." I take a couple more steps toward her.

Issy steps back, fire burning in those eyes. "Just because I'm alone here today doesn't mean I'm alone."

Oh. "Are you seeing someone?" What the hell am I doing asking her that?

"That's none of your business," she snaps back.

"Why isn't he here then?" I push her on the subject because I want to know what kind of asshole doesn't accompany his girl to her father's funeral.

"I could ask the same thing about your fiancée."

Touché there. "She had to work." Honestly, I didn't want her here because she would say something that would irritate the hell out of me, or she would try to get me to leave early. I mean, she's spent the entire day asking me stupid wedding questions when she knows where I am, but that's Kitty, self-absorbed as they come.

"I think you should leave," Issy says, glaring at me as she struggles to keep her composure.

I take a step toward her. "No. I think you need me."

Issy rears back as if my words slapped her. "Like hell I do."

What the hell am I doing? This is her father's funeral, but now I'm angry about the past and I can't stop myself. "You're right, you don't need anyone," I tell her as I run my hand through my hair. "But maybe I need you." The words are out before I realize what I've said. An overwhelming sense of grief hits me as if someone is sitting on my chest on a two-hundred-pound boulder. I can't breathe. I try to hide it, but I'm failing as a sob rips from my lips. "I miss him." Issy's face softens for the briefest of moments.

Alberto was like a father to me, especially as my own father left a long time ago, thinking a family was holding his hockey career back. He never became anyone great in the league. He was a solid player, but that didn't change the fact that he never came back for his family either. He filled his life with women and booze until he died many years ago, which we found out through the news.

"I can't be the one, Pierre, not today, not now, not ever. I need to leave. I can't be here with you." Issy shakes her head, unable to contain her sob as she walks toward the door.

She's right. But I thought, for one day we could put all the past behind us and honor her father. "You're good at doing that," I bite back, the wave of anger lashing at my conscience.

Issy stills before whirling around, the grief suddenly vanishing, it's replaced with her own anger. "Excuse you."

I chuckle darkly as I take a couple of steps toward her. I'm guessing today is the day I decide to poke into our past, a past she won't ever talk to me about. "At least this time you're not running halfway across the world to get away from me."

Issy gasps. "Fuck you," she yells, taking a couple of hurried, angry steps toward me. "How dare you say that to me?" she hisses, poking a hard finger into my chest.

Ouch.

"Today isn't about you, which I know might be hard for Mr. Hockey Superstar to appreciate." She continues to push her finger into my chest.

"It's not about your hate toward me either." I scowl at her. "Would you stop poking me," I snap, grabbing the offending hand and moving it behind her back so she can't bruise me anymore. Unfortunately, that brings her dangerously close to me, the closest she has been since our breakup. I'm six foot five and she's only five foot five, and the height difference between us has never felt this large until now.

"Get your fucking hands off me," she barks at me before punching me in the chest with her free hand. Does she forget I'm a hockey player? I'm an immovable object.

"No," I tell her.

"You arrogant fucking asshole, let go of me," she yells as she huffs and puffs. Her cheeks are bright red with anger as she continues to push herself against me. "Just let me go," she pleads, her punches becoming weaker against me. "Please, Pierre." She hiccups on her tears.

Fuck I'm an asshole. What the hell am I thinking? She doesn't deserve my anger, not today. It hurt when she left me all those years ago, especially because she's never let me apologize to her. I needed her to know how sorry I was for fucking up so badly. She's right, I am a self-centered asshole.

"I've got you," I whisper against her ear.

"I don't want you to." She sobs.

"I know," I tell her, letting her hand go as I cup her face and wipe her tears away.

"Let those tears out. You need to let them out. Otherwise, you're going to drive yourself mad." I didn't when my own father died, and instead, I took my anger and grief out on the opposing teams. It was great for the fans, not so great for my mental health, not when the golden boy of hockey got into trouble for punching another team's fan when I was drunk. That was before Kitty. I cleaned myself up before her, that moment was my rock bottom and unfortunately, I had mine publicly. Issy relents for the briefest of moments as I wrap my arms around her. "I've got you," I whisper again as I pull her into me, and this time, she doesn't fight as she breaks down.

"It's not fair," she mumbles against my chest. "I told him he needed to look after himself more. Why didn't he listen? Why did he leave us?"

I stroke her hair. "Your father was stubborn. It runs in the family."

"He didn't have to die. It was preventable," she says, looking up at me, those brown eyes red rimmed with tears, and she's never looked more beautiful.

"Sometimes it's not. Your father had an aneurysm, there was no way of predicting that."

Issy shakes her head. "I told him to stop drinking coffee, to have a better diet to ..." her words catching on a sob.

I hug her tightly again. "Your father loved you girls, and he would have done everything in his power to not leave you, but sometimes the universe has other plans."

"I'm not strong enough to deal with this world without him," she confesses.

I look down at her. "You are the strongest person I know, Isabelle Alessi. Your father loved you. He was so proud of you. Anytime we talked he would tell me about everything you were up to, how many new clients you had brought over to the agency. How many multi-million dollar deals you secured, that you didn't take shit from any of the guys at work."

"He told you all that?" she asks, sounding surprised.

I nod. "He did. And I liked hearing it too. I always knew you were destined for big things. Just always thought I would be by your side when you achieved them." She frowns. "Listening to him talking about all the great things you've done in your life made me feel like I was still a part of it." We stare at each other for a long moment, as my hand comes out and cups her face, my thumb slides across her cheek. "If I never messed up all those years ago, I'd be by your side right now. I wish I could go back in time and change things," I confess as I continue stroking her face.

"Don't," she whispers.

"It's the truth."

"Please, Pierre, don't." More tears fall.

"I know it's not the right time. For years I've been trying to tell you how sorry I am for hurting you. I fucked up, Issy."

"No," she whimpers.

"You are the biggest regret of my life." Issy gasps as we stare at each other, the unspoken truth now out there.

Next thing I know, I'm leaning forward and kissing her. And even more shocking is that she lets me. The first sweep of my tongue forces her mouth to open, and I feel her tongue against mine. I'm done for. As if muscle memory has taken over, her fingers dig into my suit as she kisses me back.

"Fuck, I've missed you, Issy." I groan as I press myself against her and deepen our kiss until she bites me. "Ouch," I say, jumping back, a metallic taste in my mouth.

"Fuck you," she shouts. I'm so surprised by her biting me that I stumble back a couple of steps. "You fucking asshole. You're engaged," she screams at me.

Shit.

What the hell did I think I was doing?

"Why the hell did you kiss me?" she asks, looking angry.

"I don't know," I yell back at her. Shit. This isn't good.

"I see the leopard never changes his spots." Her eyes narrow on me as she folds her arms in front of her.

"I'm not a cheater." She scoffs. "Issy, come on. That's not fair. What I did to you was years ago, I was a kid. It still haunts me."

"You're not a kid now."

"I know, but that was different."

"You broke my heart into a million pieces that night. I will not be an accomplice to inflicting that pain on another woman." She points at me angrily.

I have no recourse. She's right. I'm engaged. What was I thinking? *You weren't thinking.* I shouldn't have touched her, but having her back in my arms after all this time, in her childhood bedroom, it felt as if all those years of us being apart vanished. For the first time, the tension in my shoulders released, the thing in my chest started beating as if she had awoken it from a slumber. Having Issy breaking down in my arms broke me, and all I wanted to do was make it all better. By kissing her. Not the brightest of plans, but she kissed me back. Then attacked me for cheating on my fiancée. True. But she doesn't know how bad things are between Kitty and me. Everyone says it's the stress of the wedding, that it's natural to have cold feet, but I'm not so sure. Something is going on with Kitty. She's disappearing more on work trips when I'm on the road, she's attending a lot more red-carpet events instead of spending time with me when I am back home, and we hardly have sex. Still, not reason enough for you to cheat on her. I know, okay. I don't feel good about what I've done but also ... fuck ... I feel alive for the first time in a long time.

I run my hand through my hair. "You broke me, too, when you fled to London," I throw back at her. Issy gasps. Yes, I messed up that night, but then she disappeared, totally ghosted me, and I never saw her again.

"W*HERE IS SHE?*" *I scream at Harper.*

"A long, long way from you," she spits back at me. I heard she left for Europe for Spring Break. I had to create an anonymous profile so I could follow her. It killed me watching her and Harper have fun with all those men. Seeing their hands all over her made me see red. Imagine what it was like for her seeing you with Missy Jenkins. *Fucking torture. I hated it. I thought I would see her again, that she would come back after Spring Break, and we could talk. Sort it out. Maybe start again. I will never touch another woman ever again. I know how much I fucked up. A week had passed, and she hadn't returned, then I heard around the school that she had transferred to somewhere in Europe. I didn't believe it. There's no way she would have left her family.*

"I need to talk to her."

"What are you going to say, sorry you found my dick down Missy Jenkins throat? Sorry for fucking all her friends," Harper throws back at me.

She's not wrong. I fucked up. I wasn't faithful to Issy, and the stupid thing is, I don't understand why I did it.

"What happened to you?" Harper asks, looking at me with disgust.

"I don't know," I say, running my hands through my hair.

"Really?" Harper says, crossing her arms over her chest, glaring at me.

I throw my hands up in the air. "I let my fucking ego take over. Are you happy?" I shout my confession at her.

"None of this makes me happy. You broke my friend. She is devastated. I will never forgive you for what you did to her."

"I don't need your forgiveness, Harper. I need Issy's."

Harper scoffs. "There is no way in hell she is ever going to forgive you. I hope she finds a hot English man who's happy to heal her broken heart."

"English man, she's in England?"

"Shit," Harper curses, knowing she's let slip Issy's secret. "There's no way you're ever going to find her, England is a big place."

"Watch me. I love her. I messed up and I need her to know I will do anything and everything to make it up to her. She's the only person that I love," I declare.

"Issy is stubborn, you know once you've hurt her, that's it. There are no second chances," Harper warns me.

"I will spend eternity making it up to her."

"Eternity isn't long enough," Harper states.

"Issy isn't as cold-hearted as you are."

Harper's eyes narrow on me. "Because she's never had her heart broken until you. You are the reason she will be forever changed, all for a couple of quick meaningless fucks to fuel your ego."

She's right, but I'm not about to give her the satisfaction of knowing that she is. "I will get her back. This isn't the end of us."

"You're delusional, Pierre."

"Maybe, but this isn't the end of our story."

"I came after you," I tell Issy. "I saved up as much as I could to buy a return ticket to London. I spent part of the summer searching for you." Issy stills as if my revelation is the first time she's hearing this. "No one would help me. I even asked your father."

She gasps at that.

As another memory flashes before me.

I stare at his office door. Suck it up. You messed up, if you want to fix it, you are going to have to ask him for help. Reluctantly, I knock on his door.

"Come in," he bellows. My heart beats wildly in my chest as I turn the knob and open the door. "Pierre, this is a surprise." His eyes narrow on me.

Shit, does he know?

"Do you have a moment?" I ask him timidly.

"I have one," he answers curtly.

I'm dead, I think as I solemnly walk into his office and take a seat. "Sir, I really need to speak to Issy, and I was wondering if you could tell me where she is."

He stills as he leans back in his chair and rubs his chin. "Send her a message, I know she has her phone."

"She's not responding to me."

"And why would that be?" he asks, his eyes narrowing on me.

He knows. Now is the time to be a man, Pierre. "Because I broke her heart."

Alberto stills.

Oh shit. He didn't know.

He stands up abruptly and slams his hand on his desk. A pile of papers on the left rattle and a couple flutter to the floor. His cup of coffee wobbles, and the contents slosh over the lip and drip down the ceramic mug. "It was you who cheated on my girl. You!" His voice rumbles like a volcano. "I trusted you. I brought you into my home. Treated you like my son, and this is how you repay me, by breaking my little girl's heart."

"It was the stupidest thing I have ever done. I love your daughter, sir. I, just ..."

"You fucked up," he yells at me as he slams his hand on the desk again. "You fucked up so badly that my girl fled to the other side of the world to get away from you."

"I wish I could turn back time and not make those stupid decisions."

"You've disrespected me in my own home."

"I never meant any disrespect."

"But you did disrespect me," he says, pointing his finger into his chest, "you made my little girl fall in love with you behind my back." Tears well in my eyes. I hate the way he looks at me like I am dirt. I deserve it, but it still hurts.

"How could I not fall in love with your daughter? She is the most extraordinary girl I know."

"And yet you cheated on her." I nod as a tear falls down my cheek. I feel like the worst person in the world. *"Why?"* he questions.

Swallowing hard, I confess to him, *"I got swept up in the fame."*

He shakes his head, disappointment lacing his face. *"I thought you would be different, Pierre. This is going to be a hard lesson to learn. The fact that you hurt my baby girl to learn it kills me."*

"I'm so sorry, Mr. Alessi. Please, I need to make it right with her," I plead with him.

He shakes his head. *"I'm sorry, son, I won't tell you where she is. The best thing I think is for the two of you to be apart."*

"I have to tell her how sorry I am," I exclaim.

"Now isn't the time. She needs space."

"I don't want space. I love her."

"Too little, too late, boy. I will not let you hurt her again." My stomach sinks. No. I won't give up. *"I think it might be best if you go back to Quebec for the summer."*

"You're kicking me out?"

"Out of my house, yes. Out of school and training, no. I am still your manager," he states.

§

"You asked my father. He knew about us?" Issy asks.

"Yes, I asked him where you were. I was desperate to find you. He refused to tell me and then he kicked me out."

"He kicked you out of New York?"

Did she not know? "Yes, I spent that summer in Quebec after coming back from London. I returned to school in the fall, but was never welcomed back for family dinners for a long time. He continued to manage me, but I was no longer like a son."

Issy shakes her head. "He knew all this time, he never once said anything to me."

"Guess that's why he took pride in telling me about your accomplishments, he liked letting me know that I messed up. He didn't have to remind me, the fucking ache in my chest that's never gone away is a constant reminder."

Issy gasps at my confession. "Until Kitty."

"Not even Kitty can fix this. We aren't in a good place. I'm having second thoughts about the wedding." I don't mean to blurt the last bit out, but I need her to understand I'm not the bad guy here, even though it looks like I am.

Issy shakes her head. "You shouldn't be telling me this."

"Perhaps not," I say, my shoulders sagging. "Everything is a mess at the moment, and I don't know what to do."

"That has nothing to do with me," Issy snaps.

She's right, the problems Kitty and I have are nothing to do with her. "I'm sorry, Issy. I'm sorry for the way I treated you when we were younger, you never deserved that. I hope my immaturity and foolishness didn't change you. I couldn't live with that."

Tears fall down Issy's cheeks before she angrily swats them away. "Don't flatter yourself. I haven't thought about you at all."

"Your father was a great man. I will miss him with all my heart," I explain to her as my voice breaks with emotion. "If you ever need anything, let me know."

"I won't."

Right, of course I'd be the last person she contacts. I give her a nod and walk out of her bedroom and head back downstairs.

2

PIERRE

I had to leave right after the wake to get back to South Dakota for an important game, which we won, moving us into the playoffs. And the one person I wanted there by my side for it, wasn't. Kitty has spent the day blowing up my phone, yet she never came home after work. I don't know where the hell my fiancée is. All my other teammates' partners were there by their sides, cheering them on while I was left wondering where she was. Especially as she isn't answering her phone anymore.

The door opens to our home, and in walks Kitty with her bags, plus a mountain load of shopping bags, which she puts down in the foyer before kicking off her heels. Where the hell has she been for the past couple of days?

"Oh, you're home," I call out from the living room where I'm sitting, watching the highlights from our game. Frankston is beside me, snoring away.

Kitty stills. "You're still up, I thought you'd be asleep it's ..." she looks down at her watch, "eleven."

"I should be out celebrating the team's win ..."

Her eyes widen. "Oh my gosh, you won, you made the playoffs." She gasps as she rushes toward me, before jumping into my arms and hugging me.

"Yeah. I thought you would have been home for it, I needed you there," I tell her, pulling her to me, but my mind instantly starts comparing how different Kitty and Issy feel. I try to shake it off.

"I'm sorry, baby, but I knew you would win," she says, pulling away and kissing my cheek. "Honestly, I thought you were still in New York for some reason. I must have got my dates mixed up."

Kitty isn't a ditz, her entire life is highly organized. Why is she acting like one now? "That was yesterday. I had to come back to prep for the game."

She nods. "That's right. Did you have fun in New York?"

I still. Did I have fun? "I went to a funeral."

"Oh, that's right. I'm sorry, this wedding prep has me all scatterbrained." She giggles.

"Are you drunk?" I ask her.

She giggles again. "Maybe. Barbie and I might have had a couple of bottles of champagne on the plane home."

"Where have you been? I thought you were only going away for the one night, not two."

Kitty stills. "Oh, yeah, you know what it's like when Barbie and I get together, we just have so much fun. I was telling Barbie how stressed I was about the wedding with all the planning and stuff, so she suggested we go to Vegas to destress."

"You've been in Vegas?"

"Yeah, we went after Dallas. My photoshoot ended up being super quick so instead of coming home to an empty home ..." Frankston was here, I'd hardly call it empty. "... Barbie and I decided to go and have some fun, so we took the plane to Vegas."

"You're telling me that while I was at a funeral for a man who was like a father to me and then playing one of the biggest games of the season, you were in Vegas having fun because you're stressed out about the wedding?" I ask her, my voice rising as I push her away from me angrily.

"Pierre?" She gasps, surprised by my response.

I get up from the sofa and start to pace, running my hands through my hair. Maybe my sister is right. Things have changed between Kitty and me, and I don't know if it is all wedding-related or if it's something else.

"I don't know if I can do this ..." I mumble to myself as I continue to pace the room.

"Pierre!" Kitty squeals.

"I needed you," I yell at her.

"You won," she answers, looking up at me, all wide-eyed.

"Yes, but it would have been nice to have you in the box cheering with all the other wives and partners."

Kitty stands and places her hands on my chest. "I'm sorry, baby. I'll never miss another game. I didn't realize how much my being there meant to you."

"You didn't realize how much I would want my fiancée there?" I question her.

She shrugs. "Yeah."

"You're my fiancée!"

"Pierre ..."

I push her away and start to pace again. "You're my fiancée, Kitty. We are about to pledge our love for each other, through sickness and health, through good times and bad. I don't know if you're willing to do that for me."

"You're getting upset because I missed one game because I had to work," she yells at me.

"You were in Vegas!"

She waves her hand at me. "That was after."

"If you had time to go to Vegas with your friend, you should have had time to come to New York and be by my side during a really difficult time."

Kitty scrunches up her face. "I told you I don't do funerals. All that sadness is upsetting."

"I needed you."

"Babe, you had your family. I would have been in the way," she says, shrugging off my feelings. I stare at her, and she's serious.

"Do you still want to marry me?"

Kitty stills. "Excuse me?" she asks slowly.

"It's a simple question, Kitty," I say.

She tries to frown but her forehead is baby smooth. "What a stupid question to ask me."

"If it's so stupid, why are you not answering it?" I push her.

"Because you're trying to hurt me, and I don't appreciate it." She huffs.

"I'm trying to hurt you?"

"Yes," she says, folding her arms in front of her. How the hell is this now my fault?

"All because I want to know if the woman I love wants to marry me?" I question her.

"I know what this is." She giggles. "You're getting cold feet. My mom told me this would happen, every groom goes through it, it's natural."

"You think I've got cold feet?"

"Yes, baby," she coos.

My shoulders drop, and exhaustion hits me like a freight train. Maybe now isn't the right time to be having this conversation when she is clearly intoxicated. "I'm tired, baby. I'm going to head to bed. Are you coming?"

"Oh, um, I'm still amped up from traveling. I was going to get changed and head to the clubs with my girls."

Of course she is. "Have fun," I tell her as I turn and walk away from where she is standing in the living room. Frankston stretches, jumps off the sofa, and follows me, at least he's got my back.

THIS IS IT, Pierre.

Everything rides on this goal.

Make this, and the South Dakota Devils go to the final of The Cup.

I shoot.

Everything is in slow motion as the puck flies through the air. My teammates are frozen in anticipation. If this goal makes it, we draw, and that pushes us into overtime. I can feel the seconds ticking down, the buzzer is moments from going off, signaling the end of the game and our hopes. My heart thumps in my chest, sweat drips down my face as I watch in agonizing slow motion whether I've given my team a second chance.

Goal.

I can't believe it.

My teammates all jump on me as I've just given them a second chance at the finals.

Yes!

I look up into the crowd and every one of our supporters is going wild.

We all regroup and get ready to play overtime. This is do or die, now whoever gets the first goal wins.

"This is it, boys, no fucking mistakes, we do this, and we do it right," I scream at them before we get back on the ice. We are pumped. This is my chance to take the team to the finals.

I should have taken my own advice.

Because I make a rookie mistake.

I fuck up big time.

I trip the opposing player during a breakaway as he heads toward the goal, my stick catches him around the legs, and he goes flying.

Fuck.

I just lost us our chance.

My team is screaming at me, and the fans are booing.

I fucked up.

Hanging my head, I take myself off to the penalty box for tripping and pray that nothing happens while I'm sitting in it. They restart and my stomach sinks as the opposing team breaks away again, and then I watch in terrifying slow motion the puck sink into the back of the net.

The opposing crowd goes wild.

Our chance is gone in seconds.

Because of me.

Our fans lose their minds with anger. I can feel their pissed off eyes boring into the back of my head as they smash the glass around the penalty box. I smash my fist against the board as I watch my teammates deflate, and they slowly, one by one, skate off the ice and back to the locker rooms. As I stride off down the players' tunnel, I hear the fans shouting at me, threats of violence against my name as I pass, all are warranted. My stupidity cost them their hopes and dreams of our team winning the cup.

"What the fuck, Cap," Sinclair says as soon as I enter the room.

"I'm sorry, fellas, I ..." There is nothing that I can say right now that will take away the anger my team is feeling toward me.

"We wouldn't have been in this position if Captain hadn't won us that goal," Gustafsson states. That man always looks on the positive side of everything. I give him a small appreciative smile.

"Thanks, Gus. I fucked up, guys. I lost us the chance. There's nothing I can say that can take away how you all feel right now."

"Who knew you could be a hero and a villain in one game?" Coach says, clapping me on the back.

"You're gonna have to give us time, Cap," Smith the rookie grumbles.

He doesn't know it yet, but he will have plenty of chances in his career to get that cup, but he can't see that right now. This old guy, his chances are becoming slimmer and slimmer. I take a seat and start to undress.

"Where is he, where the fuck is he," a booming voice echoes through the locker room. Then seconds later, I see the team's owner, Bill Reeves, come in. He picks me up by the scruff of my neck, and for an old guy, he's pretty strong, still got some of that past hockey strength in him as he slams me against the lockers. "You motherfucking asshole," he spits in my face. "I should fucking trade you for that."

The room goes silent.

Bill Reeves created the South Dakota Devils three years ago, the league's newest team, using the billions he's made in soybeans since retiring from professional hockey. We built this team together when he brought me in as Captain on an extremely lucrative deal, and this was the closest we have been to making the finals and getting a stab at the cup. I've been lucky enough to win it many times before with my former teams, but to do it with this one would have been a dream.

"Bill ..." Coach Barrett says as he watches the team's owner accost his captain in front of everyone.

Bill's eyes narrow on me, and I see nothing but anger behind them. I've never seen this side of him before. "You have no fucking idea." He chuckles darkly at me. I've seen him hot-headed before, but in this moment, I feel like if he could strangle me, he would. We've become good friends over the years, building the Devils. I considered him family, and we attend Sunday family lunch once a month at his home. But this man I see now, I don't know. "Looks like my golden boy is nothing but fool's gold." With that, he slams me back into the locker and storms out of the room. Everyone stares at me in shock but remains silent as if they can't believe what they've just witnessed.

"Are you okay?" Coach asks once everyone gets back to getting changed so we can do cool downs.

"I let everyone down."

"Emotions are high at the moment, and like Gus said before, we wouldn't have been in with a chance if you hadn't grabbed us that goal."

"Until I fucked up."

"You did in that moment, and the other team got lucky. Any one of you guys could have fucked up on the ice landing us in the same situation we are now, it's just unfortunate it was you."

"I knew better. What the hell was I thinking?"

"You can make yourself crazy debating the what-ifs over that play, none of them are going to change the outcome. Shake it off. Enjoy your time off, you're getting married, you have so much to look forward to. Then next year win the fucking cup. That will shut all the haters down. Now, come on let's get these old muscles cooled down. Don't want to pull a hamstring on your honeymoon now do we?" he jokes.

After cooling down and having a shower, I get dressed and head out to the press conference. One of the toughest things I ever had to do was sit there and have one person after another asking me in various ways what the hell I was thinking messing up like I did. It was torture. But I get through it and head up to the owner's box where there are drinks for the players' and staff families. I'm greeted warmly as I walk in by my sister, Collette.

"I'm sorry," she says, hugging me tightly.

"Me too," I tell her.

"Pierre, there you are. You look like you've been through it." Michelle Reeves, Bill's wife, walks over and greets me warmly.

"You could say that."

"We'll get 'em next year," she says, giving me a wide smile

before looking over at Collette. "Look, I'm sorry about Bill ..." she starts to say.

"Nothing to apologize for," I tell her.

"He's passionate." She chuckles.

"That he is."

"I'm sure nothing he says is going to be worse than what your inner thoughts are saying," she adds quietly.

"You'd be right."

"Things will get better. Something will happen and the news cycle will move on, maybe not the fans, their memories seem to be long, but the media will. Plus, you have your wedding to look forward to."

"Speaking of weddings, where's my beautiful fiancée?" I ask, looking around the suite.

Collette's face falls. "She went home with her friends."

"Oh." My sister's words sucker punch me.

"Things got a little rowdy in the suite, it was probably for the best. Keep that chin up, things will get better," Michelle reassures me before going back to her family.

"Did Kitty seriously leave?" I ask my sister.

"Yeah, but to be fair, I think it was her friends that pushed it."

I nod. "I need a fucking drink."

"Come on, let's get you one or two." My sister smiles as we head over to the bar.

Eventually, I make my way home, the crowds have dispersed, and thankfully, people are not waiting for me to get their pound of flesh. My driver drops me off at my door, and I walk in and drop my gear the moment I enter. Frankston rushes toward me and jumps into my arms, at least someone is happy to see me tonight as I hug him tightly, he licks my face, and I didn't realize how much I needed the affection.

"You're home early," I hear Kitty call out from the living room.

"Wasn't much to celebrate." I sigh as I walk toward her, desperately wanting to fall into her arms and hear her tell me everything is going to be okay.

"Not after you messed it all up." I still. "Do you have any idea how embarrassing that was for me?" For her? "I had my friends with me."

"Wasn't thinking about you while I was out there," I snap back.

"Looked like you weren't thinking at all."

"What the hell, Kitty? I had a fucking shit night, and I come home expecting my fiancée to be consoling me, except I get nothing but this attitude."

"I'm not going to stroke your ego when you mess up." She huffs.

"Wow," I say, shaking my head, this is utterly unbelievable.

Kitty rolls her eyes. "Do you have any idea how many people have tagged me in shit about tonight. The comments on my photos I took at the game are full of hate."

I can only imagine how horrible they are, my phone has been going off all night. "I'm sorry."

"So, you should be."

I hate fighting with her. I walk over to where she is sitting and take the seat beside her. I reach out, and after a couple of attempts, she eventually crawls into my lap. "I'm sorry I'm putting you through this."

"They are so mean." She sniffles.

I hug her tighter. "They will move on."

"I sure as hell hope so. I will not tolerate this when it comes to my wedding content." She looks up and warns me.

"Baby, they wouldn't do that."

"You promise." She pouts.

"I won't let them," I reassure them.

This makes her smile. "I knew you wouldn't. I wrote a statement that you can post to your fans about their harassment of me. I've emailed it to you."

Oh. "I'll check in the morning if that's okay?" She doesn't look happy with that answer. "It's been a long night, I kind of want to chill."

"Sure. That's what I thought you would want to do. I knew you would want to be alone to brood about it so I'm heading out with my friends. I just wanted to see you before I left."

I still. "You're not serious?"

"Um, yeah. They all flew in to watch the game. I have to make the trip worthwhile somehow."

"Of course you do," I mumble as I pick her up and place her back on the sofa. "Go do whatever it is you need to do."

"See, this attitude is the reason why I don't want to be around you tonight. I knew you would be in a mood, you're always a grump after losing a game," she says, getting up from the sofa.

I'm too exhausted to fight with her. "I'd rather be alone anyway."

Kitty gasps. "I know, but you don't have to be so mean about it." She turns on her heel and storms toward our room to get ready. Frankston jumps up onto the sofa and takes Kitty's spot. He paws me, asking me to wrap my arm around him before snuggling in beside me. At least I know he has my back.

3

ISABELLE

MONTHS LATER

strange text from Harper woke me up super early this morning.

> Harper: SOS. Just landed in NYC see you soon.

This can't be good. She's supposed to be in Italy with Felix for Pierre's wedding. As soon as the message comes through, I check her socials, then Felix's, and as a last resort, I check Kitty and Pierre's to see what is going on, but there doesn't seem to be anything. Of course, there wouldn't be, they're probably in the middle of getting married. I heard they got a million dollars from some magazine to shoot their Italian wedding so I doubt they will post anything online to jeopardize that. I don't know what's going on, and my anxiety is in overdrive.

Heading into the kitchen, I grab a bottle of champagne from the fridge because if it's bad news, like she's broken up with Felix, she is going to want to drink her sorrows away no matter how early it is. Then I order a breakfast platter from the café next door. I don't cook. I'm hopeless at it. They should probably revoke my Italian citizenship hearing that. I know my nonna is turning in her grave hearing I can't cook. Look we can't be good at everything all the time. I hear the front door open and rush out of the kitchen to greet Harper.

I still.

No.

This has to be a nightmare because there is no way in hell I am staring at Pierre St. Fucking Pierre in the entrance of my home, all six foot five inches of him. Harper wouldn't do this to me. She wouldn't bring this man into my home.

"Don't freak out," Harper says.

Don't freak out? Oh, I'm most certainly freaking out.

"Nope. No. Get the hell out of my home," I yell, pointing at the front door.

"Issy," Felix pleads.

I shake my head. "No. I don't care what the reason is, he needs to go."

"Issy, give me a sec ..." Harper says as she tries to advocate for this asshole, but I'm not interested.

"Aren't you supposed to be getting married?" I stare at the man I swore I would never see again. The man who broke my naïve heart into a million pieces. *The man that I can't seem to let go of.*

"Yeah, about that," he answers awkwardly as he rubs the back of his neck. This was always his nervous tell growing up. My eyes narrow and that's when I notice the disheveled dark hair as if he's run his fingers through it all night, the dark circles under his eyes, the tie on his suit is loosened and pulled to the side haphazardly, his square jaw is covered in stubble, and those hazel eyes look haunted.

"Welcome to operation runaway groom," Harper states, giving me jazz hands.

I stare at my best friend, the traitor. "Oh my god, you left Kitty at the altar. And you two helped him?" I'm dumbfounded. Who the hell does that to a woman? Who am I kidding, it's fucking Pierre, of course he would do that. What I don't get is Harper entertaining the illusions of this fuckboy. I get why Felix would help him as his brother but her, she's my friend.

"It's not what you think," Harper argues.

"You have no idea what I'm thinking," I tell her before glaring daggers at Pierre, those familiar hazel eyes quickly looking away from me. Good, I hope I make you pee your pants in fear.

"I can see it on your face," Harper says.

Of all the people, she is the one who knows what this man did to me. The pain he caused, and now he's doing that to someone else. I will not be a part of it. I'm not helping this man wreck another woman.

※

"*Come on, let's go to that party,*" *Harper pushes.*

"*I'm tired.*" *I groan.*

"*We are going, come on. You don't want to leave Pierre with all these puck bunnies prancing around,*" *she warns me.*

"*I trust him.*" *I glare at her. I know Harper doesn't, but I've been with Pierre for years now. We love each other, we are planning a future together, he wouldn't jeopardize that.*

"*You might, but I sure as hell don't trust those girls that hang around the house.*"

I roll my eyes and reluctantly get off the couch and get ready.

Moments later, we head into the frat house. People spilling out of the house onto the street, and the music is pumping. Harper takes my hand and pulls me through the crush of people.

"*Do you see him?*" *she screams over the music. I shake my head because I can't, and usually it is easy because Pierre towers over everyone.* "*What does his location say?*"

Pulling out my phone, I stare down at the app. "*He's here.*"

Harper nods and pulls me up the stairs toward his bedroom. He's probably in his room, Pierre takes his hockey seriously and doesn't usually party with the other players, his sole focus is to be the best.

"Which room is it?" she asks.

"That one." I point to his door.

Harper continues to pull me toward it, but instead of knocking, she barges right into his room. Before I have a chance to stop her, she flicks the light on, and I gasp at what I see. Missy Jenkins giving my boyfriend a blowjob.

"Hey, assholes, don't you knock, I'm kind of busy." Pierre groans before looking up. "Shit, Issy," he curses, pushing Missy off his dick. I can see her spit glisten across his cock. I'm going to be sick.

"And this is why I don't trust him. She's not the first," Harper informs me.

"What the fuck, Harper?" Pierre screams at her as he tries to get himself dressed.

I am in utter disbelief. I can't believe he would do this to me.

"Issy, please, it's not what it looks like," Pierre pleads.

"Not what it looks like? It looks a hell of a lot like you're fucking over my friend," Harper tells him.

"This is none of your business, shut the fuck up," he screams at her.

"Whatever lame ass excuse he's going to give you, remember she's not the first," Harper says to me.

I stare at Pierre, and I don't see the boy who held my heart anymore, I see nothing but a stranger.

"Issy, please, let me explain," he says.

But I don't want to hear it, nothing he says can make me forgive this, nothing. And with that, I turn and disappear out the door in tears as my heart breaks in two.

"Babe, I'm so sorry," Harper says, running after me.

"You knew." I stare at her as tears run down my cheeks.

"Not one hundred percent. I had heard girls boasting about it around campus, but I could never catch him. I knew you wouldn't believe me unless I showed you the proof," she explains.

My stomach turns. "Do I know these girls?"

Harper nods. "Some are friends," she confesses.

Oh.

My stomach sinks. "Friends?"

"Obviously, not real friends," Harper adds.

"Why did he do this? Was I not enough? Am I not pretty enough? My boobs not big enough? Am I bad in bed? What did I do?" I sob to her.

"Nothing, you did nothing. It's his ego. He's got caught up in the hype of himself. He thinks he's a fucking king," Harper explains to me.

"I don't know that guy in there," I say, pointing toward the frat house.

"That's the real Pierre when you're not around. The womanizing hockey star," Harper adds.

"If that is what he wanted, why didn't he break up with me?"

"Because boys are assholes."

"I never thought he could be one."

"He has a dick, they are born that way," Harper adds.

I never understood Harper's men-hating attitude, but I guess I've never had my heart broken before.

"I thought he was different," I sob to her. Harper comes over, wraps her arms around me, and pulls me into a tight hug.

"I'm so sorry," she says, holding me as I break down.

"IT'S NOT what you think, he's not the asshole doing the cheating this time," Harper explains, pulling me from the past.

"Hey," Pierre protests, but I glare at him, and he shuts up.

"We caught Kitty screwing someone in the garden the night before the wedding," Harper explains.

I'm dumbfounded.

"Not just someone but Bill Reeves," Felix adds.

As in the owner of the South Dakota Devils. That Bill Reeves. Isn't he like sixty-something, and she's late twenties? Hasn't he been married forever? I just stare at them all. They must be messing with me.

"I have video," Harper adds.

I scrunch up my face, I don't need to see that. I reach out, grab Harper by the arm, and pull her into the kitchen. "What the fuck were you thinking?" I hiss at my friend. If what she is saying is true, why the hell is she bringing this to my doorstep, especially him? I want no part of this. No way.

"I was thinking of what was best for my client and bringing him somewhere the media wouldn't look for him," she whisper yells at me.

"In *my* home," I say, thumping my hand on my chest.

Harper's brows pull together. "It made sense in my head, but I see now, in practice, it might not be such a great idea."

"I can't believe you did this to me." I try to hold in the emotions that are threatening to erupt.

"I had no choice," she argues.

Of course, she had a choice. She has a house. Her family own a fucking hotel empire there are so many other options. "And why should I do this for him?"

"For closure. Because I don't think you have ever gotten over his betrayal, and I don't think you will ever be able to move on until you do."

I can't believe she said that to me. I don't need anything from this man. "Don't you hate him?"

"We're friends now," she says, giving me a smile as if everything is okay in the world. I'm stunned. "Honestly, it's going to be the best therapy. Face your fears."

I glare at my friend. Is she so dickmatized by Felix that she would do this to me? "You're asking me to shock therapy myself with my ex while he is hiding from his ex because she's been boning his boss," I throw back at her.

"I can tell you it's not a visual you would want to see," Pierre says, stepping into the kitchen and interrupting our conversation.

"This is a private conversation," I snap at him.

"About me," he argues.

Felix walks in behind his brother. "Sorry, I couldn't stop him," he says, giving us a guilty look.

"He's your client, why can't he stay with you?"

Pierre crosses his arms and glares at me. "You're going to have to get used to me being around you, Issy, seeing as my brother is dating your best friend."

"No, I don't have to."

"I'm also going to try to get picked up by The Mavericks," Pierre declares.

"You're doing what?" Have I fallen into The Matrix or something. He wants to jump ship when he probably has years left on his contract and at his age, but now wants to move to a team that just signed his brother, his much younger brother. I turn to Felix because this is crazy. "I didn't think you ever wanted to play on the same team as him. You said he was too competitive against you."

"I push him to be better," Pierre argues.

"You bulldoze over him because your fucking ego is uncontrollable. And it looks like nothing has changed since college," I yell at him.

"My life has blown up. I was supposed to be getting married this weekend. My career is circling the drain over this. Everything I have worked for could vanish," he says loudly. We glare at each other. Silence falls around us. I hate his stupid face. "Please, Issy, give me one week and then I'll be out of your hair. I promise."

One week. One hour, no, one minute is too long. "Can't you go back to Quebec with your mom?"

"She's staying in Italy with my sisters, they are having a

holiday," he explains.

"I don't feel comfortable," I tell him.

His face softens. "I promise you won't see me. I'll stay in my room." Just his presence alone is enough. I can't have him roaming my home, my private space. I shake my head. No. This man is not staying here with me. Pierre's face tightens. "Fine, I'll play hardball then. I thought my agency would try to help their client get out of a contract and find them a new one. That's what managers do, don't they?"

Is he fucking serious? My eyes narrow on him. The asshole. How dare he use my business against me. "One week and then you are fucking out of my house." I point my finger at him in warning before I turn and leave the kitchen. I have to get away from this man. I hate the stupid spicy cologne that he's wearing, which swirls around my head, messing it up. And I still hate his stupid, perfect face.

"Oh, one more thing," Pierre calls out to me. Seriously, there's more? I stop and look at him angrily. "I need to go get Frankston."

"Frankston? Who the hell is Frankston?" I ask.

"My dog."

"Your dog."

"He's my baby, I can't leave him," he explains.

"And you want to bring him here, to my home?"

"He's house-trained. He's a good boy."

Pierre's being serious. He wants to get his dog and bring it to my house. *My house.* But I'm not a heartless bitch and it's not the dogs fault his dad is the world's biggest asshole. "Fine, but if he destroys anything you are paying for it."

"Promise." He grins as I walk out of the room.

"Issy, wait," Harper calls after me.

"Don't talk to me, you traitor," I say as I stomp through the house trying to get away from everything just as the front door-bell rings. Shit. That's breakfast. I head over to the front door and greet the waiter, I grab the platter and shut the door behind me. "I ordered food, I knew you would be hungry. I even had champagne chilling because I thought you might need it. I thought you and Felix had broken up, and I knew you'd be sad."

Harper's face softens. "You did that for me?"

"Of course I did, because I'm a good friend, unlike you."

"How about I take this from you?" she says, walking over and taking the platter from my hands. "And we can talk. I'll explain everything."

"Fine, but bring the champagne, I think I'm going to need it," I say, rolling my eyes.

4

PIERRE

"That didn't go so well." Felix grimaces as the girls leave the room.

"Didn't think it would," I tell him. Especially not after what I did to her at her father's wake. She hated me before it, she sure as hell hates me after that.

"I think Issy is going to be the least of your problems this week." My brother chuckles as Harper walks back into the kitchen with a platter of food.

"Help yourselves, I have to smooth things over with Issy," she says, grabbing the bottle of champagne from the bucket.

"Maybe I shouldn't stay here, I don't want to cause Issy any more problems than I already have," I tell her.

"This is the best place for you. There is no way anyone will look for you here. Once the shock has worn off, everything will be fine."

"Why are you doing this for me, Harper?" I ask her.

Harper looks over at my brother before looking back at me. "She never got over you, and I want her to. It's time."

Oh.

And with that, Harper disappears.

Felix gives me a sad smile. "That sounded worse than how she meant it," he tries to reassure me.

"Oh no, Harper meant it," I tell him as I dig into the fruit platter she placed down.

"She's looking out for her friend, from what Harper has told me, Issy's never really dated long term, I guess since you," my brother explains to me.

"Really?"

"Yeah. I mean, she's dated, but no one special."

"And you think that's because of me?" I ask, popping a strawberry in my mouth.

Felix shrugs as he starts feasting on the food, too. "You're her baggage. Just like Harper's ex is her's, Cynthia is mine, and now Kitty is going to be yours."

"The difference is, I don't know if I'm that devastated about Kitty. I feel more upset at Bill and what that all means for my future than losing the love of my life. What the hell do you think that says?" I ask.

"That you had a lucky escape." I think he's right. "Were things that bad between you and Kitty?"

"Yeah. They weren't great."

5

ISABELLE

"**B**abe, I'm sorry about springing all this on you this morning, but truly, I did think it was the best place for him. His life is about to implode and not in a good way either," Harper explains as we sit in my bed, sipping our champagne while the boys stay downstairs.

"You could have stuck him in one of your hotels, the security would be better."

Harper sighs. "You're right, I could have but if I'm being honest, I'm worried about him being by himself during this time."

"You think he'll hurt himself?"

She shakes her head. "No, but shit is going to start hitting the fan, we won't be able to contain the news for much longer. And I kind of need someone to keep an eye on him."

"And you think that's me?"

"Honestly, no, but like I said in my mind I thought it was a brilliant idea. I now know it's not."

"What happened at the wedding?" I ask her.

"Pierre wanted to talk. You know, give the whole don't mess with my little brother speech to me," Harper explains with a roll of her eyes. "And then suddenly he started freaking out about getting married, he asked me if he should do it. Me!" I gasp. "It was weird. Maybe things between him and Kitty were not at all what they seemed. The loving façade may have just been that, a façade," Harper explains.

"You think it was a fake relationship?"

She shakes her head. "No. I don't think so or maybe it started off real and gradually turned fake. I've seen it so many times in the influencer space, once their platform grows, reality turns into fiction. They want to show that everything is perfect because perfection gets likes. Perfection gets brand deals. Perfection makes money." I nod, that makes sense. "She was a complete Bridezilla in Italy. Seeing Pierre and Kitty together, you could see the strain looking back on it. I think he was going through the motions like maybe if he marries her, everything will get better. Anyway, the more he freaked out the further he started to walk into the garden. I had to run to keep up with him. Then we heard moaning. There was no mistaking what was happening. We heard Kitty's voice. It was awkward as fuck. It was Pierre who made me record what was happening."

"Insurance policy," I muse.

"He was smart. He knew Kitty would turn it around on him if he didn't have evidence. That if he left her at the altar, she would play the victim. I'm sure she will still after this."

"I can't believe she was screwing Bill Reeves." I shudder.

"He's not even a cute billionaire," Harper says, making us both laugh. "I'm sorry for dropping this bomb in your lap this morning. But we need to protect Pierre right now, especially as he is our client."

"Don't remind me." I scoff as I throw back the rest of my champagne.

"I really do mean it when I say get closure with him, Is. You deserve happiness but I think holding on to what he did to you all these years ago isn't healthy."

It's hard to find closure when your heart has a permanent scar on it, and no one has come close to healing it.

§

"Issy?" My father stares at me as I burst through the front door of my home, tears falling down my cheeks. I can't believe it. Harper was right, I would never have believed her if I hadn't seen Pierre cheating with my own eyes. He is not the same boy I fell in love with. "Issy," my father calls my name again, concern lacing it. "What's going on?"

"I don't want to talk about it," I scream at him as I take the stairs two at a time toward my bedroom. All the memories of the two of us together assault me as I slam the door to my bedroom and collapse on my bed, screaming into my pillow.

There's a gentle knock on my door, "Issy." It's my father again and I can hear the pain in his voice.

"Mr. Alessi, I've got her," I hear Harper's voice.

"Harper, I'm worried. This is not like her. She is upset, I need to know she is okay," my father asks her.

"She's suffering her first case of heartbreak," Harper explains delicately.

"Oh," My father answers, seemingly surprised. "Do I need to make this boy hurt?"

Harper chuckles. "Maybe. I'll let you know. And when you do, I'll be right by your side."

"Good. I'll be in my office if you need me," he tells her.

Then I hear the door to my bedroom creak open. "Issy ..." I shake my head, I can't. The bed dips as Harper sits beside me. "... I'm sorry you had to find out that way. I never meant to hurt you, I didn't know how else to tell you."

Turning my head, I look up at her through tear-soaked lashes. "I would never have believed you." I sob.

Tears run down Harper's cheeks, and she never cries. "He's changed, Issy. That boy in there isn't the same one from high school."

"Why did he do it?" I sob.

"Ego."

"I can't go back to school. I'm a laughingstock." Harper's face softens. "All those girls looking me in the face after doing whatever the hell they did to my boyfriend. How can I trust anyone ever again?"

"They were not your friends, and this is a real shitty way of finding that out. You don't deserve this. You are the best human in the world, and I hate the fact that he has tainted the world for you," Harper tells me.

"I'm sorry for not being more understanding when you went through your own heartbreaks."

"Babe, my heartache is nothing like this. He threw away years, years of a loving relationship for desperate puck bunnies who are probably sucking his best friend's dick tomorrow." My stomach turns replaying the image of Missy Jenkins with her mouth around Pierre's cock. I will never ever be able to scrub that from my soul. "He will rue the day he ever fucked up. There will come a moment in his life when he is going to look back at the choices he made and realize cheating on you was the biggest mistake of his life." My phone vibrates beside me. "Is that him?" Harper asks. I pull it out of my pocket and give it to her, I don't have the energy. She takes it, looks down at the screen, and scrunches up her face at it. "He's called you like twenty times."

"I never want to speak to him ever again," I tell her.

"Consider it done," she says, tapping away on my phone, "he is now blocked."

Relief fills me. "Thank you." I give her hug, something I know she isn't a fan of.

"That's what friends are for. If you need to go away for a bit, just say the word and I'm down. Need to head to Paris for the weekend, shopping always makes me feel better. Maybe Spain, we can drink Sangria and laze on the beach checking out hot Spanish men or we could go to Italy, you will never feel more desired nor wanted than *from the men in Italy. It helps the ego."* She chuckles. *"Spring break is next week."*

That sounds nice, getting out of New York might be what I need. The thought of going back to school and having everyone look at me with pity makes me sick. Also, the thought of running into Pierre again fills me with dread because I don't know if I'm strong enough to say no to him, and that scares me.

"I'm in."

Harper stills. *"Excuse me, what did you say?"*

"I said I'm in. Let's go to Europe. Screw school, screw hockey players, screw everything."

"You're being serious."

"Yes."

AND I NEVER CAME BACK. It was the best decision for me. Some might call it running away from my problems, namely Pierre, but it seemed like a problem for him not me. A clean break was for the best.

"SWEETHEART, are you having fun over there?" my father asks.

"I love it here," I gush, who wouldn't? The sunshine, the partying, the hot men with accents.

"You're sounding happier, that's for sure." I can hear the smile in his voice.

"I am. That's what I wanted to talk to you about." I swallow the knot in my stomach churning inside of me. *"I want to transfer schools."*

"What!"

That's what I thought he would say, but I came prepared. *"Please, hear me out."*

"*You want to change schools all because of some insignificant guy? No. I won't allow it. You need to come home and be with your family,*" *he argues with me.*

"*Papa, please listen. I can transfer easily to a school in London, I can work in the London office. Wouldn't it be good to have an Alessi keeping an eye on things over here? Wouldn't I be getting a broader education on the business if I learn how the entire company runs, not just how the American side does?*" *Silence falls between us. This is good, it means he's thinking it over.*

"*You know nothing about European sports.*"

"*Then wouldn't it be good if I learned all about them? I'll happily start back down as an intern again and work my way up,*" *I plead with him. There are a couple of gruff huffs.* "*I could live in our apartment here, go to school, learn about a new side of the business, be your eyes and ears over here.*"

"*You are making a compelling argument, Isabelle.*" *Yes. I knew if I spoke to him from a business point of view rather than an emotional one, he would see it my way.* "*And this isn't because of a boy?*" *he asks.*

"*It may have started off like that, but I love it here. It would only be until I finish my studies and then I'll come right back home.*"

"*What about your sisters? They will miss you,*" *he asks.*

"*They hardly see me now as it is. They're both growing up and doing their own things, they don't want to hang out with me. If they do need me, it's only a six-hour flight. I will come home for holidays, birthdays, and anytime you need me.*"

"*I don't like this. You are all alone in a city that you don't know,*" *he states.*

"*That's what I love, no one knows the Alessi name here, I can be normal.*"

"*Is it that bad being an Alessi?*" *he asks, sounding hurt.*

"*No, I love it. It's just that people know who you are there. Sometimes people try to be my friend because they think they can get tickets to the bowl or the Cup, or as an athlete they can get a deal* from you. I'm always on edge, wondering if people like me for me or for what they can get from me or from you."

"I had no idea."

"It's not your fault, it's how the world works. It's just nice knowing I can meet people, and they like me for me, not the season tickets I have access to," I explain.

"You're my firstborn, sweetheart. I will miss you," he confesses to me.

Tears well in my eyes. "I'm going to miss you, too, but I need this, please."

"I can't deny my girls anything. If you need this then I can't see why not," he says. Really? I can't believe he's giving in so easily. "But I want you home for Thanksgiving and Christmas. It would be great to see you during the summer too."

"Deal," I tell him.

"Isabelle, you're the future of my business. You will be the one taking over when I'm too old to continue." I know my father, he is never going to retire. "Seeing how all our operations work is a smart idea. And the fact that you researched everything before coming to me makes me so proud. If this is what you want, then I am fine with it."

"You are?" I still can't believe it.

"Yes. I better not find out who this boy was who broke my baby's heart because I will knock him out, and then I will thank him for making my baby stronger. He was a lesson you didn't need to learn, but I think you will be better for it, my love, as horrible as it is to have your heart broken. I'm proud that you want to spread your wings. I've always wanted the best for my girls, and I may be overprotective, but only because I never want to see anything bad happen to you girls. That was the promise I made to you all when the doctor placed you in my arms when you were born, that I would never let anything bad happen to you all. But they don't tell you how hard that is when your babies start to grow up and turn into three extraordinary independent girls." Tears fall down my cheeks. *"I guess I can't shelter you any longer, and I have to deal with the fact that you're an adult now and can make your own decisions. Whether they are good or bad, just know you can come home any time you want. You need me night or day, I am there for you."*

"I love you," I sob to him.

"I love you too, my sweetheart."

"Will you forgive me? Harper asks, shaking me from my memories.

"Eventually, once that man has left my home. Still can't believe you've changed your tune about Pierre," I say, shaking my head.

"He's still a dick, but I'm not about to kick him when he's down, plus, you know Felix ..." She grins. "I'm asking a lot, but being with Felix has changed me. That man downstairs has surprised me, and he's so patient and understanding about my past that I feel like he's slowly teaching me how to be whole again." Harper deserves that. I will never understand how someone as beautiful, intelligent, and wonderful as her picks the reddest flagged guys in the world. Ever since high school, she has had bad luck regarding relationships. It's like she's cursed.

I feel like I've been cursed lately. The men I've been dating have been jerks, I haven't had much luck since breaking up with Pierre. I've dated, but they never liked the fact that I would always put work first. I had to, though, because no one respected me as a woman in a male-dominated field. I worked twice as hard to be given the same respect as a man, plus I was the boss's daughter, too. That earned me even less respect behind my back, of course, never to my face.

"It's nice to see you in love," I tease.

Harper rolls her eyes. "Hold your roll there. I'm very much in the lust stage, lots and lots of lust." She giggles.

"Ew, he's like a brother to me." I groan, pretending to gag which makes her laugh.

"Speaking about his brother ... after this weekend, when the press finds out about his non-wedding, things are going to explode for him and not in a good way. Did you know Pierre gave me his phone on the plane?" I shake my head. "Kitty was a complete bitch to him as was her family and friends. She said some horrible things in her text to him, which I would get if she was left at the altar for no reason, but she was busted screwing someone else and yet she's blaming him. That woman is crazy, and it's hard to control crazy," Harper warns. "I told Kitty to explain to everyone at the wedding that there was a family emergency back in Canada and Pierre and his family needed to leave, and if she didn't, I would release the footage. This would give us time to plan what we needed to and keep people from speculating anything untoward. They will eventually, but hopefully not until Monday. We've sent Bill Reeves an email from Pierre's lawyer and his agent asking to be let go from his Devils contract, so he can be a free agent."

Shit. That isn't good, not at his age. Pierre was the highest scorer this year in the league and is consistently up there, but that is a huge risk to go free agent just before a new season. People are going to have questions, and I'm not sure if anyone is willing to answer them.

"You seriously think Bill is going to let him go?"

"We have evidence of his infidelity, and I'm sure his wife, who he has no prenup with as per media reports is going to cost him more than releasing Pierre out of his contract. Of course, we have asked for his contract to be paid out for his silence," Harper explains.

"And Pierre is okay with this?"

"He pushed for it. His agent tried to talk him out of it, but

Pierre is adamant that he never wants to play for South Dakota ever again. He might be willing to retire if he must, we've started to put feelers out for that option too." Wow. I don't know what to say other than this is going to be a shit show. "I'm not trying to guilt you into anything, but his life is about to implode, maybe ease up on him a tiny bit." I give my friend a side-eye. "I know it's a lot to ask, especially with him living here."

"I get it." I groan, throwing back the rest of my champagne. "Can you believe he wants to bring his dog to my home?"

Harper bursts out laughing at the change of topic. "He loves that dog."

"And this is my home." I moan. My home is my sanctuary, and yes, I am anal about things, but I like structure, it makes me calm when everything is in order. Pets are chaos.

"I understand how much you like things a certain way in your home, and that when you can't control things in your life, it makes you anxious, but maybe you need to spice up your life a little," Harper teases me.

I glare at her. "Spice up my life? Is that a PR word for I need more chaos in it?"

Harper chuckles. "It should be. I might use it. I love you, Issy, but you're all work and no play."

"I play. You've just been too busy with Felix to see it."

"When was the last time you went on a date?" I don't remember, but it was a disaster. "See, it's been so long you can't remember," Harper points out.

"Because I'm choosing to forget it, it was a disaster, my mind has blanked it. You know I don't have time to date. I work sixteen-hour days. Don't you come for me over my work-life balance when you're the same."

"It's not healthy," she argues.

"Look at you changing your tune now." I raise a brow at her.

Harper rolls her eyes at me. "I don't need to date when I have Paradise."

"Paradise is great to fulfill your needs, but don't you want more?"

I shake my head. "No. I'm happy as I am."

Harper nods. "Okay, I'll stop pestering you about your love life." She then goes on to sniff her arm pits. "Ew, I stink, I need a shower, and I need to call Meadow and fill her in on our newest client. Are we good?"

"I'll let you know in a week," I grumble.

Harper laughs and gives me a hug. "I'll message you. Come over to my house later so we can all talk about what the plan is going forward."

"Okay."

6

ISABELLE

H arper texts me to let me know Meadow is on her way, and to head over to her place so we can start strategizing. I've been holed up in my bedroom for the past hour, not wanting to leave and run into Pierre. But I have no choice now.

I walk down to the guest bedroom and knock on the door.

"Harper messaged, we have to go," I call out.

Nothing.

"Hey, did you hear me?" I call out, knocking on the door.

Nothing.

"Pierre, we have to go. We're trying to save your fucking career."

Still nothing.

He might have fallen asleep, he used to sleep like the dead and would always sleep through his million alarms. He did just fly in from Europe so he's probably exhausted. My hand turns the doorknob, and I step into the spare bedroom and freeze.

Shit.

There, standing in all his naked glory running a towel through his hair, is Pierre.

Holy shit.

I blink a couple of times as I take him in, my eyes running over his large frame, across his tanned skin, the beads of water sliding down his broad chest through the dark hair down his pecs and across his six packed abs until it vanishes beneath the other towel which hangs low exposing the deep V of his hips.

He's bulked out heaps since I last saw him naked.

What am I thinking?

No.

Don't react. Please, you traitorous bitch of a body stop tingling. You are not turned on by this man. Pierre looks up, and a wide smile falls across his pouty lips. Lips that not so long ago touched mine in a kiss that I haven't stopped thinking about. That I should never think about.

"Déjà vu, isn't it? Just like the first time we met." He smirks.

THANK GOODNESS IT'S FRIDAY. I stomp up to my room after another exhausting day of school and throw my bag onto my bed, I walk into my bathroom to get ready to go meet my friends and scream.

"Who the hell are you?" I ask, staring at the near-naked boy in my bathroom. My eyes roam over his hard, lean body, my cheeks warming as I take in every hard muscle on display. My eyes drift further down to the deep V on his hips before they disappear into the towel hanging loosely. My eyes make their way up the naked body, and still when I see the hottest guy I've ever seen in my life, the square jaw, the dark hair, and the clearest blue eyes. He is gorgeous. Why is he in my bathroom?

"Hey, you must be my new roomie, Isabelle. I'm Pierre." He smiles, introducing himself with a touch of a French-Canadian accent as he holds out his hand for me, giving me the brightest, whitest smile.

"Roomie?" I stare blankly at him as I ignore his outstretched hand.

"Yeah, I'm in the room next door, your father said it would be cool," he explains.

"Dad," I scream out his name as I make haste out of my bathroom and away from the naked guy in it. "Dad, what the hell?" I call out, stomping through the house, making my way downstairs. "Dad," I call again as I storm into his office. He looks up from his desk and gives me a bright smile.

"You're home, sweetheart. Look, there's something I need to talk to you about before you go upstairs," he says.

"Why there's a boy in my bathroom."

He stills. "Oh, so you've already met Pierre."

"He was in my bathroom," I reiterate.

"It's his bathroom now, too." He grins as if finding a strange boy in your home is normal. I'm used to random athletes being in my home, but not my personal space.

"Dad!" I squeal.

"Issy, sweetie, listen. This boy is a rising star in hockey, he is the next big thing in the sport, and he's signed with the Alessi Agency. I promised his mother that I would take care of him, educate him, train him, and give him everything he needs to become the biggest star. That I would treat him like a son. You always said you wanted a brother," he adds with a grin.

"Not him," I argue.

"Pierre is a good boy. Promise me you will be nice to him. I told his mother that she wouldn't have to worry, that my girls would treat him just like his sisters back home would. That we would be family."

I glare at my father. Has he lost his mind? "Why couldn't you put him on Vee and Eve's floor, why mine?"

"Because that is where the spare room is, plus I thought the two of you would get on. You're the same age. You'll be going to the same school, it made sense."

"You know I like my space," I whine.

"I know, sweetheart, and you still have it," my father tries to reassure me.

"I don't because he's in my bathroom. I'm about to head out to catch up with my friends, I need to freshen up," I tell him.

"Perfect, why don't you take Pierre out with you? He can meet your friends before he starts school on Monday."

"No."

"Issy." His voice drops low with a disappointed tone.

I roll my eyes and cross my arms. "Fine," I grumble as I start to leave his office.

"Be nice," he calls out after me.

"Be nice," I sneer, stomping around the corner and back up to my room.

"GUESS it's been a while since you've seen me naked, have I changed much?" He smirks again at me.

His words pull me from memories as I continue staring at his naked body. "Asshole," I sneer, turning around and walking out his door. All I can hear behind me is his laughter. What a dick. *Actually, what a dick.* I forgot how nice Pierre's dick is. *Bet you all the girls from college don't forget how good his dick was.* My stomach turns remembering how I felt seeing Missy Jenkins' mouth on it, my champagne from earlier wanting to come up and revisit me.

Moments later his door opens, and he steps out.

"Good, you're ready, we have to go. Harper called a meeting, that's why I was looking for you and no other reason," I snap just so he's clear as I storm toward the front door.

"May not have been the reason, but you certainly did stay longer than you should have." He chuckles, teasing me for checking him out.

I whirl around. "Fuck you. I am doing this as a favor for Harper, and because you're a client, there is no other reason. I couldn't give a shit about you. I don't care if you have a broken heart. What I care about is my business, and unfortunately, that includes you, for now."

Pierre holds up his hands. "I hear it loud and clear, but you were the one who invaded my personal space."

"I had been knocking for ages, and you couldn't hear me. I thought you had fallen asleep. You were always hard to wake up if you fell asleep," I explain to him.

"Nice to know you still remember things about me. You always knew how to wake me up no matter how hard it was." He smirks, raising a brow.

My cheeks flush at his innuendo, I flip him off and storm out of my house. The driver is waiting as we walk down the stairs and get into the car. Pierre comes around the other side and gets in.

"Kevin, just going to Harper's place, please," I tell my driver, who nods and merges into traffic.

"It's weird being back in the city again," Pierre muses as he looks out the window. I ignore him. "Everything is so tall and everyone looks so busy. Guess I've gotten used to the wide-open spaces of South Dakota." I continue to ignore him and play on my phone. "Are there any parks nearby to take Frankston to? I don't know if he is going to love all this concrete," he asks.

"No, I don't know," I grumble.

"He's going to hate leaving his cushy home for all this," he says, continuing to talk to himself.

"You can always go back." I huff.

"And work for the man that was screwing my fiancée." He hisses as he continues to look out the window. Guess he does have a point there. "You're probably thinking I deserved it, karma finally found me." He turns and looks at me, I see the fire of emotions in his eyes. Maybe a tiny portion of me might have thought that, finally, now he can understand what it feels like to have your heart ripped out by someone you love, but it was only for a moment because I don't want karma to find me too.

"I would never wish that for you," I answer quietly.

He scoffs and continues to look out the window. I don't like that he thinks I'm a horrible person. *You were hardly empathetic when he arrived.* That was shock, and I still think I am in shock. "Have you heard from Kitty?"

"Yes," he grumbles.

"And?" I push.

He looks over at me. "She told me I had embarrassed her. That I'm a piece of shit for walking out of our wedding. That I'm a coward. I'm a loser. That she never loved me. Shall I go on?" he says. I get the picture. "Somehow, I'm the bad guy in all this. Me. She's blaming me, as are her friends."

"When the truth comes out no one is going to think that," I try to reassure him.

"You think this is coming out?" he questions me. "Bill Reeves to the world is the happily married hockey legend. No one would ever suspect what Kitty and Bill did. No one. He's almost three times her age. Plus, he's a billionaire. He can pay anyone to make all this go away. To make me go away."

"Is he threatening you?" I ask, slightly concerned.

"Of course he is, he has much to lose," Pierre snaps.

"Guess it's good that we are coming up with a plan for you then."

"You really think Harper is going to be able to help with this?" he asks, and it's the first time I see fear on his face.

"Harper is brilliant at her job. She knows people. There's no way she is going to let anyone come for you. I mean it, she will fight for you," I reassure him.

"And what about you? Will you fight for me if things go south?"

"Are you doubting my work ethic?"

"I know you're good at your job. Will you be good at it for me?" he asks. I'm offended that he would question me like that. *Why? You have made it clear all these years you want nothing to do with him. Why would he think now you'll care?*

"Of course I will. You are one of our top clients ... plus, Dad would want me to." Tightness in my chest takes over. I look out the window, trying to rein it in.

"Thanks," he says as we fall silent again.

IT'S NOT long till we arrive.

"Morning," Harper say cheerily, greeting us. She pulls us into her living room where Meadow is sitting with her, but I see no Felix anywhere.

"Hi, I'm Meadow, second in charge of The Rose Agency. Sorry to meet you under these circumstances," she says to Pierre in greeting, giving him a wide smile as her eyes rake over him. What does she think she's doing checking him out like that? I glare at her, but she doesn't notice it.

"Have your lawyers heard back from Bill's lawyers?" Harper asks him.

"Not yet," he says, shaking his head.

"Looks like Kitty is playing nice and has kept to the script. You're just going to have to stay low, so the media doesn't find you here. At the moment, they think you've gone back to Canada," Harper explains.

"Aren't they going to question why she's not with me?" Pierre asks.

"We can say she is dealing with the wedding stuff," Harper advises.

"Won't they see Pierre's family traveling around Italy?" I question.

"I've asked them not to share anything online until we have sorted all this," Harper adds.

"This buys us some time. Don't you think they are going to have questions if I'm released from my team?" Pierre asks.

That's my thought too. The public is smart and will likely put two and two together. They are also going to think Kitty did something wrong because Pierre fled the wedding and is asking to move from the team. They will probably think it has something to do with one of his teammates which sucks for them but is probably a win for Bill.

"My hope is you can get signed with The Mavericks. Felix has gone for a run with my brother to get him on board to help convince our father, who is on the board of The Mavericks, to push for a deal with you. But we can't do anything until we find out what is happening with Bill," Harper states.

"Fucking Bill," Pierre curses.

"Okay, say this all works out. Don't you think they are going to wonder why Kitty hasn't moved to New York?" I ask because right now, there is no talk regarding a press release announcing their break up. Is Pierre going to pretend they are still together until the dust settles?

"If Bill agrees and lets me go, I'm happy to say I got cold feet and that I think Kitty and I are better off as friends," Pierre states.

"Women will crucify you. Actually, everyone will. The golden boy persona will be tarnished, which will make it hard for your sponsors, which could mean they drop you, and once that starts happening, it's all downhill," Meadow explains.

"I'm going to be crucified either way," Pierre says.

"Not if you tell the truth. I'm surprised Bill didn't respond straight away to your request which is a fricken nice request. I think he thinks he has you over a barrel and that you won't blow up everything," Meadow states.

"You think?" Pierre asks Meadow.

"Men like him think they hold all the power in the world because of their money. He knows you do not want to ruin your career. He knows how much your image probably means to you, and I bet Little Miss Gold Digger is in his ear telling him, he's Canadian, he's too nice, he's not going to do shit. The question is, how far are you willing to go?"

"All the way. I want out," Pierre says confidently.

"Think about this, Pierre, don't let your anger or revenge sway you. This could mess up your career," I warn him. Look, I hate the bastard, but he has worked hard for this career.

"And what happens if Bill decides he's going to punish me and make me stay playing for his team? Two years of utter hell, I will give him my worst, I will not let him win any silverware. Me playing shit is going to ruin my career also," he explains.

"We need to speak to Jackson and find out if his wife knows about his affair," I ask Harper.

"Already on it. He said he should have something for me by lunch," she says.

"You sure about this, Pierre? Because once this gets out, your world is going to implode," I ask him again.

"I will go anywhere in the world as long as I don't have to stay there," he says, and I can see the determination on his face. Nothing is going to sway him from this.

"Right. Okay. Guess we wait and see if Bill is going to come play," I say.

"Pierre, if you need my plane to get your dog you can use it," Harper tells him.

I glare at my friend, she really has lost her mind over Felix because that is awfully generous of her.

"Harper," he says her name in surprise, "I ... I don't know what to say."

"Thank you, is a good place," she says.

"Of course, thank you. I don't know how I'm going to repay you for your kindness."

I want to throw up seeing these two be nice to each other.

"There's one condition," Harper adds.

"Anything," Pierre answers quickly.

"Take Issy, she's been working hard, and I think she needs to get out of the city."

Excuse me. Did I hear her correctly? "No," I shout at Harper.

"Yes." She smirks

"Fuck you, Harper. I agreed to him staying for the week, and I agreed he could bring his dog there, but I am not jumping on the plane and going to pick it up. You have just increased my workload," I yell at my friend.

"That's my condition," she tells me.

That is some bullshit. "That's not fair. You're being a real bitch you know."

"I know." Harper grins.

"You can work from the plane," Meadow adds.

"Stay out of this," I snap at her.

"I can rent my own, Issy, you don't have to come," Pierre says.

I throw my hands up in the air. "How am I now the bad guy? This is so unfair. Come on, let's go get the fucking dog and whatever else you need from your home," I shout as I stomp out of the room. I will not cry. I will not cry.

"Oh hey, Issy." Felix grins as he steps inside Harper's town-house, looking all sweaty.

"Fuck you," I says as I push past him. He looks confused.

"Issy, wait," Pierre says.

"What's going on?" Felix asks his brother.

"Don't worry about it," Pierre tells him. He grabs my arm and pulls me back to him.

"Don't touch me," I yell at him. *Don't cry.* My emotions are all over the place right now. This has been one messed-up morning.

"Issy."

"Don't," I warn him.

He rubs the back of his neck, he's nervous. "I'm not trying to complicate your life."

"Well, you are," I snap at him as a ball of stress sinks its teeth into my shoulder blades.

"I don't deserve your help, but I sure as hell appreciate it and you right now," he says.

Damn him. That was nice. I ignore him and walk out of Harper's home toward the car, and Pierre follows. He gets in the car with me, and we are silent all the way back to my apartment.

It's not until we are back inside that he finally speaks again.

"Issy."

"Yes," I answer irritated.

"I'm going to head to South Dakota tomorrow," he explains, his hand rubbing the back of his neck, and I hate the way his arms flex when he does it. His biceps tense, his forearm veins expose, urgh, I shouldn't be looking. "I know you don't want to go, but I could really use your help. I don't know if I can do this on my own."

Oh. I wasn't expecting that.

Then I watch as Pierre clutches his chest. "I can't breathe," he says, gasping for breath.

Do not have a heart attack on my watch as I rush toward him.

"You're going to be okay. Quick, sit down," I say, dragging him into the living room where I pull out the dining room chair for him. "Just breathe." He continues to gasp, the panicked look on his face is terrifying. "You're having a panic attack." I realize, and make him put his head between his legs as I drop to my knees and rub his back. "It's going to be okay," I reassure him as he continues to freak out.

"It's not," he says through strangled breaths. I'm surprised he hasn't had a breakdown earlier, he's been too collected since arriving this morning. Maybe the adrenaline of the flight has finally worn off, and the reality of what's happened has hit him. I stay with him, talking gently until his breathing returns to normal.

"Shit, I don't know what happened," he says, looking down at me.

"You had a panic attack," I explain to him.

"I haven't had one of those in a while," he confesses.

"It's understandable, you've just flown in from Europe on a day that is supposed to be your wedding day. You've been running on adrenaline, and your body is now crashing. You probably didn't get much sleep on the plane either. I can't imagine what's going through your mind, not only about your relationship but also your career."

"You mean that," he asks quietly.

"Yes." I nod. I'm not a total monster. He gives me a small smile.

We stay there looking at one another, and I hate that my eyes are clocking every change on him since the last time we were this close. I notice the tiny creases on his eyes, the freckles across his nose, the squareness of his jaw with the odd bit of peppering coming through on his five o'clock shadow. The way his body fills out his tee, the muscles upon muscles, his dark hair which has grown longer and the way it curls up on the ends, I hate how silky it looks.

Pierre reaches out and cups my face. I still. Hating the way one touch from him still makes my body tingle. It's not fair. "Thanks for coming to my rescue," he says as his thumb slides along my cheek. I swallow hard because my body betrays my heart.

Instantly, I stand up and put distance between us. "I'll grab you a water." I quickly disappear.

This week is going to be hell.

7

PIERRE

"Hey, how are you going?" Collette asks.

"I'm okay. Still haven't heard anything from Bill's lawyer. Marcus is on his way home from Italy. I told him there would be a big bonus for him to make up for cutting his Italian holiday short. I know his wife has been looking forward to it, but she understands why." I owe my agent big time. "Hope you guys are having fun though?"

"Don't worry about us, we are having a great time. We're worried about you."

"Had a panic attack today in front of Issy, so that was great," I confess.

"Oh no. Are you okay? And why was it in front of Issy?" she questions.

"That's where I'm staying, with Issy."

Collette squeals. "You're staying with Issy. How? When? I don't understand. There's no way Issy would let you stay with her."

"Harper convinced her. She isn't very happy about it, but I promised her it's only for this week. I'm going to head back home to grab Frankston tomorrow."

"Oh, poor Frankston, he's going to have no idea what's happening," Collette states.

"Once I've gotten him back, I think everything is going to feel better."

"And then what's your plan?"

"I've asked Marcus if he could find out if The Mavericks would be interested in me."

Collette gasps. "The team Felix is signed with?"

I don't like my sister's tone. Why is everyone freaking out? Am I that bad? Does Felix not want us to play together? "Thought it might be a great way to end my career playing with my brother."

"That's sweet. Don't you think you will kill each other? Don't they already have a captain? Are you okay not leading a team? Is Felix okay about this?" she peppers me with questions.

"Felix seems fine about it, but the way everyone is carrying on I'm not so sure," I say.

"You guys are brothers, you're going to bring to the team some family stuff, so people are just wanting to make sure it's the right stuff," Collette explains.

"Am I that bad?"

"No, it's not that. But you're the big brother, and sometimes you can be bossy."

"I like things a certain way."

"Exactly." She laughs. I frown. "But I do think it would be kind of cool if you two played together, and you're not that old."

"I'm fucking old for a player, thirty-five. I'm in the older bracket of the league but I'm not ready to hang up my skates just yet, unless I get injured and then fuck who knows, that's my biggest fear."

"You are at the top of your game. You're running circles around those younger guys. Don't count yourself out yet," she reassures me.

"What happens if Bill doesn't let me go?" I ask her, voicing my ultimate fear.

"I don't know. There's no way in hell you would be happy sitting on the sidelines doing nothing for your team."

The petty in me would, but the hockey player in me couldn't. "He doesn't deserve the cup."

"I know, but your teammates do," Collette reminds me. "But I'm putting out positive vibes that Bill would rather protect his billions than have you on the team."

"Me too," I say in agreement. "What about you? This affects your job, too."

"I'm not worrying about that. I don't have a contract like you do with the team. I can resign whenever I want."

"Are you going to stay?" I ask.

"I don't think so."

"What about all your friends? It would be hard to leave them."

"It will be, but you're my brother. You mean more to me than the job."

I love her loyalty. "And if I go to New York, you'd come?" I would miss having her with me. Collette and I have gotten tight since she started working at the Devils. It would be great if she, me, and Felix were able to work together.

"The three of us together, not sure if New York is ready for that."

"That's true. Look don't make any decisions regarding your career just yet, not until I know where I'm going."

"I'll worry about it later because I'm in Italy," she says happily.

This makes me smile. "Glad you guys are having fun."

"We are. I'd better go, we are off to dinner," she says.

"Isn't it late there?"

"Yes, but we are living our dolce vita life now. Plus, no one eats here until late evening anyway," she explains.

"Have fun, love you all. Bye," I say, hanging up before collapsing on the bed, the day finally catching up to me.

"PIERRE ... PIERRE," I hear Issy's voice beside my ear.

"Hhhhm, I wonder what it would be like to taste your lips again," I say, reaching out to Issy as I thread my fingers through her hair.

"Pierre," she shrieks, pushing me away.

Huh.

I sit up, shake my head, and rub my eyes from the dream I'd been having. The darkness of an unfamiliar room slowly comes into focus, and the sounds of sirens echo across the walls as reality returns and I look at a pissed off Issy.

"You're in my room again." My eyes narrow on her.

Issy rolls her eyes at me. "I'd been knocking for the past ten minutes and heard nothing, so ventured in, and next thing I know you're accosting me."

"That's what you get for coming into my bedroom in the middle of the night."

Issy glares at me. "It's eight o'clock at night. I was trying to tell you dinner was ready, but maybe I should have just left you to sleep and starve," she says, folding her arms across her chest. She's gotten changed and is dressed in a white tee that molds to her curves and exposes her taunt nipples through the fabric. Maybe she's not as unaffected by me as I think. She's also got on a pair of gray sweats and no shoes. Her dark, straight hair is shoulder-length and loose, probably why I was able to run my fingers through it. She has no makeup on, that's when I notice the freckles she still has on her nose, the ones I used to count when we were in bed together. She hated them, but I loved them, so I'm glad she never got rid of them and only hides them with makeup.

"Thanks, I could do with a feed," I say, rubbing my taut stomach.

"Good, it's in the kitchen," she says, then turns and disappears out of the bedroom. Her scent fills my room, she smells like dessert with her berrylicious scent.

A couple of moments later, I'm walking out of my room and head to the kitchen, when I enter, she is pulling my plate out of the food warmer box she has and places it on the kitchen counter. When she looks up, those dark eyes widen as she skims my body.

"Why are you naked?"

I run my hand down my abs. "I'm not naked."

"You don't have a shirt on."

"You said to make myself at home."

Her dark eyes narrow. "Manners would dictate wearing a shirt when coming for dinner at someone else's home."

I smirk at her, loving the way her cheeks heat as she argues with me. "You're worried you won't be able to resist all this," I say, running my hand over my body, teasing her. "Your eyes don't lie, princess."

"Your ego knows no bounds, does it?" She huffs as she grabs cutlery from the drawer.

"And you're only lying to yourself."

Issy ignores me. "I ordered a steak and some steamed vegetables, I hope that's okay. I didn't know if you still ate like this during the off-season."

"Thanks," I say as she shoves the plate toward me.

"Are you not eating?" I ask, noticing there's only a plate for one.

"I'm heading out."

"Out?" I question her.

"Yeah, out."

"With whom?"

"None of your business," she snaps.

"You've got a date?" I ask.

"Again, none of your business," she says, and the tips of her ears are bright red.

"Oh, did it work you up earlier, seeing me naked, that you have to go to your little sex club and rub one out?" Issy gasps and her face turns a bright shade of pink as her mouth falls open. "Felix told me. You sent him to a sex resort to sort himself out after Cynthia. He said you like to go to the city clubs."

She glares at me, slack-jawed. "I don't know what you're talking about." Lies. She busies herself with cleaning up the spotless kitchen.

"What happens in the club stays in the club type thing, isn't it?" I push, loving the way I'm making her uncomfortable. She ignores me. "What kind of things happen there? Do you like being tied up and spanked? Are ball gags involved? Does everyone walk around naked?" I continue to tease. Issy's eyes flash with annoyance and anger at my questions. "You probably get off seeing a man on his knees. I know I used to love getting on my knees for you."

"Stop it," she shrieks. "What I do outside or even inside this house is none of your business. Don't think because I'm doing you a favor that you and I are friends, we're not. I'm doing this for a client, nothing more. Keep out of my way when we are at home, do you hear me?" she says angrily.

Guess I pushed her too far. "Loud and clear." I shouldn't be surprised by her anger. Issy still hates me. I was trying to lighten an awkward mood, but I guess I'm making things worse. She nods and storms out of the kitchen. I feel bad because I can see it on her face, me being here is hurting her. *She's doing you a solid, you should respect her boundaries.* This is true, but ... being around her again is confusing. I feel like no time has passed between us, yet I can feel the chasm that is there. *You should be worrying about your future, not whether Issy likes you.* That feels like it's out of my hands. I have no control over my future right now, it's in Bill Reeves' grimy hands, but the Issy situation, that I do have control over, and I'm determined to win her back *as friends*. We are going to have to learn to be around each other, especially with the way Felix and Harper seem to be traveling. My brother has it bad.

I've finished my meal which was delicious and am tidying up in the kitchen when Issy comes in dressed like sin. *Oh hell no.* She's not going out looking like that. She has a tiny black mini dress on with a slit up the side, sky high heels, and her hair pulled up in a ponytail.

"Oh, sorry didn't realize you were in here," she says before walking over to the drinks fridge and pulling out a bottle of water.

"You're seriously going out dressed like that?" I ask her.

"You have a problem with what I'm wearing?" she asks, looking down at herself.

"Damn right I do."

"Too bad," she grins, turning on her heel, "don't wait up," she calls out.

Don't wait up. What the hell? I rush after her. "What the hell does that mean?" I call out. She ignores me. "Issy." She grabs her coat and puts it on in the foyer, continuing to ignore my questions. "Are you seriously leaving to go fuck some guy?"

Issy whirls around. "Oh, I'm not fucking just one guy, I'll be fucking many." And with that image in my head, she slams the front door in my face.

※

I COULDN'T SLEEP all night. Images of Issy and what she is doing with faceless men at some sex club are keeping me up, along with a bad case of jet lag and everything else going on in my life. When I hear the front door open and the click clack of Issy's heels, I'm up and out of bed and rushing out the door.

"Shit." Issy gasps as I surprise her in the kitchen. "What the hell are you doing up at this time?"

"I couldn't sleep," I answer as my eyes roam all over her. I can't tell if she's been fucked within an inch of her life or not and it's annoying the hell out of me. She shrugs, opens the fridge, and pulls out a bottle of water.

"I'm going to bed, I'm exhausted."

"Bet you are." The snide comment falls from my lips.

"Are you shaming me for having fun?" She whirls around, giving me a dirty look.

I fold my arms over my naked chest and send a dirty look right back at her. "I'm not shaming you. Just didn't expect this new version of you. You were always shy about sex," I tell her.

Those dark eyes flare with anger. "I grew up."

"Obviously," I say, looking her up and down.

"I'm not the naïve girl I once was. You don't impress me anymore," she says, waving her hand in front of her.

"Are you saying my dick doesn't impress you? Could have fooled me when you caught a glimpse earlier." I raise a brow at her.

"Do you want to know what impressed me tonight?" She smirks as she takes a sip of her water. I'll bite. Nodding, I implore her to continue. "Not one dick but two." My jaw clamps shut as I grind my molars. "You want me to tell you how much I loved being fucked from behind while I choked on the other man's dick?"

Shit.

"Or how I fucked them in front of a room full of people? Hearing the audience moan and groan while I got spit roasted by two men."

"Enough," I growl, my dick standing to attention in my sleep shorts, I subtly try to rearrange it so it's not a fucking tent as I slide the waist band over the tip. Which doesn't work because it pops out of the top of my shorts. Obviously, I'm not as subtle as I hoped and Issy's eyes follow my movement, they widen as she sees the tip of my dick pointing out of my shorts.

"Does hearing about how other men satisfy me turn you on?" Issy smirks, raising a brow at me. "Would it kill you knowing how wet they got me. How I gushed around their dicks as they made me come so many times I couldn't move."

"I don't believe you. You look the same as you did when you left, not a hair out of place. You hardly look thoroughly fucked. And I should know because I've seen it. Done it to you, even."

"You know nothing about me anymore. Fuck you." She sneers.

"Anytime, princess, say the word and I'll fuck you, thoroughly. Seems like you might need it after that colorful story."

Those dark eyes blink at me a couple of times. "I would rather fuck glass than touch you ever again." And with that, she turns on her heel and stomps up to the second level where her bedroom is located.

Screw her. Now I'm going to have to do something about this in my pants. Who knew Issy had such a filthy mouth on her? I loved her imagery. Did that really happen to her, or did it happen to someone else? And if so, did she watch? Did it turn her on watching them?

Fuck, now my balls ache.

8

ISABELLE

"**M**orning," Pierre sings happily as I walk into the kitchen. I grunt my response as I start making myself a cup of coffee. How the hell does he have so much energy this morning? I had a terrible night's sleep last night, stupid images of Pierre playing in The Paradise Club kept me up all night. *Don't lie, it was the throbbing between your thighs that did that.* I had to call on my battery-operated friend to finish me off. Even though I went to The Paradise Club last night, nothing happened. I was too angry to let go. Then when I got home, he was on me like the damn Spanish inquisition. *Does that man ever put on a shirt?* I snapped last night in sexual frustration. He pushed and pushed until I let him have it. What I thought I was doing was hurting him, but instead it looked like I was turning him on, judging by the large bulge in his pants. Him being turned on shouldn't have turned me on, but I may have gotten off to the image of him in shorts with his dick sticking out the top last night. This week can't end soon enough.

"I thought after all your orgasms last night, you would be in a better mood," he teases.

I flip him off, which makes him laugh. "You have a funny way of thanking me for helping you today. I have better things to do with my time than fly to South Dakota," I snap.

"You're right, I am thankful for everything you are doing for me," he says. I give him a glaring side-eye. He stops in front of me. "I'm serious, Issy, thank you. Me being in your space is a lot to ask. Me being in your business is uncalled for. If you wanted to get railed by two guys last night at a sex club, that has nothing to do with me." Damn right it doesn't.

"You're not supposed to know about that place. Felix could get into a lot of trouble. You need to stop joking about it. I mean it, Pierre, keep your mouth shut about it."

"Okay. I'll stop," he says. I don't believe him. Because seconds later he is still questioning me about it. "Do you like going there?" he asks after a couple of long moments of silence.

"I thought we weren't talking about it," I tell him as I finish off the rest of my coffee.

"I'm curious, that's all ..."

"I'm not talking about this with you," I say, placing my coffee cup in the sink. "We are going to be late, come on." I walk out of the kitchen and grab my handbag, he follows.

"How long have you been a member?" he asks.

"Not answering." I walk down my front stairs.

"Have you always been kinky?"

I suck in a deep breath and try to ignore his large, looming presence which is hard when he blocks out the fricken sun. Ignoring his questions, I jump into the car and greet Kevin warmly, with Pierre following.

"If you ask one more question, I swear I will call TMZ and out you myself," I warn him.

He shakes his head. "You always blushed when people spoke about sex, and now here you are going to a sex ..." I quickly shove my hand over his mouth.

"Shut the hell up would you? Felix could be fined millions

of dollars if they find out he told you. I could get into trouble too, and I will not let you take away my happy place. Do you understand?"

"Yes," he mumbles behind my hand. I pull it away and slide my hand along my jeans. Ew. "I have emails I need to work through, so if you don't mind," I tell him. Pierre holds up his hands as if to say he's not stopping me from doing what I need to do. He's so annoying.

IT'S NOT until we are up in the air that Pierre starts talking again, well actually, it's not until he's had two glasses of whiskey that loosen him up that he starts talking again.

"Thanks for this. I appreciate it more than you realize," he says, rubbing his neck. His nervous tell.

"You don't need to keep thanking me," I snap at him.

We sit in silence for a couple more minutes until he speaks again. "Issy, can we talk?"

"No. I'm busy." Ignoring his presence.

He pauses for a bit but continues, "Please, Is. I have enough on my plate without arguing with you every two seconds. I'm exhausted."

"I'll make it easy for you. Let's not speak to each other for the week, that way we can't argue." I go back to my phone.

"You're too hard to ignore," he says quietly.

I let out a huff. "Fine. Say what you need to say so I can get back to work." I don't mean to be a bitch but I am. I'm exhausted. Frustrated. Irritated. Confused. Wary. All the things.

"I want to talk about our past," he states.

My stomach turns and flips flops. "No," I say, shutting that down quickly.

He raises a brow at me. "There's still a lot of animosity between us and I guess ..." he continues rubbing his neck, those stupid thick biceps tensing as he does. "I guess I'm trying to sort out my shit. My life has blown up and I feel like it's out of control, and well ... I'd like us to be friends again, Is. I miss you. Miss your friendship, and I could really use a friend right now," he confesses.

He can't just say nice things and think that absolves him of everything he did to me.

"Why?"

My question stuns him for a moment. "Because of Harper and Felix," he says safely. "And because it's been fifteen years, I want bygones to be bygones."

"Of course you would. You want a clean conscious."

"No. It's not that at all. I'm fighting for everything right now, and I don't know how long I'm going to have to fight. I don't need another person to fight me in my life, Issy," he explains, looking broken.

Well, don't I feel like the wicked witch? Just because his life has blown up, it doesn't mean I have to like him or forgive him for anything.

"I'll make sure to stay out of your way so that I don't add any more stress to your life," I tell him before looking back down at my phone.

"Are you serious?" he asks, sitting forward in his seat.

"Yes, it's one week. The house is big enough that we shouldn't run into each other," I answer before looking back at my phone.

Next thing I know, he snatches my phone out of my hand and holds it above his head.

"You fucking asshole, give that back to me," I yell.

"No," he says stubbornly.

No? Is he serious right now? I jump up out of my seat and charge toward him, trying to get to my phone, which is stupid because the man's entire job is to run into other men. I'm not about to topple this man mountain over, except I do, catching

him off-guard because he's had one too many whiskies, as he
loses his footing, and I land on top of him in the aisle of the
plane.

"Ouch," he groans, holding the phone above his head while
I am splayed out over him, hating how much my body likes
being pressed against his. I can feel every ripple of muscle,
every hard plane of his body against mine.

No. Stop it. Nothing about this man should make me tingle.

"Stop it," he shouts.

"Give me my phone back or I'm kneeing you in the balls," I
yell as I try to grab the phone from him.

"Not until you talk to me. I'm not going to let this fester for
another fifteen years," he says.

"I don't care what you want." I try to snatch the phone.

The flight attendant walks out and sees us rolling around
on the floor and turns right back around. Traitor. No tip for her.

"We are going to be in each other's lives, or are you going to
ignore me every single time we are at a function with Felix and
Harper? Because those two are getting married. Are you going
to ignore me at work? When I come in and see Marcus? What
happens if I get a contract with The Mavericks? Are you going
to ignore me when I'm in the city?"

"New York is a big place." I grunt as I try to grab my phone.

"Keep rubbing yourself on me like that and you're not going
to like what pops up." He grins.

"Ew. You pig." I roll off him and get up. "I don't want your
dick anywhere near me." Pierre smirks, and I go back to my
seat, irritation dripping off me. It's just one week. Seven days.
Eighty hours. I mean, if I have to go to work on the weekend to
avoid being near him, I will. He spins my phone on his finger,
taunting me. I call over the flight attendant who finally shows
her face again, and ask for something strong like tequila to put
up with this idiot for the next couple of hours.

"Issy, come on, let's talk. Let me have it. I'm sure there are things you have wanted to say to me for the past fifteen years and never got the chance to." He smirks.

"If I had wanted to say anything, I would have but I don't," I say, folding my arms as I impatiently wait for my drink.

"You're so fucking stubborn." He curses. I ignore him and look out the window. "This is ridiculous. You obviously still have feelings for me, otherwise, why would you still hold a grudge?"

"Screw you. No, I don't," I bite.

"Weird. If you have no feelings toward me, then you would be indifferent, not this ball of hate. Why won't you let us put it all out on the table and clear the air, not just for us but for Harper and Felix." I side-eye him. "Give it to me. Please."

There are some things I should say to him, he deserves to hear them.

"Fine," I hiss, just as my drink arrives. I'm going to need it to get through this talk. There is nothing he can say that will make me forgive him.

Pierre stares at me in surprise that I agreed. "Right, um, yeah, where should we start?" he asks.

"Guess at the point where you started cheating on me," I say, levelling him a glare.

He nods. "That would be a good place to start." Pierre looks uncomfortable. "I think I'm going to need another drink for this." He calls the flight attendant over and orders himself a whiskey.

"You wanted this," I tell him.

"I did," he says.

Moments later his drink arrives, he takes a slow sip, neither one of us knows where to start.

"Why did you do it?" I ask him. It's a simple question that should be easy for him to answer. "I was a good girlfriend to you." He was my first boyfriend. I had nothing else to gauge it against, maybe I sucked. "I thought we were happy. I thought we were in love as much as two teenagers could be. Was I not pretty enough?" I know I wasn't like those blonde bimbo puck bunnies that hung around the frat house with their big boobs and short skirts. "Did I not put out enough for you?" I thought our sex life was good. I mean, we were at it all the time. "Were you embarrassed that I was your girlfriend?" With each question, my throat tightens with emotion. I will not lose it in front of this man.

"Shit, Issy, is that what you have thought all these years?" He curses, running his hand through his hair. "Have you thought that this was all your fault?" Is he dumb? Of course, I've thought this was my fault because he cheated on me. I was obviously lacking something for him to do it. "Fuck, I'm an asshole." He gets up out of his chair and kneels beside me, he's so tall that we are almost eye to eye. Why is he so close? He doesn't need to be this close to me. "Issy," he says, looking at me, "this was all on me." He starts to explain, and I don't like the way he is looking at me. I pick up my emotional support tequila and take a sip. Being this close to him is intense. "I was the one lacking." Damn right. "You were perfect. *So, fucking perfect.*" Bullshit, otherwise he wouldn't have cheated. "Once I joined that frat house, we were never going to make it." That was my concern, but he told me he needed to be with his teammates, it's a bonding thing. Lies. "I valued what other people thought about me more than you. I started to believe the hype around me. I believed in my own legend that I was untouchable, unstoppable. I loved the fact that people worshipped me. My frat brothers would fuel that ego." I continue to sip my tequila, he's not telling me anything I don't already know. "I watched how they treated their girlfriend's and thought that was normal. I mean, it was exactly how my father treated my mother. I thought I was a fucking god. I started to party more, and I enjoyed the adulation, and then came the puck bunnies." You could have said no. You could have talked to me. You should have broken up with me if you wanted freedom. I would have understood. But I don't say any of that because I'm lost in the past. "None of this is an excuse for what I did to you. I was dumb and young and was so caught up in my own ego that I turned into someone I didn't like." Someone I didn't fall in love with. "I should be thanking you for leaving my ass. You were the wake up call I needed to get my shit together. If you hadn't left, I don't think I would be here today, nor have the career that I have." *You're welcome,* I think. "The guilt of what I did to you haunts me." It haunts me, too, but still he has no idea the damage it did to me. "It's a festering wound that never seems to close." Mine too. The more he tries to explain, the angrier I'm getting. He still doesn't get it. "I wish we were able to have this conversation years ago." What conversation? You just gave me line after line of bullshit. "I fucking missed you, Issy, didn't realize how much until you left. You were my other half, and I was lost without you." He means none of this. It's just words. Words that he thinks I need to hear. I'm gripping the tumbler of tequila so tightly I swear it's about to shatter beneath my fingers.

"From what I heard, after I left, you didn't stop partying," I say through gritted teeth. He wasn't wallowing with a broken heart like I was.

Pierre hangs his head. "I was angry for a long time. Wish I could say I handled it maturely, but I didn't. When you didn't come back after spring break, and no one would tell me where you were, I lost it. I sank into a dark hole of drinking and women, but realized that if I ever wanted to get you back, that hearing about me being a ho was not the way to go." He chuckles. "That rhymes."

This man is a moron. He thinks he can give me some basic bullshit excuses and throw me a smile and be coy with his nervous neck hold thing, then he's an even bigger idiot than I thought.

"You fucked my friends. Do you have any idea how humiliating that was to find out? That these girls I would go to class with, hang out with, had all been with you."

Pierre gives me a sheepish look. "I wasn't thinking."

No shit, dipshit. "Could you imagine if you had found out I had slept with your entire hockey team?"

"That would have devastated me." He stares at me intensely with those hazel eyes. I hate him. "I'm surprised you didn't after we broke up."

"They were all morons. But maybe in hindsight, I should have taken them up on their offers. You know they offered, all your friends." He stills. "Yeah, your boys, the ones you valued over me, they kept sliding into my DMs. They would always tell me that you didn't deserve me, that I was the perfect girlfriend, and that you didn't appreciate me."

"What fuckers," he says, shaking his head.

"Stupidly, my heart was yours, and no one could tempt me away from you, and I thought you felt the same. How wrong was I."

"Issy ..."

I shake my head, now I'm worked up, and let him have it. "You broke me. You ripped my heart out. It took me a long time to be able to date again. I didn't trust men, still don't. You ruined my self-esteem. I thought there was no way anyone would ever find me attractive enough to date. That they would always find someone better because I knew I would never be enough." Tears escape, and I feel them slide down my cheek. Dammit. No. He doesn't deserve them.

"Issy," he says, reaching out to wipe the tears away.

"Don't," I say, getting up abruptly, "I need a moment." I head toward the plane toilet.

9

ISABELLE

"**I**ssy." Pierre knocks on the toilet door.

"Go away," I yell at him. I will not let him see me like this. He doesn't get to swoop in now after all these years like a white knight.

"Issy," he says, knocking on the door again.

"Leave me alone, please," I plead with him.

"No."

Fuck this man. I open the toilet door and shoot daggers at him. But the devastated look on his face halts me.

"I'm so sorry. I had no idea I made you feel that way about yourself," he says, rubbing his neck.

"Don't worry about it, it is what it is," I tell him.

"Fuck, Issy. I damn well will worry about it. You were my best friend. My first love. And I hurt you beyond anyway I knew I could have. All because I was an egotistical jerk who put their needs and ego above the one person they vowed to love and protect."

"We were kids."

He shakes his head angrily. "No excuse. I made you believe you were the problem. I changed you, Issy. Me. Fuck," he says, punching the wall. What the hell is he thinking? "You didn't deserve that. No wonder you haven't spoken to me in all these years. Shit." Pierre looks distraught, maybe I was too honest with him. "Then I go and fucking kiss you at your father's funeral. I yelled at you because I was hurt, because I missed the hell out of you. And again, there I was being an egotistical jerk and taking what I wanted, and that was you." I'm shocked by his confession. "Seeing you there in your childhood bedroom again, looking so fucking beautiful, made me realize how much I fucking missed you. Everything in that moment of my life felt out of control. Things with Kitty were not good. I had been having second thoughts about the wedding for a long time, way before the funeral, and then seeing you again, all the feelings I thought had vanished, hadn't. You still have a piece of my heart, Issy, and I don't think that will ever go away." I swallow hard at his confession. "I know there's no hope for us romantically, especially not after what you told me. But I really hope there's a chance that maybe you and I could be friends because I miss the hell out of you and your family."

I stare at him in shock. I try to process everything he is saying to me. "I don't know if I can," I tell him honestly.

Silence falls between us. "I understand." His shoulders sag and his face falls. "I truly am sorry for everything, Issy. Let's get through this week, and then you don't have to ever see me again." He turns away and starts to walk back to his seat.

"That's not fair, you asshole." Pierre stills and turns back to me. "You can't say sorry and think that makes everything okay. I hated myself for years. Hated myself because you made me believe I was less than. How can I forgive you when I can never forget how you made me feel?"

Pierre looks at me, and that's when I see a tear fall down his cheek. "Issy."

"No," I point at him, "you don't get to care now."

"I never knew," he tells me.

"You never knew that I loved you with all my heart," I yell at him.

Pierre runs his hand through his hair. "I don't know what you want me to say, Issy, because sorry isn't enough it seems. What do you need from me to make it right?"

"I don't need anything from you."

"Why not?" he questions me. I ignore his question and go to step around him, but his hulking mass steps in front of me and stops me. "Why won't you let me make this right with you?"

"Move," I hiss at him.

"No." My mouth falls open in shock at his audacity. Anger bubbles to the surface, and the next thing I know, I am barreling into him, but this time he's ready for me and grabs me and pushes me up against the wall. "What the hell, Issy. Would you stop trying to fight me."

"Let go of me," I growl at him as my hands pummel his hard chest. The next thing I know, he has my wrists cuffed with his hands and stretches them above my head, pressing himself against me. "Don't fucking touch me," I curse at him.

"You could have hurt yourself. Look at me and look at you." I may be small, but I can handle my own.

"The only person hurting me is you." The barbed sting lands. Pierre sucks in a deep breath before letting it out. "Let go of me before I knee you in the balls," I warn. He spreads my legs wide with his own so I can't destroy his crown jewels as he presses himself against me harder.

"I get it, Issy. You hate me. But I think what you need to do is let me have it. Say everything you need to say to me, get it off your chest, yell, scream, fight me, but get it out. I hate that my stupidity is still festering inside you."

"Don't flatter yourself," I throw back at him.

"And yet you are just as angry with me as you were all those years ago. I'd say that's some festering," he says, staring down at me. I swallow because he's right. We broke up a lifetime ago, but it still cuts deep. "Let it out."

Tears well in my eyes, I hate being vulnerable, and I hate even more that I like the feeling of him pressed against me. That his muscles ripple with each of his movements against me. I close my eyes and try to steady my heaving heart.

"Issy, please, I need to fix this. I need to fix us."

"Why? My life was going great until you crashed back into it."

"Well, mine isn't. It's completely out of control right now, and this situation is the only thing I have control over," he explains.

"You don't have control over me."

He raises a brow. "Really, because our current position would say otherwise." He smirks. That motherfucker smirks.

"Get off me. This isn't as cute as you think it is," I say through gritted teeth.

"Probably not. In my mind, if I ever got you in this position, we wouldn't have any clothes on and we wouldn't have an audience," he murmurs.

What! I can't believe he just said that. "You're still an egotistical jerk."

"Fine," he says, letting go of me as he moves away. I miss feeling him against me and that is a problem. He storms away and takes his seat as I give myself a shake before walking back to my seat. "Us arguing back and forth isn't going to help things." He huffs as he takes a sip of his drink. He's right. "I appreciate you coming with me today to get Frankston. And don't worry, I'll make sure to find somewhere by the end of the week. I hate the fact that my being around you is triggering. I don't want to be your trigger."

He is a trigger. I didn't realize how much until now that he's back in my life. Harper is right, I need to let this go for my own mental sake. We don't have to be friends, but we should be able to co-exist without fighting. For fifteen years you've been harboring this, it's not healthy. Plus, Harper and Felix are becoming serious, and that means he is going to be sticking around, especially if he gets a contract with The Mavericks. If you keep fighting him at every step, then no one is going to want to hang around you. Pierre is Felix's family, and he will choose him over me. I will not let him take away the friendships I've built for myself in New York. He doesn't get another thing from me. I throw back a big gulp of tequila and feel the burn as it slides down my throat.

"Fine."

Pierre looks at me, not understanding what I'm saying.

"I'm prepared to put the past in the past and leave it there for the sake of Harper and Felix because as much as you might not like it, she is so going becoming your sister-in-law at some stage. This means you will be her family which means if I want to stay in her life I'm going to have to put up with you in it." He raises a brow at me. "I'm doing this for them."

"Not you?"

"Fine for me, too. I'm sick of hating you even though you deserve it. You're right. Everyone is fucking right I need to let it go. It isn't healthy for me to harbor this much hate toward you after all these years. I forgive you." The words are like razor blades against my throat, and I cannot believe I am saying them, but as soon as they are out of my mouth, my shoulders feel lighter. Is this some kind of placebo effect or something?

"You forgive me?" he asks skeptically.

I suck in a deep breath. "Yes. I'm letting go of the past. As much as I can, but these lingering feelings won't vanish overnight. I will try to be civil toward you, going forward. We won't be best friends or even friends ..."

"Acquaintances?" he asks.

"Yes."

"Guess that's better than what I was before." He smiles. Urgh. Stop being so Canadian with that smile.

"It's one level up from where you were, and the jury is still out, you could be relegated again," I warn him.

He holds up his hands. "I won't let you down. Maybe we can start again. I'm sure we are not the same people we once were. We don't really know each other anymore." There might be some truth in that. "Hi, I'm Pierre St. Pierre, Captain for South Dakota Devils, and the league's top scorer. Whose life has imploded and is on the brink of retirement," he says, holding out his hand to me, which I eye suspiciously.

He's serious? He waves his outstretched hand for me to take. I am doing this for me, not him.

I take his hand and shake it. "Hi, I'm Issy Alessi, CEO of The Alessi Agency, Sports Manager to the stars, and I'm not going to let you retire," I tell him seriously.

"I don't doubt that, but it's not up to you. It's all in Bill's hands and the lawyers."

We both take our seats again, and I can handle this change of subject more than the one about our past. "Honestly, Bill is going to let you go, even if that means you're a free agent for the year. As you said, you're the league's highest scorer. Now to be fair, most teams in the league have great centers, but we all know you can easily score from any position you play, and that is the real bonus."

"Think that's the first nice thing you've said to me." He smirks.

I roll my eyes. "I'm trying."

"I appreciate it." He nods.

"Do you think Bill's wife knows about Kitty?" I ask him.

Pierre shrugs. "I don't think so."

"Unless they have an arrangement," I add.

"Michelle doesn't seem like the type that is into sharing, but who knows what happens behind closed doors."

"Bill is a billionaire. This kind of scandal could tank his company's stocks, also destabilize his team, and of course, implode his family. He has more to lose than you do right now. The video you have of him and Kitty is leverage, and if he's smart, he will take what you are offering. I've reached out to The Mavericks personally to let them know that you want to move from South Dakota to Manhattan to play with your brother. They are interested, but they need to discuss it. Is there another team you would be interested in playing for if The Mavericks don't work out? I mean, we have the overseas leagues like Scandinavia or Russia?"

"I might as well retire if they are my options," he grumbles.

"And what happens if you do have to retire? What is the next step?" I ask him.

"Coaching, that's where I want to go next," he advises.

"Want me to put that on the table too with The Mavericks?" I ask.

"Sure. But it would be Plan B. I'm not ready to retire, and it certainly isn't like this. I have another cup in me and that's what I want to do. If I can do it with my brother, then that would be the icing on the cake for me."

"That would be pretty cool if you could achieve that," I tell him.

He smiles. "It would, it's something we always talked about growing up," he then frowns, "unless that isn't what he wants anymore. You said that he didn't want to be on the same team as me."

"Think it's more a sibling rivalry thing. You were hard on him growing up," I tell him.

"Because I wanted him to be the best."

"I know, but Felix is more sensitive than you, as the baby of the family. He used to idolize you, always did, and following in your shadow his entire career has been hard on him. You are one of the greatest players in the game, and everyone automatically compares the two of you. That can be hard to live up to. Don't forget you forged the way for him," I explain.

"But he got in all on his own. I never helped him. You don't think people compared me to Dad?"

"Hardly a comparison between what your father achieved and what you have. He wasn't a champion like you. Yes, he was a good player, but that was all he was, good. Felix is in the shadow of a legend. It's normal for everyone to compare two brothers when they play, it happens in all sports."

"I don't want to mess up his career. If he doesn't want me in New York, let's look for somewhere else," Pierre says.

"Let's worry about that if it happens. Felix will be okay with it, he's probably worried about starting with a new team and you might undermine him in front of his teammates, then he's lost their respect before he's even started."

"I would never," Pierre argues.

"Not on purpose, but as a brother, you know what it's like."

"I get it." He nods. "What do you honestly think about Felix and Harper dating?" he asks, changing the subject again.

"Honestly, I was weirded out by it at first, but now ... seeing them together it kind of works."

"What were you thinking, sending them to the same resort?"

"I didn't do it on purpose. Felix should have known better than to tell you about it."

He smirks. "Felix didn't want to tell me, but I got it out of him, he was freaking out."

"The place is huge, I didn't think they would run into each other," I explain.

His eyes widen with curiosity. "You've been there?"

"Yes."

"And is that something you like doing? I mean, you went there last night, too," he asks.

"Who wouldn't want to go to Paradise and have all your

fantasies delivered? Most men in the city are self-absorbed and there for their own pleasure, not yours."

"Sounds like you've been dating the wrong men. I was never selfish in that department." He smirks. My cheeks heat at the memory. No, he was most certainly not selfish, and again another reason why he has ruined my life. "So, this place lets you do anything?" he asks when I ignore his remark.

I smirk. "Anything, within reason."

"What were your fantasies then?" he questions.

"I'm not telling you that. We are not there in our friendship," I snap.

A big smile falls across his stupidly handsome face. "You just called what we have a friendship. I'll take it."

I roll my eyes, but a stupid smile pushes against my lips. "Keep asking me questions about my sex life and you will be demoted," I warn him.

He grins. "Noted. No personal questions, yet." He arches a brow at me.

I shake my head. "Speaking of personal questions, can I ask what went wrong between you and Kitty?"

"So, you can ask about my sex life, but I can't ask about yours?"

"I wasn't asking you about your sex life. I was asking about your relationship," I remark.

"Same thing. That's the million-dollar question, isn't it?" He lets out a deep sigh. "Honestly, I don't know. I thought we were in love, but now I think she loved the idea of us more than she loved us. Since getting together her online presence has grown, and I was happy for her at the start as she has been working hard on building her modelling brand. As her following grew and the more opportunities she got, she made new friends, and I saw the girl I thought I knew start to change. She was partying a lot behind the scenes, she stopped coming to my games, she started spending money on extravagant things, and she became distant. For example, after your father's funeral, she didn't come home for two days. I needed her, I was a wreck, and we had a do-or-die game. When she came home, I found out she had been partying in Vegas."

Oh wow. They always looked so happy online, not that I was stalking them or anything.

"And when we lost our last game, she left the stadium because she was embarrassed. She had the audacity to tell me that my losing the game embarrassed her in front of her friends." Damn that's cold. I saw that game, it was brutal. "She left me that night and partied with her friends."

"I'm sorry." And I mean it.

"I don't know what I did wrong for her to cheat." He stills. "Shit," he curses, raking his fingers through his hair. "That just hit me. I get it now. I don't understand why Kitty cheated, just like you didn't know why I did it. I'm sorry. This sucks being on this side." No shit. "I know dating a hockey player is hard, we are always away working, and I'm constantly training, but I didn't think it was enough to break us up."

"Maybe the two of you started growing in different directions. Her career was taking off while you're at the height of yours," I suggest. Pierre ponders this. "Is that why you kissed me?" I ask him.

Pierre sits there quietly mulling over my question. "I kissed you because I wanted to." Oh. He then looks uncomfortable as he rubs his neck again. "I've been thinking about this for months. Why would I kiss you if I was happy in my relationship? Kissing you made me realize that my feelings for Kitty had changed." Wow. "You know I'm sorry for kissing you. That wasn't the right thing to do, especially then. It was an emotional day, and my emotions got the better of me, which is still no excuse." Wasn't expecting that apology. "Was a good kiss, though." He looks up at me, giving me a heated stare.

My cheeks suddenly turn red reliving that kiss in my mind.

It was good. And I hated how much I liked it. "I didn't appreciate you making me the other woman, though."

Pierre rubs his chin. "Yeah, I see how that looks now."

"Why do you think Kitty fell for Bill? It's such an unlikely coupling other than money," I ask him.

"Honestly, I think that's all it is, money. I remember her telling me about one of her girlfriends dating a billionaire and he was buying her all these extravagant things."

"It's not like you're poor. Did Kitty get anything extravagant recently?" I ask.

Pierre frowns. "I don't know, she always seemed to be shopping. She was making her own money, so I never questioned what she spent it on. Maybe Bill was financing her. I just don't understand why he would do that to me. We used to go over once a month for family lunches on a Sunday. Bill would take me and some of the boys golfing. Kitty used to shop with Bill's daughters, they were friends." Wow. I had no idea they were that close, it kind of makes it worse.

"Do you think Kitty is going to try to get you back?" I ask.

"She is going to try to save her image. Most things at that wedding were in exchange for publicity. I have her muted on everything right now, so I'm not sure what she's up to. Harper told her that she needed to say there was a family emergency. I'm not sure what's going on because the thought of checking my messages gives me a panic attack, as you've bore witness to yesterday."

"Do they happen a lot?" I ask him.

He shakes his head. "Not really, but they started to happen more frequently since the funeral."

Am I giving him anxiety? Now that makes me feel shit and I shouldn't feel shit, but I do. "Want me to check your messages?" I ask before I realize what I've said.

Pierre seems as surprised as I am. "You would? Harper's

checked yesterday's but mainly she was focused on Kitty and her family's texts."

"I'm sure your teammates will have questions," I tell him.

"You're right. I haven't even thought about them. Shit," he says, running his hand through his hair. "Here," he says, handing me his phone. "Pin code is 6969." I raise a brow at him. "Harper gave me that same look." He smirks.

When I open his phone, the number of notifications from people is immense. I scroll down through them and a lot of his friends are checking in on him, asking if he is okay. They are sorry to hear about the emergency he's had, and they are thinking about him. There are some horrific texts from Kitty abusing him for being a coward and leaving her to deal with the mess he created. Then texts from Bill attacking Pierre, telling him that threatening him is not what he wants to do and blah blah blah. There are also messages from journalists who want him to comment on the rumors that he called off his wedding. Shit. Yeah. I would have a panic attack if I read all this, too. It's wanting to give me one now and it has nothing to do with me.

"Your teammates, I'll send a message letting them know you will reach out soon, you hope they enjoy their time in Italy, and thank them for making the trek," I say as I start to type out a message.

"Yeah, that would be great, thanks," he says, watching me work.

"I've also put an out of office style message on your phone so it will tell people that you are uncontactable and if it's urgent to call Marcus or The Alessi Agency, and if it's PR related, they need to contact The Rose Agency. I've given them Harper's office details. So, it's all done," I say, handing him back the phone after twenty minutes.

"You can do that? Thanks," he says, staring at his now clear phone.

"Hope it helps. Maybe these panic attacks are something we should keep an eye on. Should I tell Marcus to maybe look at a sports psychologist? You might need to speak to someone. Things are about to get rough for you depending on which way it all falls."

"Once I've got Frankston with me, all my worries will cease to exist."

Not sure how a dog is going to save him from his problems, but I don't say anything. "About Frankston. Do you think Kitty is going to fight you for custody of him?" I ask.

"She wouldn't dare. He is my baby. She knows that," he argues.

"Exactly, she knows how much Frankston means to you."

"He's mine. Always has been. I got him after we broke up the first time. I caught her cheating with an ex, and I got him to help heal my heart, but then a month later we got back together," he explains.

"Kitty's cheated on you before?" He nods. "And you took her back?" I stare at him in disbelief.

"In hindsight, maybe not the greatest idea. But she was remorseful and really made it up to me, and I know what that's like to not get a second chance when you mess up. I thought that was my karma for what I did to you. And I knew how it felt not being able to apologize." Our situations are completely different. I am not taking responsibility for this disaster. "She will have a fight on her hands if she dares try to take Frankston away from me."

"Maybe speak to your lawyer and make sure you get all your paperwork in order in case she wants to fight." He nods. "This could turn nasty with Kitty. Are you prepared to go public with this?"

"I will do what I have to, don't you worry about that," he says seriously.

10

PIERRE

That was a rollercoaster of a plane ride. The ending was unexpected, but I'll take it. Working back to being friends, and no funny business, I'll take. I'd rather have her in my life as something than nothing at all. It was hard to hear how much my betrayal hurt her. I knew I broke her heart, but I didn't realize how much I changed her outlook on relationships. I feel horrible about that. My stupidity hurt the one person in the world who didn't deserve it. Now that she's giving me a kind of second chance at friendship, I'm going to show her that I'm not the dumbass she remembers. The fact that she was willing to fly across the country to help get my dog and sort through my messages so I wouldn't have to see them meant a lot. I know being around me reminds her of our past, but I'm hoping we can create new memories together that will change that for her.

The car winds its way up the long driveway toward my home.

"This is huge." Issy gasps.

"That's what she said," I tease, which earns me an elbow to the ribs.

"There's so much nature, look at all the trees. I don't know if you'll be able to return to city life since you've been living here. You hardly have neighbors. I get why you were worried about Frankston now."

"Yeah, he loves going for a run. It's a nice home, or it was a nice home. I'm not sure how I feel, it was only last week I left it thinking my life was going one way, and now it's taken a turn the other."

"It's not far to commute from Connecticut into the city or Long Island, even Jersey has nature, there are options," Issy explains.

I called the pet sitter and said that we were missing Frankston so much that we are flying him to Italy to be with us, and that a friend was coming to collect him, and he didn't have to wait for them to arrive. I don't need the pet sitter asking questions.

We pull up to the main entrance and get out of the car. I'm going to pack some things that I'll need for the next month. I don't know what is going to happen with this house. Is Kitty going to fight me on it? I bought it, the house is in my name, but can she legally try to take it? We aren't married, but we were engaged. This is a shit show. I type in the code, and I can hear the patter of Frankston's feet as I swing the door open. His happy face is the first thing I see before he jumps right into my arms and licks my face. I fall to the floor and roll around with him.

"Who's my good boy? I've missed you, buddy. It's so good to see you. I'm never ever leaving you ever again. You and me, buddy," I tell him.

Once Frankston greets me, he rushes over and launches himself at Issy, who screams as my dog accosts her.

"Oh my gosh, ew, doggy slobber." She cringes as Frankston gets her with his tongue.

"Easy boy, you need consent before doing that to a woman."
I laugh.

"And maybe dinner before digging into the main event."
Frankston shoves his nose in her crotch. *Lucky bastard.*

"Sorry, he's just excited," I tell her as I pull him away
from her.

Issy laughs. "It's okay," she assures me. "Why don't you
show me around?"

"You want a tour?" I ask, surprised.

"Yeah." She shrugs as if it's a normal request.

Okay then. I show Issy around the house. It's very much a
luxury log cabin-style home, which is most of the home vibes
around here. It's four bedrooms, five bathrooms, a formal
living room, a dining room, a great kitchen, and there's also a
beauty room for Kitty. We then go downstairs to the base-
ment where the cool stuff is. I have a games room with a pool
table and bar set up, a home theatre, and of course, a mini
museum with all my achievements, awards, and memorabilia
in it.

"This is awesome." Issy gasps.

"Yeah, the boys would come around, and in summer we
would have BBQs out by the pool. I also have a year-round ice
rink in one of the sheds out back," I tell her.

"Of course you do." She chuckles.

"I'm always training." I grin. "Look, I'm going to go pack
some bags to take back to the city with me. Go explore, and I'll
call out when I'm ready to leave.

An hour later, I've packed five suitcases, and the driver's
come to collect them and put them in the trunk of the car. I've
also packed my equipment and anything sentimental that
could be taken by an angry partner, which was Issy's sugges-
tion. For the other items that I couldn't take with me, I took
photos and sent a message to my lawyer saying that the house
is off-limits until we come to an amicable solution on it. I don't

want Kitty coming in and destroying my shit in a fit of rage, or her dumbass friends ruining the home to spite me.

"Okay, buddy, we are off on an adventure. It's going to be a long flight to your new home or your semi new home. Dad's working shit out." Frankston stares at me and gives me a big ruff as if he understands.

"Guess he understood that." Issy chuckles.

"Of course he did, he is the smartest boy," I say, smooching his face.

"Wow, you really are a dog dad."

"Can I claim myself as a DILF then?" I wink at Issy.

She shakes her head but laughs at my joke.

WE EVENTUALLY MAKE it home after the huge day, and Issy excuses herself to bed as she has work in the morning, while I help Frankston settle in. Because it was late, I took him for a walk around the block where his little nose was working overtime with all the smells. He didn't like the traffic or the constant honking or sirens, but he was a good boy and tried his hardest.

"Frankston," Issy screams.

He comes running into my bedroom and hides behind me. "What did you do boy? You are supposed to make a good first impression," I ask him. He just gives me his innocent look. Issy comes walking into my bedroom with a mangled shoe in her hand.

"I thought you said he was house-trained. He ate a pair of very expensive shoes," she shouts, waving the shoes in her hand.

"He is. He doesn't normally eat shoes," I explain. "Buddy, what the hell? What were you thinking?" I ask him. He gives me a lick. "Now is not the time to be cute. I think the upheaval has made him lash out."

Those dark eyes narrow on me and then my dog. "Marcus and Jordan are on their way, and you're not even dressed. We are going to be late for this meeting, and it's in my home. You just have to walk two steps," Issy says angrily. "Tell your dog no more eating my shoes or we are going to have a problem." She points them again at Frankston, who wags his tail happily before she walks out of my room.

"Dude, you're supposed to be on my side. I know this is a big adjustment, but it's only temporary. I'm sorry I'm making you a child of a broken home, but it's for the best, buddy. You have no idea how much Issy has gone out on a limb with us being here. We've just called a truce between us, and you are going to make her hate me again." Frankston gives me another lick. "I love you, buddy. I think I'll need to call Uncle Felix to come and take you for a walk while we have this meeting. Would you like that?" I ask him. When he jumps in my arms, I know the decision is made. I pick up my phone and call my brother.

"Hey, is there a chance you can be on doggy duties? Frankston ate one of Issy's shoes this morning, and I have an important meeting with Marcus and Jordan at the house soon. He's used to being able to roam free around the yard and not be couped up. Plus, Issy's agreed to a truce, and he's going to ruin it before it's even started," I explain to him.

Felix laughs. "Yeah, I think I can do that. I'll take him for a walk. I've already done my run this morning. You should join Sam and me on those, you'd have to wear a disguise though."

"I can't risk it, not yet, maybe you could take Frankston in the mornings with you."

"I could do that."

"Thank you."

"So, the flight back home went well between you and Issy then?" he asks.

"We settled on starting over. It was hard listening to her tell me how my actions changed her outlook on relationships, but I needed to hear it. I messed up so badly with her and I feel awful over it, but I'm choosing to be positive that she is willing to give me this second chance at friendship. Right now, I need positivity and friends, shit is about to hit the fan," I tell him.

"Harper got notifications about some blind items that have been posted online about the wedding," Felix says.

"Really? What did they say?"

"They said that a certain hockey wedding in Italy didn't get called off because of a family emergency, it was called off due to cold feet," Harper calls out.

"You could have told me we weren't alone," I grumble to my brother.

"Don't worry, Issy filled me in on your plane trip," Harper calls out again.

"Felix!"

"I'll be over in twenty."

We say our goodbyes and hang up. I walk out of my room and into the kitchen where Issy is grabbing her coffee. "Sorry about your shoes, I'll buy you some new ones." Issy gives me a dirty side-eye as she continues making her coffee. "Felix is coming over to take Frankston out today while we have the meeting."

"You didn't have to do that," she tells me.

"He needs it. It will wear him out, and he will crash for the rest of the day," I explain. "Again, I'm sorry about the shoes. He hasn't done anything like that in years."

"Look, I get it, he's flown across the country and is now in a new environment," she says, continuing to sip her coffee. "I appreciate you asking Felix to take him out while he is unsettled. I'll make sure to lock up all my shoes so he can't get to them."

"You shouldn't have to, this is your house. I can lock him in my room when I'm gone so he doesn't destroy anything."

She frowns over her mug. "You don't need to do that, it would be cruel." She reaches down and runs her fingers through Frankston's fur, who has come by to say sorry.

"I'll buy you all the shoes," I tell her.

"I'll keep that in mind." She grins.

11

ISABELLE

The buzzer goes, and I head to the front door to answer it. "Marcus," I greet Pierre's manager warmly. "And you, too, Jordan," I say, greeting Pierre's lawyer. I hold the door open and let them both in.

"Fellas, good to see you," Pierre says, welcoming them.

"Man, what the fuck is going on?" Marcus says as they embrace each other.

"Please apologize to Sonia for cutting your trip to Italy short. Tell her to pick anywhere in the world, my shout for you both," Pierre tells him.

"You don't have to do that, but I appreciate the sentiment. It was lucky we had our holiday before the wedding, so we got to see what we wanted to," Marcus tells him.

"Good to know, but the offer is there. And same to you, Jordan. I appreciate you coming all that way with your busy schedule," he tells his lawyer.

"Don't worry about it, like Marcus, I had some time traveling before the wedding. We are both here because we are worried about you." The boys take a seat in the living room.

"I'll grab us some bottles of water," I say, getting up and

heading to the fridge while the boys talk. I walk back in on Pierre telling them about catching Kitty and Bill in the garden, and then how Harper and his family sprang into action, getting him out of Italy and back to New York.

"That's why you have Harper Rose as your new PR. She's reached out and said she will loop us in on anything she finds online, so we are aware. She's been great. There has been some chatter online about the wedding. I'm not sure if she's told you," Jordan advises.

"She mentioned something this morning about a couple of blind items, but that seems to be all there is right now. I haven't had a chance to catch up with her again since getting here. Issy and I flew home to grab Frankston yesterday. You're looking into making sure I have custody of Frankston, aren't you?" Pierre asks his lawyer.

"Yes. And as South Dakota doesn't recognize common-law partnerships, Kitty isn't entitled to anything that you have. Now, of course, her lawyers could decide to fight but we aren't there yet. I haven't heard anything from Kitty's lawyers, but today we are here to discuss what we need to do regarding that. I'm assuming you and Kitty are over?" Jordan asks.

"Oh yeah, we are most certainly over," Pierre states.

"Just needed to check. There's no chance of reconciliation or anything like that?" he continues to question Pierre.

Pierre shakes his head. "I'm done."

"I understand you are angry now, but some people are able to work through infidelity to get back together," Jordan explains.

Pierre's eyes meet mine. "Kitty isn't who I want," he tells Jordan.

Why is he looking at me? He better not be talking about me. Hell no. This is a second chance at friendship, nothing else.

"Glad we sorted that. Why don't we sort out your career first before worrying about your relationship? I think that's more important right now," Jordan adds as he looks over at Marcus.

"Jordan's right. As you know, we sent an email to Bill and his team requesting that your contract be paid out for the two years remaining. That you've lost faith in the team and leadership, and that the team no longer aligns with your values."

"Executive speak for you're a cheating asshole, I like it." Pierre chuckles.

"Honestly, I can't believe Bill would be so unbelievably stupid to mess around with one of his player's partners," Marcus states.

"I've seen men do stupid shit for a beautiful woman," Jordan adds.

"I don't get what Kitty sees in him," Marcus adds.

"Dollar signs," Jordan says, before stilling. "Sorry, man, no disrespect," he says to Pierre.

"None taken, I don't understand what she sees in him either, other than his billions. Look, Kitty and I were having a lot of problems, but I wasn't expecting her to seek comfort in his arms. Last time she did, at least it was someone her age."

"She's done this before?" Jordan asks.

"At the start of the relationship. She was living in LA, and I was helping set up the Devils. It was long distance and some photos came out of her with one of her exes. The media at the time didn't know we were together," he explains.

"Sorry, man, I had no idea," Jordan says.

Pierre shrugs his shoulders. "We put it in the past and moved forward. Like someone has told me before, a leopard never changes their spots." He looks over at me, it's the same words I threw at him during the wake when he kissed me.

"Issy, have you heard anything back from The Mavericks?" Marcus asks me, pulling me back into the conversation.

"Not yet, but I'm following it up today," I tell them. Little do they know that later tonight we are having dinner with Harper's dad and using his position on the board to push for Pierre. "But I've also sent out some feelers to other teams."

"I'll do the same as well, when I get back into the office. It's going to be hard talking cryptically about you, but it's not the first time," Marcus explains.

"I appreciate it, guys. I don't want to retire, but I think we might have to look at those options, too, especially if Bill is not prepared to let me go."

"We put a retirement clause in the contract, so yes, we can invoke that if we have to. But you still have a couple more years before you need to retire. This is not how your career ends," Marcus says.

"I won't play for the Devils. And if Bill wants to be an ass, then this is going to be it because either way if I stay with them, he is going to bench me to teach me a lesson, and if he doesn't, the last thing I want to do is win him a fucking cup. And that kills me because the team deserves that win," Pierre says, raising his voice.

"THANKS SO MUCH FOR DOING THIS," I say to Harper as we leave my home. We've left Felix and Pierre together to hang out while we said we needed girl time. They are none the wiser, and I didn't want to get Pierre's hopes up about The Mavericks if we aren't able to do it. After dinner with Harper's dad, we are meeting up with Kimberly and Meadow for drinks. I need to get out of the house and away from Pierre's looming presence.

"It's no problem at all," Harper says as we get into the car.

"Who would have thought this is where you would be all these years later, Pierre's advocate." I tease.

"The universe works in mysterious ways." She chuckles. "You two seem to be co-existing."

"I'm counting down the days till he leaves." I smile as I hold up my countdown app.

"Issy!" Harper laughs.

"He's annoying."

"Guess annoying is a step up from hating him."

"See, progress," I tell her which earns me a side-eye. "I'm doing this for you," I tell her.

"Me?" she questions.

"Because of you and Felix."

"You shouldn't be doing this for us, you should be doing it for you. It's time, Issy."

"I know. But what am I meant to do if I don't hate him?" I ask her.

Harper pats my hand. "Maybe you could be friends." Friends? We aren't going to KiKi over brunch together. "Judging by your face, that's a no."

"It is what it is between us. There's been too much time and too much hurt. Please don't push this," I ask her.

"Noted. No more meddling, I promise. I'm proud of you."

Her praise is nice to hear. "Thanks."

"Felix appreciates it, too," she adds.

We arrive at the restaurant where Harper's father is waiting for us.

"My girls, how are we?" he says, welcoming us with hugs and kisses. A pang of grief hits me realizing I'll never get another hug from my father. Urgh. *Now is not the time to lose it, Issy.* "To what do I owe the pleasure of two beautiful women for dinner? Not that I would ever complain." He chuckles.

"Dad, we need your help," Harper says, cutting right to the chase.

Mr. Rose's face drops from a smile to serious. "What is it, my love."

Harper launches into why we are back from Italy earlier than was planned. She explains what happened to Pierre because of Bill and Kitty. And then she explains how Pierre wants to see if there is a chance that he can move to The Mavericks to play with Felix. He sits there for a long time in silence, absorbing the news.

"That is one big mess," he finally answers.

"I know, but we thought there was a chance that you could sway the team in his favor," Harper says.

"We've put feelers out with The Mavericks, but it's hard to explain why. He technically has two years left on his contract with the Devils, but as you can understand, he does not want to stay there. Pierre will consider retirement if Bill won't let him go," I explain.

"That boy still has a couple of good years left. He was the highest scorer in the league this season."

"He thought he would be finishing his career in South Dakota, but now he wants it to be here in New York with his brother," I add.

Mr. Rose shakes his head. "Having the two of them on the same team would be a game changer, not just for the game but for the club. Could you imagine the PR and opportunities it could provide? Ticket sales would go through the roof. Is Felix okay with this?" he asks Harper.

"Yes. He is."

"Then I guess I'll see what I can do. I'll arrange a meeting with Coach Anderson to see if there is a chance that the team has space. I'm not sure who is in or out for the next season," he explains.

"Thanks, Dad, we really appreciate it," Harper says.

"Not a problem at all, my love, now fill me in on what's been happening with you two."

"THAT WENT WELL," I say to Harper as we say goodbye to her dad.

"We just have to wait now and see. It's going to start getting harder to contain the story because Kitty has been silent on her socials, and from someone who posts as frequently as she does, the public is becoming suspicious. Even her bridesmaids are silent, and they post as much as she does. All the guests have thankfully been respectful and are just showing how much fun they are having in Italy or wherever they are. I've spoken to his family, and they are still having the best time in Italy, and no one has spotted them yet, but time is ticking on this story."

"I don't get what Bill is playing at."

"Probably thinks Pierre can't do shit and is hoping he freaks out and succumbs to his threats," Harper advises.

"He's still threatening him?"

"I'm assuming he is, but Pierre hasn't said anything. I just remember seeing the messages come through on his phone while on the plane," Harper explains.

"I saw them too."

"You did?" she asks, surprised.

"Pierre's been suffering panic attacks," I tell her.

"He has? Felix hasn't told me. Is he okay?"

"I think so. He said Frankston would make things better, and I'm assuming they are as he seems slightly more relaxed. I muted the notifications on his phone from anyone who wasn't family because every ping of his phone stressed him out," I explain to her.

"Good idea," she says. "I think boys' time tonight will help too. So how about we forget all about everyone's shit and go have some fun. You deserve to let off some steam."

"I so do." I grin.

12

PIERRE

Issy is out on a girls' night with Harper and some friends. It was nice having my brother over for dinner together, catching up, drinking beers, and watching highlights of the season's goals. Which happen to feature me a lot. He left hours ago, and Issy still isn't home. Did she go out to her sex club? Like the other night. I'm obviously cramping her style being here, it's not like she can invite men over. Urgh. The thought of watching some asshole walk into her home and her take him up to her room to fuck him while I am downstairs makes me sick. I don't have the right to be jealous. I shouldn't be jealous because I'm supposed to be mourning the loss of my ex-fiancée, but instead, I'm obsessing over what Issy is doing and who it's with. That's not right. At least she doesn't hate me as much anymore and I can see she is attempting to be friendlier, which Frankston nearly destroyed this morning with his damn teeth and slobber. I took a picture and messaged Harper to ask her to help me find a replacement pair of shoes, she sent me the link, and I bought them today. They should arrive tomorrow.

I hear a key in the door as does Frankston, and before I have a chance to stop him, he is jumping out of the bed, paws the door open, and rushes out.

"Frankie," I call after him.

Shit.

I jump out of bed and rush after my dog, who is determined to make Issy hate me again. I hear a scream and then giggles and when I come around the corner, I see Issy on the ground and Frankston humping her while licking her face.

Fucking Frankston.

"What the hell, buddy," I say, grabbing Frankston off Issy. "I'm so sorry," I tell her. She waves my apology away. "Let me grab him," I tell her as I pull him away and instantly put him into air jail. He gives me a bark of unhappiness, but he's lost privileges for causing that scene. "Frankie, I taught you better than that. Are you trying to get us kicked out?" He licks my face as he continues to wiggle in my arms. I place him on my bed and point my finger at him. "Bad boy. You need a timeout." He flops down on the bed and gives me a gruff woof as I slowly exit the bedroom, closing the door behind me. "I'm so sorry about him, he's not normally that enthusiastic ..." I start to say and stop when I see Issy has stripped off to her underwear and is currently searching through the fridge. "Um, Issy?" Issy turns around quickly and screams. "It's me, Pierre," I say, holding up my hands. Her brows pull together as those dark eyes narrow on me.

"What are you doing in my kitchen?"

Is she serious? "I'm staying here."

She tries to search for that bit of information until she eventually finds it. "I forgot you were here. I'm starving, I want a bacon sandwich before bed," she mumbles, turning back and looking into her fridge. Her words sound slurred as she sways a little.

"Are you drunk?" I question her.

Issy whirls around unbalancing herself, but she recovers

quickly. "And what if I am?" she says, placing her hands on her hips.

A smile forms on my face. I haven't seen this side of Issy before. "Guess that explains why you're in your underwear unless ..." I say, walking toward her, my hands landing on the granite of the island countertop.

"Your dog slobbered all over me. It was gross." Then her brows pull together. "Unless what?"

Thank you, Frankston. My eyes run up and down her toned body, taking her all in. She's wearing a sexy set of black lace panties and a bra. I can see her dark nipples pressing against the fabric, and they are hard.

"Unless you're trying to kill me."

"Kill you. How?" She looks at me with such confusion, and it's adorable.

I walk around the island and slowly make my way over to where she is standing. "Showing me what I can't have. By giving me an image that is going to be seared into my mind and every time my hand wraps around my cock it's going to be this that I think about."

Tension swirls between us. Issy swallows as her eyes rake over my body. I'm wearing nothing but a thin pair of pajama pants that leave nothing to the imagination as I feel myself thickening with each sweep of her eyes over me.

"I hate that you still look so good," Issy whispers.

I run a hand down over my stomach cockily. "Yeah, princess, you like what you see?"

Then her brows pull together, and she looks like she winces in pain. "Missy Jenkins ..." she says, and I still. The girl she caught me with that night. The worst night of my life, one night as well as many that I wish I could do over, and choose a different path. "I see her smug face, her spit glistening off your cock. She looks so triumphant that she's the one on her knees for you."

Shit.

There was so much going on that night that I never noticed what Missy was doing. "Issy," I say her name, reaching for her. She takes a step back from me. "That's what I see every time I look at you. I can't escape that night. It's continuously on loop. I can't forget that image or the feeling I had in that moment. It's seared into my soul."

Fuck.

I rake my hands through my hair. "You know I'm sorry about that."

"I'm not trying to be a bitch, it's just what I see when I look at you. And I don't know if that will ever go away."

Her words are like daggers in my heart. I'm never getting her back. She may have forgiven me, but nothing I do or say can erase that image from her brain. Issy will never see me as anything other than that moment in her life. The realization that the woman who still owns pieces of my heart will never want those pieces again is a crushing blow.

"I get it. How about I cook you up that bacon sandwich? Looks like you had a good night with the girls, and you're going to need it. Go wash up and I'll bring it up when it's ready," I tell her.

"That would be nice," she says before staggering through the kitchen. I hear her curse and moan as she climbs the stairs to her bedroom.

It doesn't take me long to make her the sandwich. I grab a bottle of water as she's going to need that, and make my way up to her bedroom. The door is open, and when I poke my head into her room, she isn't there.

"Issy?" I call out. The bathroom door opens, and she stumbles out of it, fresh-faced and in a black slip dress that seems as indecent as her underwear. "I have your sandwich."

"Thank you," she squeals before jumping into bed.

I walk over and place the water bottle on her bedside table

and wait for her to get comfortable before handing her the plate. She takes it and takes a massive bite of the sandwich and moans. My dick thinks it's for him, I remind him she's not into us like that. "This is so good," she mumbles around her bite.

"Glad you like it. I'll see you in the morning," I tell her.

"Wait," she says. "Come, sit, talk, while I eat." She pats the space beside her. Confused, I take a seat and watch her eat. "I don't normally get this drunk," she states as she continues to inhale the sandwich. "I'm just stressed."

"Because of me?" I ask.

She chews on her mouthful before answering me, "Yes."

"I don't mean to stress you out."

Issy waves my words away. "I know. This isn't your fault. It's a me thing."

"Kind of is a me thing, too. I crashed into your life like a wrecking ball. You didn't ask for any of this, Issy."

"You didn't deserve what happened to you either," she whispers softly before reaching her hand out to me. I take it, linking our fingers together. "I'm sorry I've hated you for so long. Didn't mean for it to take over half my life, but it did," she confesses.

Dammit, Issy, my heart. "You don't have to apologize to me." I bring her hand to my lips and kiss it.

"I should have done it for Dad. He tried so many times to get us into the same room, and I wouldn't. I couldn't do it even for him and now … he's not even here to see us try," she says, bursting into tears.

Shit.

I push aside her empty plate and pull her into my arms as she cries. Issy is still dealing with the death of her father, and my being around is making her realize how much she's lost. I never meant to cause her pain or make things worse for her. I wanted to be here for my own selfish reasons, which was I can't stop thinking about our kiss. But now I see what she needs is for me to be her friend.

I can do that. I'm going to do that. I owe her that.

"MORNING," Issy says sheepishly as she walks into the kitchen and heads over to the coffee machine. "I'm sorry about last night. I don't normally get that drunk."

"You have nothing to apologize for. Hope you had a great night with the girls. Felix texted and said Harper was a little worse for wear this morning, too," I tell her as I shovel eggs into my mouth. Issy nods. She feels awkward now as she sips her coffee slowly. I know how much she hates showing vulnerability in front of people. All her life she has been the strong one so when that façade falls, she's embarrassed.

"Guess, um, I'm going to get ready and head to the office." She finishes her espresso and bolts from the kitchen.

"Issy," I call out as I follow after her. "You don't have to be awkward around me now."

She chews her nail. "I cried myself to sleep in your arms, of course it's awkward."

"You were missing your dad and having a down moment, most humans do," I reassure her.

"Guess I'm used to crying alone," she confesses.

"Do you do that often?" I ask. She nods. Dammit, I feel for her. "You don't have to cry alone anymore, you've got me," I tell her.

"For the week," she adds with a smile.

"Yes, for the week. Which reminds me, I should probably start looking for somewhere for me and Frankston to move into."

Issy bites her bottom lip. "That might be hard when no one knows you're here or that you and Kitty have broken up. If you need to stay a little longer, that's fine. Also, you don't know if you are staying in New York."

My mouth forms a wide smile. "Really?" I'm shocked. I thought she was counting down the days for me to go. I've seen the app on her phone.

"Frankston probably wouldn't cope well with another move."

"No, he wouldn't," I say.

"You have enough on your plate at the moment. Adding looking for an apartment while you're in hiding might be too much," she suggests.

"Thanks, I really appreciate it."

"It's all good. Look, I must get ready for work. Fingers crossed Bill comes to the party today," she says. I give her a nod, and she bounces back up the stairs.

※

THE FRONT DOOR opens not long after Issy leaves. "Did you forget something?" I call out as Frankston runs to welcome Issy home again. Then I hear screaming, and it's not Issy. I get up and rush into the foyer to see Violetta Alessi getting assaulted by my dog.

"Get off me, ew, stop licking me." She squeals, trying to get away from Frankston.

"Frankston, heel," I command, and he stops and rushes to my side.

"Pierre? What the hell are you doing in my sister's home?" She looks around and panic falls across her face. "What did you do to Issy? Do I need to call the cops? Aren't you supposed to be in Italy getting married?"

I guess Issy has not informed her sisters that I'm staying here.

"About that," I say, rubbing my neck, "Kitty and I are no longer together."

Violetta's mouth falls open. "Did you leave her at the altar for Issy?"

"What! No. Why would you think that?"

"Um, because you are in my sister's home with no clothes on instead of on your honeymoon," she states as if I'm the idiot. "Why the hell are you in my sister's home? She hates you."

"She did. We're friends now."

"Have you lost your ever-loving mind?" Violetta glares at me.

"No. It's true. Call her."

Violetta pulls out her phone and calls Issy. "Why the hell is Pierre St. Pierre in your house with a dog?" I can't hear what Issy says, but her sister's eyes widen. "I'm here because I needed to borrow a bag, but that is beside the point," she argues. "He says you're friends. I thought we hated him." Violetta nods. "Fine, I'll ask him, but this conversation isn't done. I'm telling Eve," she says before hanging up. Violetta folds her arms and glares at me. "Issy said you would explain it all to me." She impatiently thumps her feet for me to continue.

"Fine. Would you like a coffee?" I ask her.

13

ISABELLE

> Violetta: 911. Family meeting. Issy's office.
> 1pm.

With my hangover this morning, this is the last thing I want to be dealing with, but I probably should have told my sisters that Pierre was staying with me. Honestly, it slipped my mind. I also didn't think they would pop into my house unannounced. Now I know where my stuff goes. They have been stealing it while I'm at work. We are going to have a conversation about boundaries and personal belongings.

Moments later, Evelina walks into my office. "What the hell is going on? Why is Vi calling an emergency meeting?"

I shrug. "You don't go into my home and steal my clothes, do you?"

My sister stills. "No offence, but we don't have the same style. Why?"

Offence taken. "I'm stylish," I argue.

"In your way, yes," my sister adds.

"What does that mean?" I question her.

"Means that we have different tastes."

"No. You think my style is bad," I tell her.

"That's not what I said."

"That's what it sounds like," I argue.

Evelina rolls her eyes. "You dress conservatively compared to me. There's a lot of black."

"This is New York, everyone wears black." Sorry, not all of us can be Little Miss Sunshine.

"See you're upset now." Evelina huffs.

"Because you don't like the way I dress."

"You know that's not what I said. How has this turned into an argument, and what does this have to do with Vi's message?" my sister asks, getting angry.

"Nothing, but I just found out that Violetta has been letting herself into my home and taking my clothes," I tell her.

"Then why are you yelling at me?"

"I wanted to know if you had been doing it, too. I thought I was going crazy when I couldn't find things in my closet and now, I know it's you guys."

"It's Vi not me," Evelina argues.

Before I get a chance to continue this argument, the thief herself walks in. "I can't believe you didn't tell us Pierre was living with you."

Evelina stares between the two of us.

"I forgot," I tell her.

"Forgot. That man is not something you forget. And does he ever wear a shirt?" Violetta asks.

"No. It's annoying," I grumble.

"So annoying, especially when he looks so good without a shirt," Vi states.

"Right?" But also, why is Vi checking him out?

"Hold on. Back it up. Did you say Pierre is living with Issy, as in Pierre St. Pierre?" Evelina asks Vi.

"Yeah, that one. Would you keep up, Eve?" she says, rolling her eyes.

Eve shakes her head. "I feel like I'm missing part of a conversation."

Vi sighs. "I went over to Issy's place to borrow a bag that I needed to go with a dress for this event I have tonight ..."

"Which bag?" I ask her.

"Doesn't matter." Vi waves me off.

"Yes, it does. How many bags have you borrowed? Because I'm missing some," I tell her.

"Oh. I thought I returned them. I'll bring them back next time. Anyway, I go over there and am assaulted by this giant golden fluff ball of a dog who loves smelling your crotch and slobbering all over you," Vi complains.

"A dog? In Issy's house?" Eve asks.

"Right? She is usually so anal about things, but he was there, and then I saw none other than Pierre half naked. And boy was it a shock. I was excited there for a second, thinking Issy got lucky with some random, and she had left him there to entertain himself till she returned," Vi explains.

"Wait. Isn't Pierre supposed to be in Italy getting married? Why the hell is he in Issy's home?" Eve asks.

"No, get this, apparently he and Harper busted Kitty getting her freak on with Bill Reeves in the garden the night before his wedding, and so Pierre did a Runaway Bride and hightailed it to New York," Vi explains to Eve.

"To your home?" Eve asks.

"It was a shock," I answer.

"And get this, he then makes Issy fly him to South Dakota to pick up his dog," Vi adds.

"You were locked on a plane for however many hours with him? What is going on? Are you okay? Is he okay? I can't believe Kitty is cheating on Pierre with Bill Reeves, the old guy," Eve says.

"No one knows. You need to keep your mouth shut," I warn Vi. She rolls her eyes. "We are trying to get him out of his Devils contract, as obviously, Pierre does not want to go back and play for them. He wants to play for The Mavericks."

"The Mavericks?" Eve asks, sounding surprised.

"Bill is being a dick about the contract. Pierre is adamant that he won't play for them. He would rather retire than play for that team."

"Wow, that's, wow," Eve says, sounding shocked.

"Things are delicate at the moment," I advise them.

"I was wondering why Kitty was so quiet about her wedding, not that I cared. I thought it was because they signed an exclusive agreement for the photos, but how wrong was I?" Vi adds.

"Is Pierre okay? He must be heartbroken," Eve asks.

"He didn't look too heartbroken when I saw him," Vi remarks.

"They were having problems, he said. He tried to call off the wedding a couple of times."

"And he told you that?" Eve asks.

"Was that before or after he kissed you?" Vi asks.

I still.

"Wait, he kissed you. When?" Eve asks.

I glare at my sister. I told her that in strictest confidence. "Oops," she says.

"Issy, what is she talking about?"

"It doesn't matter."

"Um, yes it does," Eve adds angrily.

"He kissed her at our dad's wake, reminiscing about old times. But don't worry, Issy told him to get lost," Vi fills her in.

"Issy! He was engaged." Eve gasps.

"I didn't ask for it. He kind of just did it. I told him it was wrong."

"And now you're living together. Tell me this, are you healing his broken heart?" Vi teases.

"No." I glare at her.

"The man looks good without a shirt on, I wouldn't blame you," she states. I don't like the way my sister keeps bringing that up.

"Vi!" Eve gasps.

"What? The man's single, he can do what he wants," she argues.

"Nothing is happening between us, and nothing ever will. I'm helping an old friend during a difficult time," I explain to them.

"The same man you have hated for fifteen years, and suddenly you're besties," Vi adds.

I glower at her as I lift my chin. "I've decided to forgive him and move on from my hate. It's not good for me," I tell them.

"I've been telling you this for years," Eve states.

"I wasn't ready, and it was easier to hate him."

"I still hate him," Vi adds.

"I can't believe he kissed you while engaged," Eve murmurs.

"To be fair, I was having a breakdown and we were arguing and ..."

"Passion will do that." Vi grins.

"But he was engaged to someone else," Eve argues.

"And Kitty was screwing his boss, so I guess that makes them even," Vi states.

My office phone rings, and it's my assistant. She tells me Marcus wants an urgent meeting in his office. Shit. This can't be good.

"Guys, I have to go, something urgent has come up. Can we continue this conversation later?" I tell them.

"Fine. I have to go get ready anyway," Vi says as she gets up and walks out of the office.

"Are you really okay with Pierre?" Eve asks as she gets up.

"Yeah, it's weird, but I'm fine."

"Good. I don't want to lose you again if he breaks your heart," she says before disappearing out of my office.

I didn't realize me disappearing during college affected Eve so much. I thought she was too young to understand, but I'm guessing it did. I don't have time to analyze my failings as a big sister as I rush to Marcus' office.

"Hey, thanks for coming over," he says as I enter his office. "Bill has asked for a video meeting in an hour, does that suit you?" he asks.

"Let me shuffle some things around and meet you at my place, yeah?"

Marcus nods. "I'll text Pierre and Jordan and let them know."

"HOW DO YOU FEEL?" Marcus asks Pierre.

"I feel like I'm going to be sick. This is it. My entire life hangs on this moment," he says.

"Positive thinking," Marcus assures him.

It takes us a couple of moments to get set up for the video call, and then we are ready to go. The screen shows Bill and his lawyer, and no one else in the meeting, while we have Pierre, Marcus, and Jordan. I'm sitting off to the side. Bill looks angry as he sits there, the audacity.

"Thanks, guys, for agreeing to meet us," Bill's lawyer starts off nicely.

"Cut the bullshit, Steve. We all know why we are here," Bill interrupts angrily. "So, you want to leave my team. A team we built together, you ungrateful little shit," Bill snaps at Pierre.

Pierre centers himself, and I can see him squeezing his hands as he tries to remain calm in the face of such adversity.

Frankston trots over, noticing his owner's discomfort, and Pierre strokes his fingers through his long, thick coat.

"If you want to paint me out to be a villain in this story, then go ahead, but we all know who the real villain is. I feel for Michelle and your family. Hope she was worth it."

Bill's face turns red. "Are you threatening me, boy," he hisses through the screen.

Pierre shakes his head. "Not yet, but I'm happy to go public with the video if you aren't prepared to talk about my future with the club."

"You fucking snake. I made you and I can destroy you," he continues to yell at Pierre.

"Whose threatening who now?" Jordan cuts in.

"That kid is trying to blackmail me," he snips.

"I don't see it as blackmail. I see it as negotiation. As it's quite evident that the relationship between the two of you has dissolved. Do you think it's in the team's interest for you to keep Pierre there after what you did to him? Also, why would you want someone who holds a bomb in their hand that could at any moment let slip to your family?" Jordan adds.

"Steve, are you getting these threats his team are throwing at me?" Bill asks his lawyer, who nods but doesn't say anything because he knows Bill doesn't have a leg to stand on.

"Why did you do it? How could you betray me like that? I thought we were family. I looked up to you like a mentor," Pierre asks, and you can hear the hurt in his voice.

Bill wiggles uncomfortably. "I don't know, it just happened."

"How?" Pierre pushes.

"Kitty is very persistent."

"She went after you?" Pierre asks, sounding surprised.

"Don't sound so surprised, boy," Bill snaps at him. Is he serious? Gloating that he was able to get the attention of the young woman, one of his players' fiancée's. He has lost his mind. I've lost all respect for this man. "I did you a favor, she was only ever after your money."

"You did me a favor?" Pierre questions him.

"Yeah, she's a gold digger through and through. She jumped at the chance to be with someone richer than you, didn't even hesitate." Bill gloats.

"So, you slept with her to prove a point. To make you feel like a stud again. Because, honestly, it's fucking embarrassing knowing Kitty is only with you because of your money," Pierre snaps.

"Still got to fuck her." He chuckles.

Pierre sees red, and he's moments away from losing it. I quickly get up, rush over, grab his hand, and link it with mine as I crouch down beside him out of sight of the screen. He looks down at me for a moment, and relief floods his handsome face. I nod and let him know it's going to be okay. Don't show that man an ounce of hurt.

"Right, well, I think we have gone off topic," Steve, Bill's lawyer jumps in.

"After this display, the response we will hear is that you are letting Pierre go and paying out his two-year contract. He will give you the copies of the video and will never speak about the reason for leaving," Marcus says.

"I could turn your life into a living hell if I wanted to." Bill sneers into the screen.

"And I could just retire," Pierre snaps, which stuns Bill. "I would put in effect my retirement clause to make sure that you never ever win the cup."

"You fucking little ..." Next thing we know Bill's screen goes black.

"Um, yeah, so we agree to your terms, Pierre. We think this is in the best interest of the team, and we wish you well. I'll send through the contract right now." With that, Steve disappears.

"What the fuck was that?" Jordan says.

I let go of Pierre's hand and stand up, dusting myself off.

"That man is vile. I'm sorry you had to bear witness to that," Marcus says to Pierre.

"I kind of hope his wife finds out and divorces his ass," Jordan adds with a chuckle.

"At least you're free of him," Marcus says to Pierre, who hasn't moved from his seat.

"Guys, um, do you want to give us a moment," I say to them as I notice Pierre is on the verge of another panic attack.

"Yeah, we'll get back to the office and officially start letting everyone know you're a free agent," Marcus says, giving me a sympathetic look, as does Jordan, as they make their way out of my home.

"Hey, are you okay there?" I ask, crouching down in front of Pierre again. He shakes his head. I push open his legs so that I can wrap my arms around his waist and hug him tightly. "It's over. You're free," I tell him. He stiffens against me, unsure about the touch, but when I squeeze him again, he relents and hugs me back. "That man is an asshole. He did you a favor taking your problem off your hands."

"My problem?" he mumbles.

I lean back and look up at him. "Kitty."

The frown on his face flattens and he bursts out laughing. "Kitty." He shakes his head. "He really did."

"Karma will be coming for Bill Reeves, don't you worry. His display today was him showing how much of a small cock he has," I tell him, which makes him smile. "I'm sorry you had to go through that."

Pierre reaches out and cups my face. "You saved me from having a panic attack in front of that man."

"I noticed."

Those hazel eyes shimmer as he looks down at me. "Thank

you," he says. My stomach does somersaults with the way he is looking at me like I did something extraordinary.

"It's what friends do," I tell him, while still captured by his gaze. Flutters rain down across my skin the longer he looks at me with those intense eyes. My heart thumps in my chest. Here I am on my knees between his thick thighs, his large hand caressing my face while he looks at me as if I just saved his life. Slowly, he leans forward, oh no, is he going to kiss me? My heart ramps up to warped speed, my mind blanks, but I'm unable to stop what is about to happen until he stills and places his forehead against mine.

"Thanks, friend," he says softly. His warm breath brushes against my skin, sending goosebumps all over it. A throbbing ache ignites between my legs, one that has lain dormant since the last time he touched me.

"Anytime," I whisper back to him, but neither one of us moves. His hand moves from my cheek and slides along my throat until it reaches my collarbone, his thumb sliding back and forth against my skin. I swallow hard because I'm unable to move from the position I've gotten myself into, and there's a small part of me that doesn't want to move.

"I like seeing you on your knees, Issy," he whispers into my ear as his hand tightens around my throat.

"Pierre," I try to say his name as a warning, but it sounds needy.

"Yes, princess." He groans, his fingers stay tight around my throat as he makes me look up at him. "Fuck, I know I shouldn't be thinking these things but seeing you like this ..." Those hazel eyes trail over me and I feel it on my skin like a tender caress. We shouldn't be doing this. I should be putting a stop to it. "... Issy, you have me so fucking hard."

"I know, it's pushing into my stomach." My answer surprises me as I bite my bottom lip.

"I'm trying to respect your boundaries. I'm trying to make a go at being just friends, but ...." His hand tightens, and a shiver runs through me.

Suddenly, Frankston starts barking at the front door, and that's when I hear the creak of the door opening.

Shit.

I quickly scramble out from between his legs.

Pierre curses. "I'm going to take care of this," he says, getting up from his chair where I see his gray sweats tented. He rearranges himself before he rushes off to the powder room.

"Hey, Frankston, it's good to see you too, buddy." Felix's voice echoes through the foyer. "Hey, brother, heard the good news." I hear his footsteps as he heads toward me. I open the freezer and stick my head in it, hoping it will cool me down. "Issy, hi," Felix calls out to me.

I slam the freezer door shut. "Hi, wasn't expecting to see you."

"Yeah, sorry about just barging in. I thought my brother was home alone and was going to take Frankston for a jog around Central Park, but he pushed it back because of a meeting. I ran into Marcus and Jordan, and they said that Bill's agreed to all your terms and he's now a free agent."

"That's right, he has," I answer.

"Is he okay about that?" Felix asks, looking around the empty kitchen.

"I'm fucking ecstatic," Pierre says, walking back into the kitchen. My eyes instantly falling to his dick which he seems to have now gotten under control. He gives me an arched brow when he notices where I'm looking. I quickly turn back and busy myself. "He let me go, I'm free. We need to celebrate."

"That's great, man," Felix says, hugging his brother. "But we can't exactly go out to celebrate, no one knows you're here."

"That's right."

"I can host it here," I tell him. The two brothers fall silent.

"You'd host it?" Felix questions me.

I shrug. "He's living here, so it makes sense. I'm not doing anything as I have to get back to work, but if you guys want to organize it, then ..."

"Oh, hell yeah, we can do that," Felix says excitedly.

"You're going to call Harper, aren't you?"

Felix grins. "No. I was going to call Sam. Harper has a lot on her plate at the moment."

"Fine, just text me the details, I've got to go." With that, I disappear.

14

PIERRE

"Can't believe you're a free agent, man, this is fantastic news. I bet you feel relieved," my brother asks.

I would have felt better if he hadn't walked in on what was happening between Issy and me. Seeing her on her knees between my thighs did something to me. The way she was consoling me when I know it hurts her being around me, but she pushed her hurt aside because she could see I was on the verge of a panic attack. We had a moment. I think she would have let me kiss her if we were able to continue uninterrupted, and now, I can't think of doing anything else. I also liked the way she eyed my dick when I got up and the way she searched it out when I came back in. Was there disappointment there when I was no longer hard for her? I mean, all she needs to do is say the word and I'll be hard for her. Shit. My dick twitches at the thought of it.

"Yeah. I feel relieved. It was a tense conversation. Bill was gloating about how he was able to get Kitty and that she's a gold digger, and I should be thanking him for taking her off my hands."

My brother stares at me in shock. "He didn't say that."

I nod. "He sure did. It was mind-blowing the level of anger he has toward me. Like, he hates me."

"You did nothing wrong."

"Right? I don't know what his problem is, but he is no longer my problem. Marcus is looking into options for me now that we have the go ahead. Fingers crossed I hear from The Mavericks soon," I tell him.

"Harper and Issy had dinner with her dad last night and have asked him for a favor."

"Issy and Harper?" I ask, surprised by this.

"Did she not tell you?" Felix asks. I shake my head. "Maybe she didn't want to get your hopes up. Harper's father is on the board of The Mavericks, so he has some sway, but of course it would only be possible if there is space."

"I'll sit on the bench if I have to," I tell him.

Felix claps me on the shoulder. "There is no way in hell they are benching you." My phone starts ringing, and when I look down it's from an unknown number. "Answer it, it could be The Mavericks," he pushes.

"Hello," I answer.

"You're leaving the Devils?" Kitty shrieks into my ear. I'm stunned. This is the last person I thought I would hear from. Felix hears her and tells me to put it on speaker, then he pulls out his phone and starts recording. Good thinking, little bro.

"I'm guessing Bill called you."

"He didn't have to call me. I'm still in Italy at his place. You know where we were supposed to get married," she answers. Of course she is. "I can't believe you are doing this to him." To him? What about me.

"I'm glad you are more worried about his feelings than mine."

"Of course I'm worried about your feelings, I just think it's a stupid move. You're going to be a free agent at this age. Good luck with that," she scoffs.

"What I do or don't do is none of your business."

"It damn well is my business. You are still my fiancé."

I'm still. "No, I'm not."

"To the public you still are," she snaps.

"One post and I can sever that," I tell her.

"What are you going to tell them? That you left me at the altar because you had cold feet. You promised Bill you wouldn't say anything. The public are going to crucify you."

"You seem to think I care what the public think."

"Oh, you will when no one wants to hire you because of all the hate you are getting. You'll be a PR liability." She chuckles.

No screw her. "I'm willing to risk it."

Kitty squeals. "Do you hate me that much?" she questions me.

"Come on, Kitty, this marriage was going to end in divorce before our first wedding anniversary. You know we weren't working. I guess I thought it was me, but now I realize it was because of you," I tell her.

"Not my fault I found a real man," she snips.

"A real man," I scoff. "Would a real man be cheating on his wife of forty years with someone young enough to be his daughter?"

"You know nothing about Billy and me. He's going to leave Michelle, he's just organizing his assets so she can't take them."

"Who are you? The Kitty I used to know wasn't this vindictive. Michelle was always lovely to us. As were their kids, you're friends with them for fuck's sake," I remind her.

"They will get over it once they see how much Billy loves me."

Is she delusional? "He called you a gold digger in the meeting today."

"Billy would never. You're just trying to hurt me."

Yep, she's delusional. "Look, now that my contract is sorted, I'm going to talk to my PR, and you should talk to yours and ask them to release a statement telling the world we have decided to break up."

"Do you have any idea the embarrassment you have caused me? The amount of money we have to pay back for services that we never used that I was supposed to post about. The mental anguish of being left here to deal with the aftermath of you walking out on me." She cries.

Usually, her tears would work on me, but they don't anymore. "You seem to keep forgetting that you cheated on me, Kitty. You did this to yourself. So many times, I asked you to cancel this wedding, and you wouldn't. You wanted this moment more than you ever wanted me."

"That's not true." I can hear the pout through the phone.

"Why did you do it?" I ask.

"That's none of your business," she snaps. I don't think I'm ever going to get closure from those two. Am I okay with that? Yeah, I think I am.

"That's fine. I think from now on it's best we talk via our lawyers," I tell her.

"I am trying to sort things out civilly," she says.

"That's not the impression you've given me."

She lets out a loud sigh. "I'm trying, but you're being very combative." I pinch my nose, and my brother claps my back. "But I'll be the bigger person and start the conversation. I'm going to stay in Europe, this entire fiasco has stressed me out. I'm going to take some well-deserved me time. And Billy said I can stay as long as I want at his home in Italy."

"You can take all the time you want in Europe, Kitty. But what I am going to do is send the following requests to my lawyer, and I hope you can understand and continue being mature about this breakup like I know you can be. I will be selling the home in South Dakota."

"You're doing what? That is my home. You can't just sell it," she screams at me.

"I can and I will. The name on the home is mine and mine only. I will contact a moving company to come in and pack up all your belongings and put them into storage or send them to a nominated place."

"You can't do that. I won't allow you to touch my things."

"Then you will need to arrange your own movers, but your things will be packed up within the month," I tell her.

"That's unreasonable. I'm not in the country."

"You have been given plenty of warning. Also, Frankston is mine. There will be no co-parenting regarding him. I got him when we were not together. If you remember, I got him when you cheated on me the first time." Kitty splutters and huffs but thankfully doesn't fight me on that. "I will also be sending over an NDA regarding our relationship. We will create a joint statement saying we are better off as friends, and we realized that in Italy, and we want people to respect our privacy at this time. I will not speak ill of you in the press, and I hope I am granted the same courtesy from you."

"This is outrageous."

"I'm happy to also release a statement that you were cheating on me and I caught you."

"You promised Billy you wouldn't say anything," she whines.

"I won't mention him, if people speculate then that's on them."

"You wouldn't," she hisses.

"Try me, Kitty."

"I don't know who you are anymore," she shouts at me.

"Ditto, baby."

"My lawyers will be in touch." And with that, she hangs up on me.

"Wow, what a bitch," Felix says.

"How the hell was I blind to who she really was all these

years? I'm a fucking fool," I tell him, raking my hand through my hair.

"Don't be so hard on yourself. She showed you what she wanted to show you. You loved her faults and all. Why did you never talk to me about how bad things had gotten?" he asks.

"I pushed it out of my mind. We had the play offs and Alberto passed, you found out about Cynthia, and I was dealing with the wedding. Things kind of just snowballed, and I tried to get off plenty of times, but I couldn't, and I guess I just pushed my head into the sand, and now here we are."

"I'm sorry, man, I think having this party tonight is exactly what you need, a freedom party. Saying goodbye to the old you and saying hello to the new you. Like you're shedding your old skin," he explains.

"Where the hell did you get that hippy dippy shit from?"

"I'm being supportive. Honestly, it will do you good. Let me call Sam, and let's make this a great night." He grins.

Maybe this is exactly what I need. Saying goodbye to the old Pierre and embracing whatever the future is going to hold for the new me.

"CAN'T BELIEVE you went to all this effort," I say, looking at Felix and thanking Sam Rose, Harper's brother."

"I knew Sam would know people." He smirks.

"Thanks, Sam," I say, shaking his hand.

Sam laughs. "Look, if I were really planning a Sam Rose party, I would not be including my sister and her friends, no offence." He looks over at my brother who rolls his eyes. "Honestly, the women would flock here knowing Pierre St. Pierre is back on the market." He grins.

"Sam is a womanizer, do not let him corrupt you," Felix warns.

Sam rolls his eyes. "I'm trading you in, Felix, for your brother. You're too loved up with my sister to be an effective wingman. What do you say?"

"Not sure if I'm ready to get back out there. I was supposed to get married last week," I remind him.

"True. The optics wouldn't look great. What is a good time? A month?" he asks.

"My brother is more focused on his career than getting laid," Felix adds.

"Speak for yourself, it's been a while." They both stare at me. "Yeah, Kitty and I were not having sex, I understand why, now."

"You're Pierre St. Pierre." Sam likes to say my full name all the time. "You should be getting laid all the time."

"You need to stop watching hockey porn, hockey players are normal people," Felix teases.

"Hey, let me live in the fantasy." Sam chuckles. "Didn't you and Issy date when you were kids? I remember vaguely Harper talking about it."

I think I met Sam maybe once at a party when we were younger, I can't remember, he was in college when Issy and I were dating in high school, and I never saw him around when we made it to college. "Yeah, but we're friends now."

"Friends with benefits?" He elbows me teasingly.

"Don't let her hear you say that she will castrate me. We've kind of only just become friends again over the past couple of days."

Sam stares at me. "You're joking."

I shake my head. "We haven't spoken since she caught me cheating on her in college."

Sam's eyes widen. "You cheated on Issy. Why? She's great. Oh shit, is that the reason she moved to London? I remember how devastated Harper was."

I rub the back of my neck. "Yeah, I'm the reason."

"Damn, man. She was there for a long time. So, you two never spoke for all that time, and now you're living together?"

"Harper kind of forced it on them," Felix adds.

Sam is surprised. "That sounds like her. And how are things going there?"

"I'm only here till I find somewhere to live," I explain to them.

"I thought you had to get out next week?" Felix asks.

"She let me stay a little longer. It's hard to find somewhere to live when you're in hiding."

"Wow, that's not at all what I expected from her. I guess that's progress," Felix adds.

"She's trying. Especially since Frankston has been playing up and eating her shoes because he's stressed. She said she didn't want to stress him more than he needs. So, guess I have Frankston to thank for not being kicked out," I explain to them.

"The old don't want to stress the dog excuse, I like it," Sam teases.

"What do you mean?"

Sam's brows raise. "Seriously, oh my sweet Canadian friend, you think she's doing it for the dog?"

"Issy hates me. No, it's more she tolerates me."

"I thought you were friends," Sam questions.

"It's fragile right now. She's being nice. I'm her client."

He nods. "So there's nothing there?"

"Issy's a beautiful woman, but there is nothing there between us. I don't see her like that. We are just friends," I tell him.

"Oh hey, Issy," Sam says, looking over my shoulder.

I still. Did she just hear what I said? I turn around and see her hugging Sam. But I see nothing on her face to indicate she heard me.

"I know a Sam Rose party when I see one. I'm surprised there aren't topless waitresses walking around."

"Felix didn't think it was a good idea," Sam jokes.

"You're home early," I say.

"I thought you guys might need help, but it seems you have it all sorted. I might go grab a shower and get ready. What time are Harper and Kimberly coming?" she asks.

"They are on their way," Felix says. She nods and disappears.

"You don't think she heard me?" I ask them.

They both shrug. "Would it matter if she did if you're just friends?" my brother asks.

"It doesn't. I just want to make sure I didn't offend her in any way," I tell him. Felix nods.

"Come on, let's grab a drink and celebrate your Freedom Day," Sam says.

15

ISABELLE

"**I**ssy's a beautiful woman, but there is nothing there between us. I don't see her like that. We are just friends." I hate that his words have been constantly playing in my mind all night while I watched him and the boys have fun, drinking, singing, and dancing. I shouldn't care. But I'm also confused because earlier he said, *"Fuck, I know I shouldn't be thinking these things but seeing you like this ... Issy, you have me so fucking hard."* When we had a moment after his panic attack. And for a microscopic second, I was about to give in. Thank goodness Felix came in when he did, otherwise, I might have done something I would regret. And I would have regretted it. He doesn't want me. I'm convenient. I heard Sam teasing him about being on house arrest, and all he has for company is his hand. Pierre told him he would rather his hand right now as he has trust issues when it comes to women. Does that mean he has trust issues with me? I hate being up in my head about this. This is why I needed to keep him at arm's length, but no, I had to try to be the bigger person and let my anger go. What has it gotten me? Now I'm angry again for an entirely different reason, and that's what's annoying me.

The party is winding down, everyone is well and truly drunk, especially Pierre who is dancing around the room with his brother and Sam. Meadow, Kimberly, and my sisters left earlier, which leaves Harper and me together.

"You're quiet tonight," Harper says.

"Been a long week."

"You two seem to be getting along?" she says, looking over at Pierre who is messing around with Sam and Felix.

"It is what it is," I tell her with a shrug.

Her eyes narrow on me. "Has something happened?"

"What! No," I answer too quickly.

"Something happened. I knew it would." She leans in.

"Nothing happened."

"You're lying to me," she says, sipping her champagne.

"Like you lied to me," I throw back at her.

She gasps in surprise at my comment. "It must have been good if you're being spicy about my questions."

I throw back the rest of my champagne. "I'm tired, I'm going to call it a night." I start to get up.

"Hey, wait, Issy ..." Harper says, tugging at my wrist and pulling me back down. "Are we okay? What's going on?"

"Nothing," I mumble.

"Right, because this is normal," she says, waving her hand at me.

Urgh. I let out a frustrated sigh. "This is all a lot, okay," I snap at her.

Harper stills. "You mean Pierre is a lot," she says slowly.

"Him being in my space. His being here in general."

"You said there was a truce," she adds.

"There is but it can still be fricken hard to be around him. Every time I look at him, I see Missy Jenkins' smug face. I hate it."

"Oh, shit."

"That night ..." I start but feel the emotions choking me.

"That night gave you Pierre PTSD. Babe, I'm so sorry for doing this to you," she says, pulling me into a hug. "I thought I was doing something to help you move on ... shit, I was so wrong. I'm sorry." Her hug tightens. "I'll talk to Felix and get Pierre moved in with us until Felix finds somewhere to live."

"Felix is still moving out?" I ask her.

"Yeah. We both agreed it was only until the end of summer, nothing's changed," she explains. Everything has changed. How does she not see it? But I'm too exhausted to get into it with her tonight.

"I can't let Frankston eat your shoes," I tease.

"He's still eating shoes?" I nod. Pierre replaced the ones Frankston ate, which was nice of him. "I love my shoes."

"I know."

"I'm sure we can sort it out," she says, grimacing.

"I appreciate it, but I can handle it," I tell her.

"You shouldn't have to handle it."

"It's fine. I'm exhausted, it's been a long day," I tell her.

Harper whistles, and the boys stop dancing. "Felix, let's go."

"See ya, boys." Felix smirks, and they all give him hell, but he just flips them off. "Are you ready?" He looks to Harper who nods, and moments later, he picks her up from the sofa and pulls her into his arms. She wraps her legs around his waist, while the boys boo him. Felix ignores them. "Thanks for letting us celebrate tonight, my brother really needed it," he says. I give him a nod as he says his goodbyes and hauls Harper koala-style out of my home.

That just leaves Sam and Pierre together, who take a seat with their beers. I get up and start to tidy up the kitchen.

"We need to go out now that you're single. I know the best places," Sam says.

"I can't go out, I'm stuck here for the foreseeable future. No one knows that Kitty and I have broken up," Pierre tells him.

"Shit, that's right you said that earlier," Sam says, taking a sip of his beer. "That's going to make it hard to get laid. I've got the best idea. I'm going to gift you a membership to The Paradise Club. I'm part owner of the islands. Nate, not sure if you've met him, but he's just got his girl back, and he's disappeared off the face of the Earth with her. Anyway, it's these secret sex clubs, everyone who is famous goes there. And it's only via word of mouth. Right, Issy, she's a member," Sam says. Why is he bringing me into this? Pierre looks over at me, and I ignore him as I continue to clean. "Don't you think him going to the club, Issy, is the perfect idea? He can get laid, and the paparazzi will never know."

"Sure, whatever he wants," I say, grabbing the empty bottles of beer and placing them in the recycling bin. Pierre frowns at me.

"I'm going to organize it for you. I'll send over the forms and you'll need to get some medicals, but it's easy. Then you are going to discover a world of fun, so much fricken fun. Anything you could ever desire is available to you, and man, they have the hottest women there," Sam says enthusiastically. Maybe this is a good thing. Pierre probably has a lot of pent-up frustration, and I'm the closest thing to him so he is misdirecting his attention toward me.

"I'm intrigued," Pierre says, sipping his beer.

"Your mind couldn't possibly comprehend the shit that goes on there. Tell him Issy." Sam grins.

"I'm always satisfied," I answer.

"Damn, right you are." Sam chuckles, which earns him a filthy look from Pierre. "That's settled. I'll send you the details tomorrow. Right. Well, I've overstayed my welcome," Sam says, getting up and walking over to me. He gives me a big kiss on the cheek and a tight hug. He's always done this to me because he knows it annoys me, and Sam Rose is fucking annoying. "Thanks, Issy, for letting us use your home. It's been great as always." Then he points to Pierre. "Congrats, to you on your freedom. And with that, I'm out." He walks out of my home with his bottle of beer.

"That man is crazy. Think I'm going to head to bed."

"Sam's very flirty with you. Did you two ever?" Pierre asks.

I still. "Excuse me?"

"You and Harper are close, and he's her brother. Have you two ever hooked up? He seems to know how satisfied you are." Those hazel eyes narrow on me. Is he jealous?

"That's none of your business, and you've been drinking," I tell him as I throw the paper towel that I was wiping the countertop with in the bin and start to walk away. I am not in the mood for this.

Next thing I know, Pierre grabs me, picks me up, and places me on to the kitchen counter, my bare ass meets the stone and it's cold. Stupid G-string.

"Issy, I need to know if Sam has ever touched you. The thought that he has will drive me crazy."

He's insane. "Why would you care? You only see me as a friend," I say, pushing against his hard body.

Pierre pushes between my legs and locks me in place with his hips. "You heard that? I thought you did, but you didn't react." Those hazel eyes glare at me.

"Yes. And I feel the same," I say, pushing against him but it's no use, the man is a fricken mountain.

"Except earlier when you were on your knees for me, I saw it on your face, you wanted me. Don't forget I know you, Issy. I know the way your eyes dilate when your panties get wet, the way your skin flushes as your cunt tingles, the way your breath quickens, I haven't forgotten any of it." He snarls.

"Please, I had my first orgasm after we broke up," I spit back.

Pierre's hand grabs my throat. "Bullshit." His fingers tighten around my throat. "I made you scream all the time."

"It's called faking it." Pierre's fingers tighten, and he glares at me angrily. "I never had to fake with Sam." For the record, I've never slept with Sam. Yes, he is good looking, but he is such a playboy, plus he's Harper's brother. Nate, on the other hand, I would have climbed that man like a tree, but it never happened. Pierre doesn't need to know that.

"You fucked him?" he questions me. I don't say a word only glare at him. "Tell me, Issy, did you fuck Sam Rose because he and I are going to have a problem if you did." Pierre looks angry, but I don't want him taking it out on Sam. He'd be collateral damage in whatever game Pierre is playing.

"Who I have or haven't fucked is none of your business. You lost any right to ask about my sex life years ago."

"You didn't sleep with Sam?" His face softens.

"No, I didn't, you asshole. Now let me go," I say, trying to push him out of the way.

"Why did you make me believe you did?" he questions me.

"Let me down," I yell at him as my fists pummel against his chest.

"Issy, were you trying to make me jealous?" His voice lowers as his thumb slides along my collarbone. I'm unable to hide the shiver that it gives me, which makes him smirk. "The thought that someone else could make you come better than I can, would drive me insane. You were right, it did."

"I've had plenty of people make me come better than you," I snap back.

"Is that so? You know how competitive I am, Issy. Seems like you have thrown the gauntlet down. Now I'm going to have to prove you wrong," he says, pressing himself between my legs. Why the hell did I wear a mini dress tonight? The hem is around my waist. Pierre's hand slides between us and over the damp fabric of my underwear. "Seems like someone likes me."

"Fuck you," I hiss.

"Maybe I will." He grins as his hand tightens again around my throat and his other slides against my underwear, and with a rough tug, he snaps the fabric as if it was nothing leaving me pantieless. He then brings the fabric to his nose and sniffs it. Why is that hot and disturbing? "Fuck. I've missed the smell of you, Issy."

"You're a pig," I hiss.

He smirks at me as he continues to sniff my panties. "I'm going to wrap these around my cock later and pretend I'm fucking you with them." My jaw falls open as he shoves them into his back pocket. "Now, where was I?" He grins as his hand slides between us, but this time his fingers slide between my wet folds. A moan falls from my mouth before I have a chance to stop it, which makes him chuckle darkly. I should be pushing him away, but I hate how much my body wants this.

"Fuck," I groan as his thick fingers slide into me.

"Still as tight as I remember." He grins as his fingers move inside me, instantly finding those sensitive bundles of nerves like he was always able to. It looks like Pierre hasn't forgotten at all how to make me come. "Let go, Issy. Don't fight me on this," he coos as his fingers continue to do indescribable things to me. No. I shouldn't be doing this. *Let the man give you an orgasm, he owes you, and you need one.* No. He doesn't deserve it. He doesn't deserve any piece of me.

"Stop," Pierre's hand stills, his fingers inside me.

"You want me to stop?" he asks.

Suddenly, tears well in my eyes. I'm ashamed of myself for letting him get this far with me. I'm ashamed that I like his hands on me. Pierre pulls his fingers from me, and his hand falls from my throat as he stands back, giving me space. I quickly pull down the edge of my dress to cover myself.

"Issy, I'm sorry." I can see the anguish on his face.

"I'm going to bed," I say, hopping down from the counter.

"I thought ..." he says, running the hand that was inside of me through his hair.

"We can only ever be friends. I can't do this, even if I wanted to," I confess as I leave him alone in the kitchen and head to bed, upset, ashamed, and worst of all, horny too.

16

PIERRE

S hit.

What have I done.

I thought after earlier today when we had a moment, that maybe she was interested. She's not. *That's not what she said. She said, she can't even if she wanted to.* What the hell does that mean?

Shit.

I have to make this right. *Not tonight you don't.* Right. I should give her space. *And you should stop flirting with her.* I can't help it, she's just so beautiful. *Pushing her isn't going to get her to give in to you. What do you want from her?* I want what we had back. *For fifteen years, your mistake has festered inside her. The wound might be too big to fix.* I've changed. *Have you? Because you kissed her when you were engaged.* But she knows that things between Kitty and me weren't good. *Not good. You were about to marry her last weekend.* Because I ... crap ... I was going to marry her and try and make it work. And now here I am trying to make things work with Issy. *You're a mess.* I am a mess. *Show her you've changed.* I have. And I will. *Don't be jealous if she dates, remember she is single.* I don't know if I can do that. *Then she will never be yours. Is that what you want?* No. I want a second chance. *A second chance, a week after leaving another woman at the altar.* Okay. You're right. I'm rushing things. *You may have gotten freedom today, but you're only halfway there. You still have to announce to the public that you and Kitty have broken up, and you still need to find a new team. Don't rush things.* It's hard being around her all the time, though. *Just like it's hard for her being around you, but for different reasons.* You're right. I need to work on myself first before I can even think about a second chance with Issy. *She still remembers you as the cocky teen.* I've grown up. *But you're still cocky.* I can't help it. *Tone it down then.* I will. For her.

§

My phone starts ringing off the hook. Urgh. My head hurts after one too many beers. Then I hear the front door buzzer and Frankston barking. What is going on? Reluctantly, I get out of bed and go outside to investigate. I'm surprised when I see Felix and Harper walking through the front doors.

"Bro, you look like shit," my brother states.

"Why haven't you been picking up your phone," Harper adds.

"I've been asleep," I grumble.

"So, you haven't seen it?" Harper gasps.

"Seen what?"

Moments later, a bleary-eyed Issy walks down the stairs. She looks so beautiful, her chocolate hair is all messy, and she's wearing a silky black slip that leaves nothing to the imagination as it clings to her body, it's short and exposes her long, tanned legs with each step. "What the hell are you guys doing here so early?"

"You haven't seen the news either?" Harper asks. Issy shakes her head, looking as confused as I am. "Shit. Okay. Well, Kitty has decided to say fuck you, Pierre, and has released a statement on how you left her at the altar as you got cold feet and then disappeared, and she has no idea where you are and she's heartbroken."

"She did what?" I yell.

"It's everywhere. The internet is going wild, and people are losing their minds. She's painting you out to be the villain," Harper explains.

"How fucking dare, she. Kitty promised yesterday that she wouldn't do anything," I yell.

"She lied. Which isn't surprising is it," Harper adds.

"How about I make us some coffee and we talk in the living room," Issy says.

"I'll help," Felix adds.

"I can't believe she did this to me. Is it bad?" I ask Harper.

"It's not good."

Shit.

"What do we do? She can't get away with this. Do you think they planned this together to take me down?" I ask.

"Possibly. Currently, you're the runaway groom, and the female demographic is very much upset with you. A portion of the male demographic think you've lost your mind for leaving Kitty, and there's a small portion who are on your side."

"That's not good, is it?"

Harper shakes her head. "We can turn this around for you, but we are going to have to make a statement."

The front door buzzes, and Felix rushes to get it. Moments later, Marcus and Jordan arrive.

"Just saw the news, fucking hell, and I sent her the NDA last night," Jordan says.

"And I have a meeting with The Mavericks today, too. This couldn't have come at a worse time," Marcus adds.

Shit.

I can't believe Kitty is fucking up my life for her gain. *Are you surprised? This is low even for her. She wanted to control the narrative, of course, she would release her own statement before you. Now she is playing the victim in this story, knowing full well you can't do shit about it because of the contract you signed with Bill. They fucked you over again.* "I want to make a live statement, now."

"What? No. This isn't a good idea. You have to stick to a script," Harper says.

"A carefully curated speech is not going to win over the public," I tell her.

"You have to be so careful in what you say, Pierre," Jordan warns me.

"I don't mention Bill, I got that. But Kitty never signed the NDA, so I am happy to expose her cheating. Let the world know I have evidence of her infidelity, and I'll release it if Kitty doesn't retract the lies she is telling."

"Rather aggressive," Harper states.

"It's the truth, though."

"Might stop the media trying to find him, we all know how they operate," Felix adds, looking over at Harper.

"A heartfelt video on your socials might work. Are you up for it, though?" Harper asks me.

"Yes. I will not let them try to destroy me."

"Kitty isn't going to expect you to fight back." Felix smirks.

"Exactly, and that's why she did it."

"Okay, if you think you can do it," Harper says before turning to look at Jordan. "Any notes on legally what he can and can't say?" she asks him.

"Yeah, I have some ideas," he adds.

"Good, now, Pierre, go have a shower, get yourself together, and we will have a plan once you've gotten out," Harper states.

I'M SHOWERED, Harper's dressed me like a fricken Canadian lumberjack with a flannel shirt, white tee and jeans, apparently this makes me look down to earth and gives the illusion I am in the wilderness somewhere and not in the city. She also asked me not to shave, so I look disheveled, making the public think I am truly upset over the relationship. I still can't believe Kitty did this to me.

"Are you sure about this? Once it's out there's no going back," Felix asks.

"She can't paint me out to be the villain when she is one," I tell him.

He claps me on the back. "I'm here for you."

My family called from Italy earlier and they gave me their blessing to do whatever I needed to do, that they would stand by me through this, and it's exactly what I needed to hear. I've gone over all the notes Jordan and Harper have given me, and I'm just going to go with my gut and hope that it translates to the public.

"Okay, are you ready?" Harper asks as she sets up the phone and stand to film me on. We've gone for a blank wall in the living room so that no one can work out exactly where I am, hopefully. I'm nervous as hell, but thankfully it's not live and I can redo the video if I mess up.

"I'm ready," I tell her as I nervously move in my chair. Just treat this like any other media interview, especially one after a bad game where you don't want to be there, but you have to be. Harper gives me a count in and indicates she's recording.

"Hi, everyone. It's come to my attention today that my ex has released a statement on our breakup before our joint statement could come out. I understand Kitty is upset and hurt over my leaving Italy, but she knows the real reason why. I was never going to publicly talk about the reason for my leaving, but she isn't being truthful about what happened. Yes, I did leave without telling her personally, but I was upset. Finding out your fiancée has been seeing someone else behind your back in the middle of your rehearsal dinner was a shock. Kitty, I was never going to tell anyone about your affair. I would have stuck to the statement we were releasing in a couple of days, that we both had cold feet and realized we wanted different things, that it was no one's fault. I would have let everyone believe that I was the bad guy to protect you, but you couldn't do the same for me. I cannot in good conscience let these lies continue in this way and damage my name. I'm not angry at Kitty, I'm disappointed in how things have turned out. We had been having problems for a while and should have called off the wedding months ago, but you feel like you can't when your wedding has been turned into a circus. But seeing Kitty with another man the night before our wedding, there was no way I could go through with the marriage. Was it a cowardly thing to do, to run away? Yes. But I wasn't thinking straight. This will be my one and only statement on the matter, so please respect my privacy at this time. And please do not harass or attack Kitty over this either, that is not what I want. I just want to clear my name. Regarding my career, it is with great regret that I inform you all that I have requested to be let go by the South Dakota Devils so that I may start a new life somewhere else. I will be coming into the next season as a free agent. I am so sorry to the Devils' fans and my team as I feel like I am letting you all down, especially being unable to bring the cup home. Unfortunately, I'm being selfish, and I need this change for me. A clean slate. Wherever I end up, I look forward to seeing the Devils thrive, they have a real chance at the cup next season. I don't know what the future or my career holds, but I know now is not the end. I still have some of the best years left in my career, and I hope that I get a chance to show them off. I appreciate your support at this time and hope to see you all on the ice again."

And with that, I sign off. Everyone is silent.

"That was fucking awesome, so Canadian polite. Everyone is going to lap this up." Harper squeals with delight.

"You did good, bro," Felix adds.

"Perfect, there was nothing in there that would get you into trouble," Jordan states.

"You are going to have so many options from teams when this goes live," Marcus suggests.

Then I look over at Issy, she gives me a small smile.

"Right, do I have permission to post this?" Harper asks as she plays around on my phone.

"If you think it's ready to go, do it," I tell her.

"Perfect." Her fingers move rapidly over the keys. "It's done. Gone. Good luck. How do you feel?" She grins.

"Slightly relieved, but who knows what the public are going to think?"

"I'm going to have to go, I have that meeting with The Mavericks this afternoon that I need to prepare for. Fingers crossed they see this, and I have good news," Marcus tells me. Me too.

"I might head out, too. You're in good hands here," Jordan says, following Marcus out of Issy's home.

"I've got to head into the office, too," Issy says.

"You're not going to stay?" Harper asks.

"Pierre isn't the business's only client," she states.

Harper frowns at her friend. "Of course. Don't worry, we've got him." And with that, she disappears upstairs. "Are you two okay?" Harper asks me.

"Sure," I answer, but it doesn't sound convincing. Harper looks over at my brother before the buzzing of my phone distracts her. She starts scrolling and scrolling.

"Holy shit, people are losing their minds."

"In a good way?" I ask.

"Like a Team PSP way." She grins.

Relief slides over me, thank fuck.

17

ISABELLE

So much for working, I've spent most of my time online reading everyone's reaction to Pierre's video. It was a damn good video. Kitty is getting slammed on her socials, and she is not dealing with it well, so much so she has turned comments off on her profile. My sister walks in with her phone in her hand.

"Wow, this is insane. He did such a good job turning his profile around. This morning everyone was Team Kitty and now they are all Team PSP, which is trending," she says, shaking her head.

"He didn't deserve what she posted especially since it's her fault."

"This has backfired on her spectacularly. I also loved how he let the hockey world know he's free too."

"Marcus has a meeting with The Mavericks right now. He mentioned before he left that teams have been calling him enquiring about Pierre. Kitty did him a huge favor by going rogue," I explain to her.

"That she did. How are you? You seemed quiet last night," she asks.

"Just a lot of my mind at the moment."

"Pierre?"

"Not everything is about him," I snap before I realize what I'm doing.

Evelina stares at me. "Guessing it is about him." I roll my eyes. "Talk to me. I know I was too young when you guys were dating, but I do remember the aftermath," she states. There's a long moment of silence before I let out a sigh.

"Fine. We keep having moments," I confess to her.

"Moments? As in *moments*," she says, wiggling her brows.

"Yes."

"Oh. Wow. Unexpected. I thought you weren't interested," she asks.

"I'm not."

"Seems like you are."

"There's a physical attraction between us, I guess, but ..." Urgh. I nervously move things around on my desk.

"But ... last week he was supposed to be getting married in Italy, and now he is living in your home with his gorgeous dog. Plus, he's the guy who broke your heart all those years ago." She's not wrong. "And you are confused by your emotions that seem to surface, not to mention the fact that he kissed you not that long ago when he shouldn't have. Guess it makes sense now why he did that." Again, Eve is making valid points. "And you can't seem to let the past go, and he's probably trying to make up for the past, and here we are."

"Every time I look at him, I see Missy Jenkins on her knees. And the stupid wound opens again."

Eve's face softens as she reaches out and pats my hand. "I was not expecting you to be so open about it. That's tough, being reminded of something so painful every time you see him. Especially if you keep having *moments*," she says, giving me a small smile. "I'm glad you're talking to me about this. Usually, you would go to Vi for this kind of stuff, not me." Do I?

"Now that you are asking for my advice, I don't want to mess up, otherwise, you will never confide in me again." That's a little dramatic, but it's also sweet that she wants to help me. "So, do you want to have sex with him?"

"Eve!" I gasp, surprised by her question.

"What? You said you've been having moments. I'm assuming they are sexual. You just said there is physical attraction still there between you both, but it's mental which means you want to, but your brain is stopping you." She's not wrong.

"I don't want a relationship with him."

"But you want to fuck him?"

"Eve!" I say her name again.

"I'm not a kid anymore, we can talk about sex," she says, rolling her eyes. "Pierre is hot, anyone with eyes can see that." I don't like the fact that she's noticed that. "But his life has just blown up so he's mentally not in a good spot." All facts. "And the two of you are around each other for the first time in years, so the familiarity is still there which is confusing." True. "And that is probably confusing you both because you don't know how to be around each other without being sexual." Didn't see it like that but she makes a good point. "Why don't you two just sleep together. It might be bad and then all that tension will go, or it might be good, and the tension will go, too."

"That is a horrible idea," I tell her.

"Sex is a great tension reliever, and you look tense. Do I look tense?" she teases.

"Ew, I don't want to know about your sex life."

"You're jealous that I have one." She pokes her tongue out at me. Mature. Evelina is a free spirit. Ever since the accident that ended her ice-skating career, she's gone from this super strict Olympic hopeful to a woman who lives life to the fullest because she is happy to be alive.

"I don't have to have sex with him."

"You don't? Seriously, look at him," she questions me. Why does she keep talking about how hot Pierre is?

"Eve!"

My sister rolls her eyes. "Was the kiss not good?" I don't answer which makes her face light up with a big smile. "It was good, wasn't it? And you hate the fact that it was because you want Pierre St. Pierre to stay in a box marked asshole but he's not fitting in that box anymore." I hate how right she is, but I'm not going to give her the satisfaction of telling her she is right. Because I want Pierre to stay an asshole because it makes it easier not to forgive him for breaking my heart and turning me into this. "It's okay to let him out of the box, and it's okay to realize he's not the same guy who broke your heart all those years ago. You can forgive, but you don't have to forget. Although, if I'm being honest, I think you should forget it. You two are different people now and a lot of time has gone by. Maybe you need to start again."

"That's what I'm trying to do."

"But you're still stuck in the past. You keep seeing him with that girl he cheated on you with."

"Because it sucked seeing it."

"Have you told him this?" she asks.

"Yes. Kind of. It's not like he can change it. What's done is done," I tell her.

"So, you're just going to live in this purgatory. It's going to drive you insane," she says.

It already is. "It's not like he's staying with me forever. The Mavericks will hire him. Now that Kitty has blasted their business to the world, he doesn't have to hide as much, so he'll start looking for a new place soon."

"I'm sorry you're going through this," she says, giving me a small smile.

"It's only short-term pain," I tell her.

"You shouldn't be in pain around someone."

"I know."

"He really hurt you, didn't he? I know I was too young to understand what was going on, but I always thought he was a good guy."

"Until he wasn't," I add.

"People make stupid mistakes when they're young," she says, giving me a knowing smile. A stupid mistake when she was younger changed her life forever. "All I'm saying is people change. You're not the same person you were at that age, and neither is he. If you truly want a clean slate with him, Issy, you're going to have to move past the images in your head. Really. Truly. Try."

Maybe she's right. "Thanks for this. I appreciate the chat. We should do it more often," I tell her

"Does that mean I gave you good advice."

"Yes, of course," I say. Eve gives me a blinding smile. "Eve, did me going away hurt you? You said something, and I guess I was focused on my own heartbreak that I didn't realize I might have hurt others in the process."

"It was confusing. No one would tell me what was going on. You went to Europe for spring break and then never came home. Dad was upset, so was Vi. Pierre was then kicked out of the house during the summer. There was a lot of turmoil. I guess I just missed my sister. And ten years was a long time to be away. You missed so many milestones, not just with me but with Vi, too." Oh wow. I had no idea. "Things that we could have used our big sister for."

"I called all the time."

"I know. Just sometimes we would have liked you to be there," she confesses.

"I had no idea." Guess that's why Vi and Eve are so close because I pushed them away while trying to protect myself. "I'm sorry."

"You have nothing to apologize for, Issy. I'm glad you turned to me when you needed help." Her words hit me, and I make a note to make more time for my sisters. I get up and hug her. She stiffens under my embrace because I'm not a hugger, but when I give her a squeeze she hugs me back. "I love you. We need more sister time."

"Does that mean I can take you shopping?" she asks.

"Again, with my clothes. Are they really that bad?" I ask her.

She bursts out laughing. "No. You are stylish, but I would love to see you less buttoned up."

You know what, it's just clothes. "Okay. Let's do it. You and me, shopping day. I could use an excuse to get out of the house." I grin.

"I've got you." She smiles back.

18

ISABELLE

Something smells amazing as I walk into my home. I hang up my coat and bag before I'm attacked by a ball of golden floof. "Hey, Frankston." I chuckle as I bend down and scratch him. "How was your day?" *Am I seriously asking a dog how their day was?* He gives me a big lick that makes me laugh.

"You're home." Pierre comes out and greets me. He has a tea towel slung over his shoulder with red sauce on it. "Hope you're hungry, I've been cooking."

"I'm starved and it smells amazing," I tell him. The smile that lights up his face over my compliment warms me. My instant reaction is to hate that feeling but I'm putting into practice what Eve said. I can't change the past. But I can change how I deal with it, and as she said, I've put Pierre in this box and now I'm opening it up and letting him free.

"When I'm stressed, I cook," he says.

"You cook?" I ask, surprised.

Pierre shrugs. "My sister bought me cooking classes one Christmas. She thought it was funny, but I went and loved it. I don't always get time to cook, plus during the season my meals are boring as hell, you know, got to keep the physique up." He rubs his flat stomach. "Did you want some wine? I thought you probably had a shit day because of me."

"Did you go out?" I ask.

He shakes his head. "Got it all delivered."

"You don't think the delivery person would have recognized you?"

He grins. "I told him I was sick, slipped a fifty to them to leave the shopping on the stoop and waited for them to go to collect it." Smart.

He gestures for me to follow him, and I do, still in awe that he's cooked a homemade meal. The bottle of wine has already been popped, and it seems he's been having some while he cooks. His phone is playing music softly and the kitchen looks like a bomb has hit it.

"What's for dinner?" I ask as I watching him pour me a glass of wine.

"Just spaghetti and meatballs, nothing fancy. We haven't had time to have a proper meal since I arrived. You order out a lot."

"I'm a busy woman and usually I'm out with the girls or at a function or on a date," I tell him.

"Do you go out on a lot of dates?" he asks, handing me the glass. Our fingers touch, and I hate the way my body lights up over it. "Or do you mainly stick to your sex club?" Oh wow. He's going to come right out and ask.

"Do you really want me to answer that?" I ask him, taking a sip to steady my nerves.

He goes back to stirring whatever is in the pot. "I do. I want to know you, again."

"So, you're starting with my sex life?" I question him.

"No, it's not like that. Sam sent over the paperwork for The

Paradise Club earlier and I started reading about it and ..." He frowns as he concentrates on his sauce pot.

"The paperwork can be overwhelming but it's not as scary as you think it is," I reassure him.

"There were some kinks on that paper that shocked me, and I thought I was kinky but maybe I'm more vanilla than I thought. Is that what you're in to?" he asks, and I can see his brows pull together as if wondering what kind of depraved things I might be into. Before I get a chance to answer, he holds up the wooden spoon to me. "Try this, let me know if you think it's missing anything ... it's hot," he adds as he blows on it before offering me the spoon.

I tentatively taste it and moan. "It's delicious. I don't think you can improve that."

Pierre looks happy with my answer. "Okay, if you're happy then I'll start plating up. Go, sit and I'll bring it out to you." He starts to move around the kitchen, when I turn around I notice my dining room table is set up for us.

"You went to a lot of trouble," I tell him, taking a seat.

"It's the least I can do for everything you've done for me this week," he shouts over his shoulder. I stare at his taunt back, watching his muscles work. This wine is going to my head as my cheeks flush. *No, it's that fine man working in the kitchen that is making you hot.* No one's ever cooked for me, I realize, which is sad. The men I've dated have always taken me out and because I don't cook, we never did anything domesticated together. This is new. *And you like it.* I do. I'm so used to living on my own that I guess I didn't realize how lonely it is now that my house is full.

"Down, Frank. You have to wait, it's too hot for you. You will burn your tongue," Pierre instructs Frankston who gives him a frustrated ruff as he watches him place the hot meatball on the counter and starts cutting it up. I watch the steam bellow from the meatball as does Frankston whose nose twitches with the delicious scent. Pierre walks over to where I am seated and places the large bowl of spaghetti and meatballs in front of us, then walks back and brings a bowl of salad and garlic bread before returning with the bottle of wine.

"Thank you so much for all this, it's unexpected," I tell him. Pierre shrugs. "You've been looking out for me this week, I just wanted to do the same." He disappears back into the kitchen to grab the cheese before taking a seat. "Dig in," he tells me. And I do, I don't realize how starving I am until I heap my plate full of deliciousness.

I wait for him to serve himself before holding up my glass to him. "Thank you for dinner," I say, clinking our glasses together. We both take a sip and look over the rim at each other before we silently dig in. We are quiet after the first couple of mouthfuls, which are amazing, it's like eating at my favorite Italian restaurant down the block. It is so good. I could get used to coming home to this.

"Good?" he asks. I moan. Which makes him fidget in his seat. "So, you um, didn't answer my question earlier." I nervously take a sip of my wine. "If you're into half the stuff on Sam's kink sheet."

"Most on there don't do it for me," I answer, and he looks a little relieved. "You don't have to join if you don't feel comfortable. If you're not ready to move on from Kitty. Don't let Sam pressure you."

"I'm ready to move on from Kitty," he answers quickly. Oh. "And I, um." He rubs the back on his neck exposing his muscular bicep. Arm porn at its finest.

My eyes widen as I realize what he is getting at. "You want to get laid." The words are out of my mouth before I register what I've said.

"I just ... you know ..." He stumbles over his words.

"Have urges," I answer for him.

"Don't you? I mean, you went there the other night to destress, and I'm really stressed right now. I know you're not interested because, you know ... anyway, I respect your boundaries ..." he rushes out to say. "Unless you ...?" He looks up at me.

"Unless you what?" I question him.

"Unless you want to destress together," he states. I stare at him shock. "Fuck, see I knew I would mess this up."

"Is that what this dinner is about? You were trying to butter me up thinking this will change my mind, and I'll sleep with you?" I question him, abruptly standing and throwing my napkin on the table. See, men are liars. My stomach turns, just when I thought about letting my guard down, he proves to me I can't.

"Issy, no, that wasn't it at all. I got Sam's email after I started cooking this meal. Please, don't leave," he asks.

"I don't trust you," I tell him, which makes his face fall.

"That wasn't my intention tonight. I was trying to thank you for being there for me during all this. I know it's hard. I know I am asking a lot from you. I see it on your face every day, you look at me like that night at the frat house. I can't get rid of the look of your broken face from my memory, it haunts me still. I just wanted to show my appreciation, but stupid me starts the conversation off about the fucking sex club instead of how was your day? Or did you hear how well the meeting with The Mavericks went or that Team PSP is trending. Instead, I've been here all afternoon drinking wine. That is the second bottle I popped, I drank the other one while I was cooking," my eyes widen at that confession, "because Sam sent me that kink list, and all I could think about was you at that club doing all these things with other men. I shouldn't feel jealous because I don't get to be jealous, but I was, and I am, and ..." he confesses.

"You're jealous?"

"Yes."

"Why?" I question him.

"Why?" He stares at me as if that is an absurd question.

"That's what I'm asking, why?"

"Because I haven't stopped thinking about you for the last fifteen years. Like I've said before, you are the biggest regret in my life. I wish I wasn't so weak in trying to fit in with everyone at college because if I hadn't done what I did, you and I would have gotten married, maybe we would have kids by now. That's what haunts me, the life I so desperately want I threw away."

"We were kids."

"I was old enough to know what was right and what was wrong," he tells me.

"I think you and I need to talk, and I think we need another bottle of wine," I say, cracking a smile at him. The tension that was there eases as he rushes into the kitchen, grabs another bottle, and meets me back at the table. "Can we talk honestly and openly tonight, no judgment, I promise," I say, holding up my hands.

"I'd like that."

"I have a wall up when it comes to you," I tell him.

"Understandably," he adds.

"Not really. You messed up fifteen years ago. That is a long time to still be angry with someone."

"I hurt you."

"And I hurt you by ghosting you all that time," I say, which surprises him. "I should have come back and dealt with you. Told you all the things I should have and then maybe it wouldn't have festered inside me for so long."

"Maybe I should have tried harder," he adds.

"I was never going to let you," I confess.

"If you could turn back the clock, what would you have said," he asks.

"I probably would have punched you," I grin as does he, "but I would have asked why? Still to this day, I don't understand what I did." Urgh. I hate being vulnerable and that's exactly what I'm doing and especially in front of him.

Pierre takes a sip of his wine, and I can see he is mulling over what he is going to say. "You loved me too much and I never felt worthy of your love," he confesses. His words tear at my walls. "I didn't believe I deserved you, Issy. I had to listen to all my friends talk about how you were too good for me. That I was punching well above my weight with you."

"We were together for three years."

Pierre nods. "I was the last person who saw my dad before he left." I didn't know that. "I had forgotten my cup, and there was no way I was getting a puck to the nuts, so I rushed home to grab it. That's when I saw my dad walking out the door with his bags packed. I was confused because he didn't have any away games. He was angry when he saw me standing on the path, looking at him taking the coward's way out, leaving during the day." I can see the pain on his face as he relives that memory. "I asked him to stay, and he told me I wasn't enough of a reason for him to stay, that none of us were. That this wasn't how he saw his life turning out. That he was bigger than this. Then he wished me luck and left."

"I'm so sorry, I had no idea."

"After you left, things spiraled for me. I went a little wild," I remember seeing images of him, and that made me hate him even more. "I knew I self-sabotaged the relationship because I didn't think I was good enough, and I was sabotaging everything else in my life, too. Coach told me I needed to shape up or ship out. I was nearly kicked out of college," he confesses. I had no idea. "Coach suggested that I talk to someone, and I thought it was stupid, but he made it a stipulation of my probation to stay on the team or he would bench me for the entire season." Wow. "It took me a while to work through my shit with my dad, but the counselor made me realize that I started unconsciously mimicking my father's behavior especially since people started comparing me to him, telling me how much I played on the ice like him. That doesn't excuse what I did, Issy. You were collateral damage against my childhood trauma."

"I had no idea."

He shrugs. "I didn't either until I started talking to someone. But it was too late when it came to you." His hazel eyes meet mine.

"I'm sorry, I guess I should have listened to you," I tell him.

"Don't you dare feel sorry for me. Just because my dad hurt me doesn't mean I get to hurt you. I did try to find you a couple of times, but your dad told me you were dating someone in London, and you were happy. I mean, you were in London, and I was in New York, it was never going to work anyway. So, I gave up," he explains, knocking back the rest of his wine.

"You tried to talk to me when I first came back during Dad's birthday, and I wouldn't listen."

"Is, you were hurt. I understood. I talked to the counselor about what I did to you, and she tried to help me forgive myself, but I never could until you forgave me on the plane."

I take a sip of my wine. "I didn't want to forgive you. It was easier to hate you and blame you than to deal with the fact that I still loved you, even after everything you had done to me." Pierre's face falls. "I wasn't prepared to ever let you get that close to me again. I couldn't take a chance on letting you inflict that kind of damage on me again. I hid away instead of dealing with it all."

"I really fucked things up." He sighs, running his hand through his hair.

"I did too. We were kids," I tell him, sipping my drink.

"I wasn't a kid when I kissed you at your father's wake," he states, looking at me.

"No, you weren't," I agree.

"I want to apologize again for that moment. I honestly can't believe I did that to you at such a vulnerable time. You were crying and I wanted to help, but being back in that room and having you hug me and ... in that moment, I wanted to pretend everything between us never happened," he tells me.

"I did too," I confess.

Silence falls between us.

"But I made things worse because you thought I was still that man. A cheater. I mean, I was. Things with Kitty at that time were rough. I tried to call off the wedding when I got back from the funeral."

"You did?" I'm shocked.

"Not because of you ... I mean kind of ... urgh ..." he says awkwardly. "Kissing you made me realize that Kitty and I were not meant to be, but I felt trapped. The wedding was a media circus, everyone kept telling me it was cold feet, that everyone goes through second thoughts. Then our team made the play-offs, and you know what it's like, that was my sole focus, it had to be. I pushed every red flag Kitty showed me away because I couldn't deal with it."

"I watched the game," I tell him.

"You did?" He seems surprised.

"I always watched your games." Pierre's mouth falls open in shock. "That penalty was a rookie move, and I felt for you. You had snatched back the chance to make the finals."

"Pretty low point of my career," he says.

"It won't define your career, though," I tell him, which pulls a small smile from his lips.

"You watched my games?"

I smirk. "Don't think anything of it. It's my job to keep an eye on the agency's clients." He sips his wine, chuckling. Which makes me giggle, a bit of tension slowly easing from my shoulders. "And things seem to be looking up for you, from what Marcus says."

"I can't believe The Mavericks are interested in me."

"Having the St. Pierre brothers on the ice together is a huge deal for the team. The added revenue that you and Felix would bring in, the merch, the fans, your skills, it's a no-brainer. Will you entertain any other teams?" I ask him.

"Not if The Mavericks are interested. I want to end my career with my brother by my side."

"You're not over the hill yet," I joke with him.

"For hockey, I am. The Mavericks have said that they would be interested in talking to me about coaching with them if or when I'm ready to hang up my skates," he explains.

"They did? And that's something you would be interested in doing?"

He nods. "I would, yeah. If I can get one season with my brother, then I'll be happy, even better if we win the cup," he adds.

"You're in with a chance. Bill will lose his mind if you guys win it." I chuckle.

"I'm highly motivated." He grins. "Are we good, Issy?" he asks. "I know we are laughing now, and I don't want to ruin it, but I need to know that you and I can try again ... as friends. I've truly missed you." His speech is heartfelt, and being around him again, deep down inside, I have missed him too. He was my best friend as well as my partner.

"I've missed you too," I confess, and I see the hope in his eyes. "It's hard, I've held onto the anger toward you for so long, I'm going to need a minute to truly let it go. And when I look at you, I see Missy Jenkins on her knees, smiling."

"I'm so sorry about that."

"I know you are," I reassure him. "I want to truly move on from our past, Pierre. Do you mind being patient with me?" I ask him.

"I'll wait forever for you," he tells me.

⁂

"You're a horrible singer," I tease him.

"I can't be good at everything." He belts out another noughties power ballad. I'm having fun and laughing with him, something I never thought I'd ever do again. The two of us may have drunk too much wine tonight, but after the conversation at dinner where we put a lot of our issues on the table and spoke honestly, I feel like a bit of the weight and tension between us is lifting.

"Oh, sorry, Mr. Hockey Superstar."

"Hockey isn't the only thing I'm good at," he says.

"Really, what else do you excel in?"

"Cooking."

That's true, he is a good cook, but I'm not about to inflate his head. "I've only tried one dish, the jury is still out on that."

"Fine. I'll cook for you every night until you realize I'm a fantastic cook." He grins.

"You don't have to do that," I tell him.

"I want to. It's the sign of my appreciation for letting me crash your life," he explains to me.

"Guess I can handle that." I take a sip of my wine. If it means I don't have to cook, sign me up.

Pierre continues to list off his other talents. "I'm good at being a dog dad." He is, he loves that floof ball. Frankston is passed out on the rug in front of the television, he's totally over listening to our bad karaoke tunes.

"You are a good dog dad."

This makes him smile. "I'm good at massages." Really? The old I'm good at massage trick. "Not those kinds, but I am good at them too. I give good foot massages, here give me your feet," he says, trying to grab my feet.

"Ew, no." I giggle as I dodge his hands.

"Don't you remember how good I used to be at massaging your feet?" he says.

That's right, he would massage my feet when I came back from Pilates, his strong fingers digging into the right spots.

"Come on, give me those little piggies," he teases. I could use a foot massage, being in heels all day hurts. Reluctantly, I move my feet into his lap, he places his glass of wine on the side table, and then grabs my feet. The first slide of his thumb along my arch has me moaning.

"Oh my ..." I groan, throwing back my head as his fingers work wonders over my skin.

"Told you I was good." He chuckles.

"So good," I moan. Who knew so much tension was being held in my feet?

"I miss hearing you moan like that," he says as he suddenly stops massaging my feet. "Did I say that out loud?" I nod. "Ignore me. I've had too much wine." He starts massaging my feet again. This time, I try to keep my moans to myself. "Fuck," he grumbles as he moves uncomfortably on the sofa. I open my eyes and realize what is happening. The tenting in his sweats is a damn giveaway, he's hard and he's trying to move his cock into a more convenient position.

"Did I make you hard?" I stare at the large tent.

"Um, yes. The sounds you were making were hot," he confesses.

"Your fingers are good."

A proud smirk falls across Pierre's lips. "You know they are."

I bite my bottom lip, remembering the other night when I let him slide his thick fingers inside me before I broke down. Thank goodness for my battery-operated friend who was able to finish me off. "Pierre!" I blush.

"Right, sorry. I can't not flirt with you. It's a habit." He grins.

"You can flirt, I guess, as long as you aren't expecting anything," I warn him.

"I would never dare." He smirks suspiciously.

"I mean it. You and I are friends only," I remind him.

"Looks like I've been upgraded from acquaintance to friend," he teases.

I roll my eyes and try not to laugh. "I have to go to bed, I have work in the morning."

"Think of me while you play with yourself, eh?" he calls out to my retreating back.

Asshole.

But he's not wrong.

19

ISABELLE

"**M**orning," Pierre greets me happily. The smell of bacon wafts through the air, and my stomach grumbles.

"Morning. How are you so chipper this morning after all that wine?" I ask him. I walk straight over to my coffee maker and start preparing my glass of energy.

"I've made breakfast, thought we could use something to soak up all that wine. We polished off a couple of bottles," he says, sliding the tray of bacon toward me.

"And my head feels every bit of it." I swipe a piece from the tray and nibble on it.

"I was thinking about cooking steak tonight for dinner."

"You're going to cook for me again?" I ask.

"Told you last night I would. I promise we won't drink as much wine tonight as we did last night."

"Don't think I'd survive if we keep it up." I smile as I take a sip of my wake-up cure. My shoulders instantly relax as I take my first sip of coffee.

"I had fun last night," he says, looking up at me as he takes a bite of his bacon.

"I did too." I think the wine helped.

"Just like old times." He grins.

"Yeah. It was. We always did have fun together." The pang of nostalgia hits me as the smile falls off my face.

"I'm sorry I broke us, Issy," Pierre says again.

He's trying. And I can hear the sincerity in this voice. "You don't need to keep apologizing to me."

"It doesn't feel like I've done enough to make it up to you."

"Making me dinner every night seems like enough," I tell him. I don't want him to keep punishing himself. That is on me, not him. He's done enough. I do still have hang-ups about him, but he's not doing anything now to warrant me not speaking to him. His life has enough turmoil in it, I don't need to add to it. I'll deal with my insecurities internally just like I have always done.

"That's it?" he questions me.

"Yeah. I'm a simple girl. Look, I have to run. I have a morning meeting. I'm sure you have a lot to talk about with Marcus and Jordan. Concentrate on finding your next team, everything else doesn't matter," I remind him.

"Okay. Let me at least pack you some breakfast to go. Two slices of bacon is not enough for you to go kick some ass at work with," he says.

"I don't eat much at breakfast," I tell him.

"That's not good. Breakfast is an important part of the day. Let me do this. Food I know." He grins. Okay, if the man wants to make me a breakfast to go, I'm not one to say no to that.

Pierre: Hey, I'm doing a load of washing. Do you have anything?

> Issy: You don't have to do my washing, the housekeeper does it.

> Pierre: You paused her, remember?

SHIT. I did too because he was staying there for the week, and now it's turned longer, I forgot to un pause her.

> Pierre: I'm happy to clean the house. I am the reason you don't have help.

I can't expect a two-time cup winning hockey player to clean my house.

> Issy: You don't have to do that. I can do it when I get home.

> Pierre: After you've worked all day. No. I'm here now doing nothing but contemplating how messed up my life is. I need something to do, otherwise, I'm going to go stir crazy.

He is basically in lock down.

> Issy: Do you know how to do the washing?

> Pierre: I had to wash my own gear growing up.

> Issy: Fine. The basket is in my bathroom.

> Pierre: *Thumbs up*

I click on my in-home security app to see what Pierre is up to, I don't want him snooping around my bedroom. I watch the cameras flick through following him as he walks through my home, up the stairs, and into my bedroom. He stops for a moment, taking it all in, he then walks into my bathroom and picks up the overflowing basket. He carries it back downstairs to the laundry room, but I notice he drops a couple of things along the way. He starts sorting through the clothes, separating the whites from the colors before putting a load on. Why is it so hot watching men do household chores? He walks back into the hall and sees the items he dropped. When he picks them up I notice it's a couple of pairs of my underwear. Oh no. That's embarrassing. He stares at the white cotton panties, and next thing I know, he is sniffing them. What the fuck? What does he think he is doing? He stops abruptly as if he can sense me watching him, and the next thing I know, he takes a seat on my sofa and pulls his cock out of his sweats. I still. My heart starts beating uncontrollably in my chest, my cheeks flush, and I nervously look around my office wondering if anyone can see the indecent images I do. I shouldn't be watching. Pierre thinks he's alone. But then he pulls my knickers to his nose and inhales as he starts sliding his hand over his cock. His hard, thick cock. I'm transfixed by the image on my phone. This is creepy. I shouldn't be looking, but I can't seem to look away either. I wiggle in my chair, a deep throbbing ache between my legs. This isn't good. I'm at work. Now is not the appropriate time to get turned on. My teeth sink into my lip as I watch his veiny forearms tug harshly on his cock as he continues to use my panties as inspiration. This is hot. So hot. Watching Pierre's dirty little secret. Has he done this before? He must have, he stole my underwear the other night. I should feel violated that he is using my underwear in this way, it's a breach of friendship, but so is watching your roommate jerk off. We're even. He continues to touch himself, his hand getting faster and faster, every muscle in his arm and body tensing as he works himself closer to the edge, until he wraps my knickers around the tip of his cock and comes. His eyes are closed, his back arches, those hard biceps straining as he releases himself into my knickers. A filthy, satisfied smirk slides across his lips as he starts to tidy himself up. And now I'm drenched.

I DIDN'T GET any work done today because I couldn't stop thinking about what I watched earlier. After spacing out in one meeting and having to reread a contract three times, I gave up and decided to leave early. This is going to be an awkward dinner tonight. How the hell am I supposed to look at him across the table when I watched him jerk off over my undies? Maybe I can quickly use my battery-operated friend while he's preparing dinner, and then I won't feel so wound up.

"You're home early," he calls out, hearing me walk through the door.

"Hey, Frankston." The golden floof jumps up and greets me warmly at the door.

"Yeah. Splitting headache," I call out to him.

He walks into the foyer wearing nothing but a pair of gray sweats. My eyes fall on his bare chest. This is not the visual I need when I'm as highly strung as I am right now. Has he always been this muscular? Have his biceps been this huge?

"Are you okay? You look a little flushed. Are you coming down with something?" Pierre asks, sounding concerned. *Yeah, a case of too hot to handle.*

"Hangovers. They hit differently as adults," I tell him, shaking the impure thoughts of him from my mind.

"Tell me about it. I think it's going to take me a couple of days to get over those bottles last night." He chuckles. "I'm just getting the salad ready. I can put the steaks on anytime you like."

"I'm just going to go upstairs and have a shower," I say, bypassing him and running up the stairs. I've never been this turned on before and it's making me crazy. I quickly pull out my remote-control friend from my bedside table, and there is no need to get myself going, I'm already there. I pull up my skirt, slide my underwear to the side, shove the wand between my thighs, and turn it on. Yes. A moan falls from my lips. That's what I needed. Yes. I can feel my legs start to quiver as the vibrations do their thing.

"Hey, Issy," Pierre calls out.

Fuck. I throw my vibrating friend away from me moments before Frankston comes rushing in. His eyes land on my toy, and I watch in slow motion as he zeroes in on it. "No," I yell at him, but it's too late. He grabs the still vibrating wand and runs away with it nearly knocking over Pierre in the process.

"Did he grab something of yours?" he asks.

Shit. I chase after the golden floof. This is embarrassing. "Frankston. You little fucker give that back to me," I curse at him. But he thinks this is hilarious as he continues to run around my home having the time of his life while I slowly die of mortification.

"Frankston, drop it," Pierre's booming voice commands, and Frankston does what he is told and drops my vibrating friend. It buzzes along the hardwood floors. "What the ...?" Pierre picks it up and turns it off. He turns and raises a brow at me. "Were you using this just then?"

"No," I snap, trying to grab my wand back.

Of course, Pierre thinks this is hilarious as my cheeks redden with humiliation as he holds it above his head.

"Issy." Those hazel eyes narrow on me. Don't know why he is upset over this. He isn't the one whose sex toy was eaten by his dog.

"That's none of your business," I snap at him.

"You weren't sick when you came home, were you?" he questions me. I splutter to find an answer for him, but it ends up dying on my lips. "Issy. Tell me. Did you come home early because you were worked up over something or someone?" My face falls. "Shit," he says as he rakes his hand through his hair. "It's someone."

"Yes but ..." He has no idea that someone is him.

He swallows as he tries to get a handle on his emotions. "Do I know him?"

I bite my bottom lip. "Please, I don't want to talk about it."

Pierre looks at me for a moment, and I see the shutters close as his hand drops and he hands me back my wand. "How do you like your steak?"

"Medium."

He nods and walks back into the kitchen. Shit. I think I've hurt his feelings.

"DINNER SMELLS GREAT," I say, trying to keep upbeat. The dining table is set again, there's a breadbasket and a bowl of salad in the middle as well as some condiments.

"Take a seat, I'm plating up," he says unable to look at me. I do as he asks and take a seat, and watch him move around the kitchen. He's put on a T-shirt which is a shame but probably for the best. Pierre places a plate down with a thick steak on it. It smells delicious. He fusses around with some things before sitting down. Silence falls between us as I fill my plate up with salad. "I've got a meeting with The Mavericks tomorrow."

"You do. That's fantastic," I say, glad that he's broken the ice.

"I'm going to start apartment hunting too. I've taken over your home, and that's not fair," he says, digging into his steak, cutting off the conversation. I do the same and let silence fall between us again. "I've ordered a replacement for your thing, too. Should arrive in the coming days. Sorry Frankie destroyed it."

I let my cutlery fall with a clank. "Stop. Please," I yell at him, throwing my napkin on the table and storming off toward the bar where I grab the bottle of tequila. I don't even bother pouring myself a shot, I take a swig straight from the bottle.

"Issy, what the hell," Pierre shouts as he watches in horror as I throw back another shot.

Fuck. "I have to tell you something. Fuck. I don't know if you are going to look at me the same. I'm disgusted with myself. I'm so sorry."

Pierre gets up from the dining table and walks across the living room to where I am standing beside the bar. He places two large hands on my shoulders.

"Breathe. Whatever it is I can handle it. I'm a big boy." Don't I know it.

"I can't look at you." I stare down at the floor.

"Issy," he says my name softly, probably wondering why I've lost my mind, and places a finger under my chin, lifting it so that I'm looking at him. "It's me. There's nothing that you can say to me that will make me think any less of you." I know he means it, but I don't know if he will after I confess what I did.

"You're going to hate me," I whisper to him.

"Try me. This is you and I starting again. You can trust me, Issy," he reassures me.

I bite my bottom lip. Do it. Tell him. It's eating you up inside. "Please don't hate me."

Pierre's face softens. "I could never." His thumb slides across my cheek. I hate how my body reacts to his touch still after all these years. Okay, here goes.

"Just so you know, there are security cameras in the living room," I say super quickly.

Pierre's hand falls from my face as he looks around the room. "Cameras?"

"Yes. I'm sorry. I should have told you earlier, but I didn't think about it. Until ... I ... didn't think you would ... you know ... um," I stutter.

"You didn't think I would ..." As if the penny drops, Pierre realizes what I am talking about. "You saw me today?" he asks. I nod.

"I wasn't spying. I was worried you were going to search through my room, and I didn't want you seeing my vibrators, but I guess that doesn't matter now," I blabber.

"Vibrators?"

I wave his question away. "Not the point. I invaded your personal space when you thought you were alone."

"When I thought I was alone enough to take care of my needs?" he states.

I want the world to swallow me whole right now. "Yes," I answer. I'm not sure what he is thinking. He's very calm which could mean he's freaking out.

"And you saw that?" he asks, those hazel eyes narrowing on me. He's upset. And rightfully so.

"Yes."

"How much of it did you see?" he asks. Shit. Do I tell him I watched it all, or do I lie and tell him I swiped out of it before I could see anymore? "Issy." His deep voice rumbles through me, making me jump.

"I watched it all," I blurt out.

"All of it?" he asks, raising a brow.

"Yes. I couldn't look away," I confess.

"Where did you watch this?" he asks.

"In my office. Alone," I add, just so he knows that his secret is safe with me.

His brows are high on his forehead in surprise. "Did that have anything to do with you coming home early?"

Lie. Issy. Lie. "Yes."

"Is that the reason you were using your battery-operated friend?" His voice lowers as those hazel eyes never move from me.

"Yes."

He takes a step toward me, his chest heaving as if he is trying to restrain himself. "Were you turned on over watching me get off to your scent?"

I swallow hard, my entire body tingling as nervous energy zips through me. "Yes."

Pierre's nostrils flare, his hands scrunch together, balling into a fist. He's upset and so he should be. I violated him. "Come back to the table, your steak will be getting cold."

Huh? "I'm so sorry."

Pierre holds up his hand. "I don't want to talk about it. I'm starving." And with that, he turns and heads back to the dining room table and starts cutting into his steak. I'm so confused. Reluctantly, I walk back to the table and take my seat. We both sit there in silence eating our dinner. Once we are done, I tell him I'll clean up, which he lets me do and disappears into his room. I don't see him again for the rest of the night.

I messed up.

20

ISABELLE

B reakfast was ready for me to take to work this morning when I came downstairs, which I appreciated, but Pierre was nowhere to be seen. I'm guessing he needs some space, and I don't blame him. He did say he was going to look for an apartment today after his meeting with The Mavericks. I bet he doesn't feel comfortable around me now. I wouldn't. Why was I such a dirty perv?

My phone beeps.

> Pierre: Are you alone?

Issy: Yes. Is everything okay?

> Pierre: Check the security cameras.

Oh no. Did something happen? Were we robbed while he was out? Did Frankston eat more of my shoes? I thought I had hidden them all. Shit. Did the paparazzi find him? I click on the app and gasp, almost dropping the phone in the process. There he is without a shirt on and with his gray sweats, staring at the camera as if he's looking right at me.

Pierre: Can you call me?

Um.

I watch as he makes the signal on the video of a phone with his fingers. Why does he want me to call him? My heart is beating outside of my chest. I press the button on my phone to call him and bring back up the security app.

"Good girl," he coos through the phone. "Is the door to your office locked?"

"No."

"Lock it," he commands. I get up, rush toward the door, and click the lock.

"It's locked."

"Good. And there's no way anyone can see you in your office?" he asks.

"The windows are behind me," I tell him.

"Can any other buildings see into your office?"

"Yes."

"Close the blinds, Issy," he demands.

I press the button to close the blinds. "They're closed."

He gives me a wide smile as he pushes his sweats down and starts fisting himself. I gasp but I don't look away. I should look away, but I don't.

"This is what you saw yesterday, isn't it?" he questions me.

I lick my lips watching him fist himself right in front of me. "Yes." My answer is shaky. "And you were so turned on after watching me touch myself to your scent that you came home early to relieve yourself because that throbbing ache between your thighs was driving you insane."

"Yes," I whimper as I watch him continue to touch himself.

"Thought so. Touch yourself, Issy."

"What! No. I'm at work," I hiss at him as he continues to slide his hand up and down his thick cock. I bite my bottom lip, enjoying the free show.

"No one will know, but you're not going to get any work done if you don't." He smirks as he stands there jerking himself off. This is insane. I've never done anything like this before in my life. I'm at work. "What are you wearing today?" he asks.

"Blouse and pants."

"Is there enough room for you to slide your hand inside?"

"Yes." The word sounds breathless.

"Good, now do it. Tell me how wet you are so I can continue." His hand stops moving as he glares into the camera. What the hell am I thinking? He's right, though, there's an aching throb between my legs, one that has been there since yesterday and now that he's awakened it again it's all I can think about. Thank goodness I chose pants with an elastic top today as I nervously slide my hand inside my pants and into my underwear, my fingers meeting the dampness between my thighs. A hiss falls from my lips. "Good girl." He chuckles darkly as he starts touching himself again. I thought this man was upset with me. I didn't realize he was turned on. This is wrong. So very wrong, but I can't stop it, nor do I want to. It's hot. Has a new kink been unlocked? "Did it get you hot watching me touch myself to you?" I moan at his words. "Will you leave your drenched underwear for me to use tomorrow?" he asks.

"Yes."

"Fuck, Issy." He groans, muscles straining as he continues to jerk himself to the thought of my underwear. It's hot. So hot. "The things I want to do to you, Issy."

"Tell me?" I moan as my fingers slide against my clit.

"Last night all I could think about during dinner was using that fucking vibrator on your aching cunt and seeing how many orgasms I could pull from you. Would I make you squirt? Would you pass out?" My hand thumps the desk as my fingers continue to circle myself. "When you walk into the kitchen in the mornings looking all sleeping and soft. All I think about is dropping to my knees, spreading your legs, and eating you until

you scream as your morning caffeine boost." Dammit. Yes.
"When you were on your knees in front of me the other day,
your lips all pink and pouty as you tried to calm me down, I
imagined what it would have been like to rub the tip of my dick
across those lips. Watching them wrap around my cock as it
slowly slides past them." I whimper at the imagery. "That damn
fucking nightdress you wear to bed kills me, you prance around
the house and all I see is your taunt nipples pressed against the
silk and all I want to do is bite them. Suck on them. Tease them.
See if I can make you come just by playing with them." This
man is going to kill me.

"Saint," I moan, using the nickname I used to call him.

"Say my name again, baby, it's been too long since I've heard
it on your lips."

"Saint," I moan.

"That's it. You're close, so fucking close." He groans as I
continue to watch him viciously touch himself, every part of
him straining as he chases his own high. "Come for me, baby,
drench those fingers for me." And next thing I know, I am
coming and doing exactly that. Moments later, I hear Pierre's
moans as he finishes off in his hand.

Shit.

What have I done? I hang up and turn off the app.

21

PIERRE

I t's most certainly been an interesting week. After one of
the hottest things, I've ever done having phone sex with
Issy, that night when she came home, I thought we had
turned the corner in our friendship and that she would let me
do all the things I said to her over the phone in the flesh.
Instead, she acted as if nothing happened. We sat and ate
dinner, talked about our day, watched sports on the television,
and then went to bed, separately. The next day I called her
again and just like the day before we had the most earth-shat-
tering phone sex, and then she comes home and again acts like
she didn't just watch me jerk off using her knickers on her security camera. She has done this all week. It's hot. Like it's our
dirty little secret, but if I'm being honest, I'm confused.

There's a knock on the front door. I check the peep hole first
and see that it's Sam Rose which is a surprise.

"Hey, man, how are you?" he asks, greeting me warmly.

"Still housebound," I tell him as I shut the door behind
him. "I should hear back about an offer from The Mavericks
next week so fingers crossed they can come through for me. I

had a sit down with the coach the other day and I want to play for them. I really like the coach, he seems like a good guy."

"That's great news. Does that mean you'll be searching for somewhere to live in the city?" he asks.

"Yeah. Felix and I are looking at getting a place together. Did you want a drink or something?" I ask.

"Water thanks," he answers. "You and Felix?"

"Yeah. I think he's thinking about what happens once your sister's ex moves on and leaves her alone. I mean, it was why he moved in wasn't it?" I ask him.

"That's true. I just thought they were doing so well." Sam shrugs.

"My brother is head over heels in love, but he has baggage too. I think he doesn't want to do anything that would jeopardize his relationship with her. When the season starts, we are hyper focused on the game, we can be quite unbearable to live with."

Sam nods. I know he is just looking out for his sister. "How are things with Issy going?"

"She doesn't hate me as much so ... I take that as a win," I tell him as I take a sip of my water.

"There's nothing going on between the two of you?" he asks.

"Um, no, why?" I ask defensively.

"Hey. I don't care if there is it's just, I come bearing gifts and I thought you've been here locked up in Issy's home for the past couple of weeks with nothing but your hand for company." He grins, sliding a box toward me.

I take the black box and open it. Inside is something that looks like a credit card with the words The Paradise Club on it and nothing else except a barcode and a number. "Oh wow," I say, staring at a key that gets me into this world of sex clubs. "Thanks."

"Don't thank me just yet. There are very strict rules to this club. A bit like fight club, no one talks about fight club," he warns me seriously. "Guard this card with your life. If you see anyone at the club outside the club that isn't like us, do not mention the club. We value our exclusivity and clientele it is the only reason something like this can succeed without the gossip pages finding out. I trust you."

"Thank you."

"And just so you know, Bill Reeves and Kitty are not members, I checked. This is kind of breaking the rules, but I just needed you to know you were safe. Now I can't guarantee you won't run into anyone else you know so remember your secret and everyone else's secrets are kept safe."

"I understand," I tell him.

"So, you going to go check it out tonight? I'd say let me take you but that might be weird, plus I have a thing so enjoy," he says, getting up from his chair.

"And again, thank you for this. I really need it."

"Go forth and have fun, you deserve it." He grins before giving me a wave and walking out the door.

Because Sam came over, I didn't get to have my jerk off session. I messaged her and asked for a raincheck, and she agreed. Issy is probably going to be in a bad mood when she gets home with all the pent-up tension, and I can't wait.

I hear the keys in the front door and Frankston rushes toward it, and moments later, I hear here giggles as he greets her.

"Did you have a good day, boy?" she asks. It's very sweet how much she has fallen in love with my boy. She found a doggy bakery the other day and now brings him home treats which he has after his dinner.

"Hey, how was your day?" I ask her as soon as she enters the kitchen.

"Okay. How was yours?" she asks cautiously.

"Interesting. I'll tell you about it during dinner. The table is set if you want to crack open the champagne and pour us each a glass," I tell her.

"Champagne, are we celebrating something? Did The Mavericks offer you a contract?" she asks excitedly.

"Not yet, they said they would be in touch next week."

I hear the champagne bottle pop and watch as she pours us both a glass while I bring over the beef goulash I made. We settle in at the table and suddenly I'm nervous. I'm not sure what she is going to think when I tell her I'm now a member of The Paradise Club.

"So, what are we celebrating?" she asks, holding up her glass of champagne to me to clink before she takes her first sip.

Spit it out, Pierre. "You're looking at the newest member of The Paradise Club." I grin, clinking our glasses together. She follows the motions but stays quiet until she realizes she hasn't congratulated me.

"Oh wow. Congrats. I'm sure you must be happy about that. Now you don't have to wonder what it's about anymore," she says, clearly affected by this news as she takes a large gulp.

"I guess not," I tell her as I start to dig into my dinner. "I was kind of hoping to go check it out tonight." Issy drops her cutlery which makes a loud sound before hurriedly picking it back up again.

"You should," she says through gritted teeth.

"You don't have anything to say about it?" I ask, annoyed that she is ignoring everything we have been doing this past week like I'm her dirty secret.

"No. You're single. You can do what you want."

Now it's my turn to drop my cutlery. "Seriously? You have no feelings about me going to a sex club and fucking someone else?" Her knuckles turn white as she grips her fork and her cheeks burn brightly. She's not happy at all about that thought. She's jealous. Good.

"Why would I care?" she snips.

I stare at her blankly. Why would she care? Has this been all one sided? I thought ... shit. "You wouldn't care if I left here after cooking you dinner and went to a sex club and slept with someone else." Issy swallows and I can see it on her face she isn't happy, but she can't bring herself to tell me that. "I get it. You're embarrassed."

"Embarrassed?" she repeats.

"What else would you call it? Every single day I bring you to orgasm at work and then you waltz into your home as if what we did during the day never happened. I'm your dirty little secret, Issy, you're so ashamed of yourself for wanting me again that you ignore it. I can't, no I won't be ignored anymore." With that, I throw my napkin onto the table and walk out of the dining room.

There's a soft knock at my bedroom door. "Come in." I'm rummaging through my clothes wondering what the hell does someone wear to a sex club because if Issy doesn't want me then I'm sure as hell not going to stay here and keep making a fool out of myself.

"Saint." Issy says my old nickname. I still. Dammit. She's playing dirty. I refuse to turn around to look at her. I hear her feet pad across the wooden floor until a hand lands on my back. "We need to talk."

I turn around. "I think we do." I offer her a seat on my bed, thankfully, I made it today. She takes it, and I notice she's nervous as she picks at one of her nails. We sit there in silence, neither one of us knowing how to start this conversation we should have had a week ago.

"Would it hurt you if I went to the club tonight and hooked up with someone?" I ask her. Turning to look at her as she sits there contemplating my question. She starts to answer then stops and tries again, but nothing but a squeak comes out. "It would hurt me if you went after the week we had." Slowly, Issy lifts her face to look at me, those chocolate eyes filled with so many unsaid words that I hope might spill from her lips. "Yes. It would hurt me," she answers quietly.

Oh, thank goodness. Relief washes over me. I reach out and take her hand in mine and she lets me. "This week has been one of the hottest weeks of my life," I confess to her.

Issy bites her bottom lip. "Mine too," she says, unable to look at me.

I give her hand a squeeze. "Issy, look at me." She looks up through thick lashes. Reaching out I cup her face. "Take me to Paradise and do whatever the hell you want to me." Her hand squeezes mine.

"Saint." She gasps.

Her using her old nickname on me is my undoing as I lean forward and rest my forehead against hers. "I want you, Issy. This week seems likes the filthiest foreplay I've ever had. Do you want me too?" I ask her.

"Yes, but ..." of course there is a but, "this doesn't mean anything. It's just sex." Not going to lie that stings a little, no, a lot, but the fact that she is putting sex on the table who the hell is going to say no to that.

"I understand."

"I can't risk anything more with you, Pierre." There it is, the wall she's put between us using my name. She may forgive me for what I did as kids but she's never going to forget it. I resign myself to that fact. My life is in shambles right now, I'm not looking to date anyone anytime soon, so if all Issy can offer me is sex than I can handle that.

"I understand. Just sex," I tell her.

She nods. "I think we can agree the physical attraction is still there."

It sure is. But what she's saying is the emotional connection isn't. Guess I'm going to have to respect her wishes. *So, you should. You never thought you would ever get Issy back in your arms. Are you prepared to give that up because she won't give you a*

piece of her heart that you broke the last time she gave it to you.
Point made. My thumb slides over her pouty lips. "It sure is."

Next thing I know she is pressing her lips to mine and kissing me. She's made the first move on me, catching me off-guard for a moment, but once my brain catches up, I'm kissing her back. My fingers dig into her hair as I pull her closer to me. She climbs into my lap and deepens the kiss.

"Fuck, Issy." I groan as I devour her, a week's worth of fore-play unleashing in a kiss.

"Shut up," she hisses, pushing me backward onto the bed. I do as I am told not wanting this to stop. I roll her onto her side, her leg curls over my hip as my cock digs into her. Issy pulls away, we are both panting. "If we do this, there's rules." What-ever she wants. Yes.

"Rules." I pant as my hand slides along her face, pushing her hair behind her ear.

"Yes. I think we need them." Issy is protecting herself, I get it.

"Lay them on me," I tell her, my eyes roaming over her gorgeous face.

"It's just sex," she states.

"We established that earlier," I tell her.

"I won't share you at The Paradise Club," she adds.

There's no way in the world I am going to sit and watch some other man fuck her. "I'm not sharing you either. Next."

"This stops when you move out."

I still.

"I mean it, this is just because we are living in the same house, nothing more," she adds.

"Are you saying this wouldn't be happening if I wasn't here?"

"Yes. Because I wouldn't be forced to be around you."

Oh. "Do you not want this?" I question her.

Her brows pull together as she bites her lip. "Yes. I wouldn't be here if I didn't." Then she slides her hand across my face and looks at me. "If we were not forced together, I would never have given you a chance. I would have continued to ignore you and held onto the past." That is true. "I know I sound like a broken record and it's nothing against you even though it is about you ..." she says, rubbing her thumb across my cheek, "but my heart is non-negotiable. If you think that this is going to change my mind about wanting more with you then let's not do it." Wow. Guess I should be happy that she's being honest with me, but that is a kick in the guts. "You have a lot going on in your life. You shouldn't be worrying about dating especially me."

"I want you, Issy," I declare.

"And I want to fuck you, Saint. But these are my rules," she explains.

"So, no seeing anyone else while I'm living here. It will just be the two of us messing around until I move out, and then what?" I ask.

"Then we stay being friends."

"You think you're going to be able to do that?" Because I sure as hell don't think I can.

"Of course."

"And you won't have a problem if I start dating then?" I ask.

"It would be an adjustment as it would be for you. I want you to be happy," she states.

"And that's not with you?" She shakes her head. "Okay. I hear you. We have fun until I move out and then friends."

Issy's face lights up. "Deal."

"Take me to Paradise, Issy." I grin as I grab her face and kiss her which makes her giggle.

22

ISABELLE

I'm nervous and excited at the same time. I want Pierre, physically. Like he said, this has been the longest foreplay, and honestly, I'm sick of using my battery-operated friend, it doesn't seem to get me off as well as he does over the phone.

"Holy shit, Issy, you look stunning," Pierre says as those hazel eyes hungrily look over me. I chose a sexy little black dress that barely covers the front and back of me, and dips low showing off my cleavage. "Is this what you normally wear to the club?" he asks, reaching out and pulling me to him. His hands run down my body until he grabs my ass in his large hand and squeezes it. "You're not wearing any underwear." He groans as he holds me against him.

"Didn't see the point." I smirk as I run my hand along his hard chest. I told him to put on a pair of loose pants and a top, something that is easy to get in and out of.

"Do you want to skip the club and just stay in?" he says, nuzzling my neck, his lips trailing down my throat, my nipples pebbling with each kiss.

"You've been waiting so long to go to it and now you want to stay at home?" I chuckle.

"Why would I need to go when I have everything I want here?" he says, his teeth nip my skin.

Oh.

I look up at him. "What do you want?"

"I want to see you bent over the sofa, legs spread, and show me what I've been missing all these years." I swallow hard as he stares at me darkly. I mean, fucking is fucking either at home or a sex club. Maybe we'll raincheck the club then. On shaky legs, I walk over to the sofa and do as he asks. I place my stomach on the edge of the sofa, slowly open my legs, feeling the hem of my dress roll over my backside until it is around my waist.

"Fuck, Issy," he curses behind me and his voice sounds strangled. "You're even better than I remember." I bite my bottom lip. "Show me how you've been touching yourself all week."

I close my eyes and let my fingers slide between my thighs, I am already wet.

"You're killing me." He groans, and when I open my eyes, I catch his reflection in the glass. He has his dick out and is slowly pumping his hand up and down his thick length. My fingers dip between my folds and circle my clit all while I watch him jerk off over me. It's so fucking hot. I've never had a man do this with me before. Yes, I get up to wild things at The Paradise Club, but outside of that, my sex life is tame. Not that I have much of a sex life outside of the club. No man has ever jerked off on security camera for me, nor made me dinner every night or breakfast in the mornings. The man is even doing my washing and cleaning my home. "You're dripping, Issy. I need a taste." Next thing I know, his tongue is pushing my fingers out of the way, while his hands grip my hips and he practically makes me sit on his face. Oh my god, my knees want to buckle as he eats my pussy like a starved man. My fingers dig into my sofa as Pierre's tongue slides all over me. He doesn't stop. I don't even think he takes a breath down there, but then he slides one of his thick fingers inside me, and I start to see stars. I'm panting. Mumbling. Cursing. Praying. As he pushes me higher and higher until I can't take it any longer, and he pushes me right over the edge, and I scream the house down. I'm so loud that Frankston comes running and starts attacking his dad, who reluctantly lets go of me as he pushes his dog out of the way.

"What the fuck, Frankie. I was making her come, man. You killed the vibe, buddy. She's good. So good. Tell him." He looks up at me, and I all I can do is laugh as I look down at the mess I've made all over Pierre's face. It's glistening with me all over him, his hair is a mess, and his pants are tented.

"I'm good, boy, so good," I reassure Frankston who gives me a woof and then walks away.

"Can't believe he attacked me." Pierre chuckles as he helps himself up. "He didn't ruin the mood, did he?"

"Hell no." I grin as I launch myself into his arms, which makes him chuckle. My lips are on his and I can taste myself.

"Fuck, I've missed your taste." He groans as he walks us a couple of steps and presses me against the wall. Thank goodness he has thick arms and can hold me like this. "I need inside of you, Issy. I had grand plans of taking my time with you tonight, but fuck it, we've been foreplaying for weeks now. I'll make it up to you next time." I couldn't agree more, I need him inside me. Stat. He pulls himself from his pants and slides his cock through my slickness making both of us hiss. "Shit. I don't have a condom on me, it's in my room."

"I'm on birth control and have regular checks because of the club. I'm clean. And I haven't been with anyone since then. It's been two months," I tell him.

Pierre bites his bottom lip and stills. "I thought you went the first night I was here."

"I did, but I couldn't bring myself to do anything."

"Really?" He seems shocked. I nod. "I just had mine done for the club. I'm clean," he tells me.

"Just this once, okay?" I tell him.

"Agreed." He hisses as he lines himself up and slowly slides into me. Yes. Yes. Yes. The delicious stretch of his thick cock. "I want to move, Issy, but I can't, you feel so fucking good." He groans.

I grab his face and make him look at me. "Fuck, Saint." And it sets him off. His fingers dig into my hips as he starts pistoning into me. Next thing I know he is speaking in French and it has me melting even more. He could be reciting plays for all I know, I don't care because he is seriously pushing all my buttons. I'm going to have bruises tomorrow, but it doesn't matter, it was worth it. I move my hand between us feeling him sliding in and out of me as I circle my clit. I'm feverish with each of his deep thrusts until we both can't take it anymore and come, me for the second time. It's been a while since a non-club person has pulled multiples out of me.

※

DAMMIT, my alarm goes off pulling me from a dirty dream I'd been having where Pierre was doing filthy things to me. I try to roll over to turn the alarm off, but I'm stuck by a muscular arm that is currently wrapped around me.

"It's too early for this much noise." That deep, timbered voice reverberates around me as he reaches over and turns my alarm off.

Shit.

No. No. No.

I try to make my way through the fog that is currently going on in my head. Last night wasn't a dream. Pierre did do dirty, filthy things to me as I look down at my naked body. What the hell was I thinking?

"Stop freaking out." He chuckles.

"I'm not freaking out."

"Yes, you are. You've woken up with buyer's remorse, I can feel the anxiety vibrating off you," he grumbles, snuggling into me so his scratchy stubble tickles my shoulder.

"I was shocked for five seconds finding you wrapped around me," I tell him.

"Naked," he adds. My eyes widen as I try not to freak out as he presses his morning wood against me. "See, very much naked and very much ready for round two or five, sort of lost count."

I slap him. "Get off me, I have to get ready for work." Pierre doesn't move except to pull me into him tighter.

"Give me ten and then you can go have a shower and I'll make you breakfast."

"I don't have time for sex, I have to get going. I'll grab breakfast on the way to the office," I tell him, shoving his immense weight off me, but it doesn't work, he's like a fricken boulder. He then rolls me onto my back and pushes my hands above my head as he rubs his naked body over me.

"Don't you think you would have a better day if you started it with an orgasm?" He grins, rolling his hips as his cock teases me, a small moan escapes me which makes him chuckle.

"I don't have time," I whine.

Pierre looks at me. "Give me five minutes to get you off, and then you can have a shower, and I'll pack you some breakfast to go." That does seem nice. "Issy, remember what we agreed to. If you need me, I'm here to service your needs. And I can feel how needy your pussy is this morning because it is exactly as needy as my cock."

Damn him and his mouth. "Fine," I say, rolling my eyes, but that is just for show because I wouldn't mind a quick orgasm before work.

Pierre smirks. "Thought you would see it my way," he says

before disappearing under the covers. His palms push open my legs, and I feel the warmth of his breath against my thighs and then the wetness of his tongue as he slides it across my folds. The deep rumble of his growl as he savors my taste has my hands digging into the covers. Yes. This is what I've been missing at home. Usually I order a morning wake-up call when I'm at The Paradise Club resort, but having it on tap at home is something I never realized I needed, *till now*. Maybe this no-strings-attached thing with Pierre won't be so bad if he wakes me up like this every morning. He slides a thick finger inside me, and my eyes roll back in my head. Yes. His fingers are so big and so thick and long, they reach places other men seem to miss. This is what I need, it's better than coffee as my body starts to tense and curl with the impending orgasm. Pierre continues to push me further and further toward the edge as he slides another finger inside me, stretching me, and when he curls them at the right angle, he sends me over and I lose myself in the all-consuming orgasm. I'm still coming down from my high as he smugly emerges from under the covers.

"You better go shower, you don't want to be late for work." He smiles before throwing back the covers and jumping out of bed exposing his large cock that is standing to attention.

"Don't you want me to look after that?" I ask him.

He looks down at his cock and then back at me. "Sweetness, you'll be late for work, I'll rub one out later while sniffing a pair of your dirty underwear."

"I don't have time to play, my day is full of meetings." I pout.

"Fine, I'll wait till you get home. You owe me. I want you on your knees while I watch the sports highlights. Okay?"

I smirk as if he is going to be able to wait until after dinner. "Fine."

"Go shower, I'll see you down in the kitchen." He throws the pillow back onto my bed and walks out of my room stark naked. Such a nice view. Why are guys asses so hot?

I'm showered and dressed and head downstairs, he's working topless in the kitchen and has a pair of gray sweats, and I can tell he's not wearing any underwear because his dick print is impressive in them.

"Like what you see?" He smirks as he packs up my breakfast.

"I do. This is lady porn right here," I tell him.

"Lady porn?" he questions me.

"Cooking, shirtless with gray sweats and no underwear on." I raise a brow at him.

"How do you know I don't have any underwear on?"

"It's the same as when a woman wears a shirt and no bra on and her nipples show through, I can see the imprint of your dick."

"Can you?" he grins as he rubs it with one hand. "What's he doing now?"

My eyes fall on the tenting in his pants. "Looks like he's getting ready to meet your hand. I have to go," I say, grabbing the container he's just packed for me.

"This is true, you owe me tonight," he warns.

"Cook dinner in this outfit and I'll owe you twice." I wink at him as I start to walk out of the kitchen.

"Consider it done. I've put together a tub of yoghurt and granola in there with an egg and bacon croissant," he calls out. That's more than I normally eat for breakfast, but it's also very sweet.

"Thanks," I call back to him as I grab my coat from the rack.

"You're welcome. Have a good day at work," he calls back as I hear him clatter around in the kitchen. I step out of my home with a smile on my face as I meet my driver.

"YOU GOT LAID," Eve says as soon as she walks into my office.

"Shh," I hiss at my sister, looking around her to see if anyone heard. "And how did you know?"

"You're glowing." She smirks.

"No, I'm not." I glare at her.

"Things seem to have progressed well with Pierre then." She eyes me suspiciously.

I know we promised not to tell anyone, but Eve kind of already knows. "You can't tell Vi or anyone, please," I warn her. "We've been teasing each other for weeks and last night it came to a head."

"I bet it did." My sister chuckles.

"Eve!" I squeal.

"Am I wrong?" she argues. No, she's not, but she doesn't need to know that.

"We both agreed there is something physical there between us, but I told him that's all it can be."

"Friends with benefits?" Eve asks.

"Yeah, like that, but only until he moves out. After that we are just friends," I explain to her.

"Why?"

"Because it's a proximity thing."

"You think you're only sleeping together because you're living together?" she asks.

"Well, yeah. I mean, if he was living at Harper's or at a hotel, I wouldn't have given him a chance."

Eve mulls this over. "That is true. Was the sex bad? Is that why you don't want to continue? Nothing worse when the chemistry is fire, but the sex isn't."

"The sex was amazing," I whisper to her, worried someone will hear me. *Not like you haven't been touching yourself in your office for the past week but you're worried someone might hear you say sex.* True.

"Then don't you want to keep having great sex?" she asks.

"Yes. But he's going to be heading into training camp soon, then the season starts. He's not going to have time."

"So, you're stopping it before he does," Eve states.

"No. Not really. Okay. Yes. I have to keep up boundaries, Eve, for my own sanity. The man has been cooking me dinner every single night. He gives me foot massages. Does my washing and cleans the house," I confess to her.

"I'm sorry. What did you say? That six-foot-five gorgeous man is wining and dining you as well as kept the home going. That's hot, Issy."

"It is. Especially when he cooks shirtless. He packed me breakfast this morning because he knows I never have time. He says breakfast is the most important meal of the day and doesn't want me skipping it."

"That is so cute, Issy," Eve gushes. "Orgasms and food, that would be a direct path to my heart."

"Your heart is more open than mine. Which is closed," I remind her.

She waves my comment away. "You're being stubborn, but I appreciate the resistance. Now that you've banged, do you feel better over the Pierre situation?"

"I don't know. It's still early days. Harper and Felix are together so I'm going to be around him whether I like it or not."

"Are you going to be okay seeing him with someone else once you stop sleeping with him?" she asks.

"Of course," I tell her, but Eve doesn't look convinced. "My heart is guarded, don't you worry."

"Okay," she says, before changing the subject and launching into work.

23

PIERRE

Honestly didn't think my life could get any better than it is right now. I've spent the past week in Issy's bed. We have our own routine which is me eating her off the kitchen countertop as soon as she gets home from work, then I serve her dinner where we talk about our day, and then dessert is usually taken in the living room and ends up with lots of orgasms, then we go to bed together. Frankston on the floor beside us. I wake her up in the mornings with more orgasms before sending her to work with her breakfast pack. Perfection.

The cherry on top is The Mavericks offered me a contract. They offered me a two-year deal, which would then turn into a yearly contract until I retire. It's not quite as lucrative as the one I had at the Devils, but I don't care as I get to play with my brother. But they did offer me the chance of joining the coaching team when I was ready to retire, which is a good deal.

"Are you ready?" Marcus, my agent, asks as I stand behind the curtain.

I'm in the green room freaking out about walking out in front of the packed media scrum for the first time since Kitty and I broke up. Guess my new life in New York starts now. The media think they are here to welcome Felix to The Mavericks, they have no idea they are getting me, too. This has been a tightly kept secret by everyone, they wanted it to be a huge surprise. After the announcement, Felix and I have a heap of publicity shoots to do to celebrate our addition to the team.

After today, the world will know I am in New York, and the quiet bubble I have been living in will end. Felix and I have appointments to look at apartments next week, now that I am out of confinement. Which I'm not looking forward to because as soon as we find somewhere, what's happening between Issy and me is going to end. And I don't want it to end. I just need a little more time to convince her that we should keep doing what we're doing once I leave. It will be good to finally be able to get out and about again. As much as I like living in Issy's home, I'm going stir crazy. My brother has asked me to join him and Sam on their daily runs around Central Park. The summer is slipping away quickly, and before I know it, we are going to be back into training camp, then it's some exhibition games, and then the season starts again.

Harper has arrived with Issy, and I must remember to keep my hands to myself. This is the first time we've been out in public together. I'm so used to being able to freely touch her that all I want to do is walk up to her, pull her into my arms, and kiss her but that would earn me a knee to the balls. She looks beautiful in a black wrap dress that accentuates her body, dipping low exposing her gorgeous tits. I am going to slowly unwrap her out of that dress when we get home. *Get your mind out of the gutter St. Pierre, it isn't a good look stepping out onto the stage in front of the world's media with a boner.* I watch in slow motion as Issy makes her way over to where Marcus and I are standing.

"You came?" I say to her, leaning in and giving her a kiss on the cheek.

"I wouldn't miss your big moment," she says, her cheeks blooming with a blush.

"I'm freaking out," I tell her. She reaches out and touches my arm and I know she is trying to keep the connection between us without looking suspicious.

"You've got this. You have stood in front of these things a million times," she reassures me.

"Not right after a scandal."

"You don't have to answer questions about you or Kitty," she says my exes name with gritted teeth. Someone ducks their head out of the curtain and gives me a thumbs up, I guess they are ready for me. "Good luck out there. Everyone is about to lose their minds." She grins before excusing herself and heading back over to where Harper and Meadow are standing.

"This is it, Pierre. The next phase of your new life," Marcus says, clapping me on the back.

"I'm ready," I tell him. Just hope Issy is too.

EVERYONE LOST THEIR MINDS. The sports media were shocked when I came out and announced I would be joining The Mavericks, after Felix's press conference. It felt amazing sitting beside my little brother as we bantered back and forth with the media. Sitting there and watching Felix confidently answer hard questions about his personal life gave me the strength to do the same when they asked me about mine. Overall, it was a huge success.

And that's how we have ended up at some club in the VIP section that Sam Rose arranged.

"Congratulations to your freedom," Sam says, raising his shot of tequila high. "And congratulations to my new wingman." He grins. Never going to happen. My eyes fall on Issy, who doesn't look happy. We all throw back our shots. Felix and

Harper are on the dance floor together in their own little world, and I wish so much that I could do that with Issy. But she's right when she says if our friends knew, they would assume we were back together again, and the pressure of labelling ourselves would be put on us and I won't do anything that will jeopardize my relationship with Issy again. Meadow, Kimberly, and Issy are in a corner talking together while sipping on champagne.

"There he is, the man of the hour, Pierre St. Pierre." Sam grins as he brings over four beautiful women to our area of the VIP section, obviously not needing any wingman help. "This man just got his heart broken, so he's looking for someone to help put it back together again." The girls all ooh and ahh as I shake their hands. My eyes always land on where Issy is sitting, and she isn't impressed. Thanks Sam.

"So, you're a hockey player?" one of the girls says, sliding up beside me.

"Yes, I am," I answer, grabbing my beer and taking a sip, feeling very uncomfortable.

"That's so cool. I love hockey." She grins.

"Oh really? Who's your favorite player?" I ask her.

"Um, oh you know ... um ... you," she says brightly. I may have been in a relationship the last couple of years, but I know when someone is bullshitting me.

"Thanks. I appreciate my fans." I grin and glare at Sam who thinks this is hilarious.

The night continues disastrously, I'm stuck entertaining these women, pretending to be interested in whatever mundane story they are telling, something about being flown out to Dubai to party. They show me their social media profiles which makes me cringe, but I smile and nod as they slide past their thirst trap photos. Something that I realized Kitty used to do to my friends.

When I look up, I notice Issy is talking to a man in a suit, and she's laughing, placing her hand on his chest, and leaning in as he talks to her. Is she flirting with this guy? My knuckles turn white as I grip my beer bottle. He looks like some finance bro. Is that her type? Sam notices the scowl on my face and follows my line of sight. He gets up and moves the girls out of his way, and sits beside me.

"Is she the reason you're not interested in these women?" he asks.

"No," I snap, throwing back my beer.

"You look like you are about to murder that guy." He chuckles.

"Just looking out for a friend," I tell him.

"Sure, it is. These women are raring to go, man, they would make a great rebound." He elbows me.

"No offence, but these women are carbon copies of my ex. I'm not interested." I sip on my drink.

"But they're hot." He chuckles.

"They are all yours," I tell him.

"You're the best wingman." He smirks. "If you don't like that guy talking to Issy, why don't you do something about it?"

"I can't do that," I tell him as I take another sip of beer.

"You can. Harper and Felix have gone as has Kimberly. Meadow is running around somewhere, no one is going to know. Except me, but I'm going to be very distracted by four beautiful women." He chuckles.

"You saw nothing," I tell him as I extricate myself from the group and walk over to where Issy is talking to the guy. "Hey, you ready to head home?" I say, placing my arm around Issy's shoulder. Issy shoots daggers at me and tries to push my arm off her shoulders, but I grip on tighter. "Oh, hi, I'm Pierre, Issy's roomie," I say, holding out my hand to the man, who gives me a wide smile and shakes my hand.

"Hi, I'm Simon. Have we met before, you look familiar?" he asks, shaking my hand.

"I have that kind of face." I grin.

"Are you staying with this man or coming home with me?" I turn and ask Issy.

Her mouth falls open before it shuts back up tightly.

Simon looks between the two of us awkwardly. "Issy, it was good seeing you again. Call me, we need to catch up," he says before making a hasty retreat.

Exactly what I thought, he couldn't handle the competition.

"What the hell do you think you are playing at?" Issy pushes out of my arms and glares at me as she places her hands on her hips.

"You looked like you were hitting it off with that guy."

"Who, Simon? He's friends with my sister, and he's gay." Oh. I've played this all wrong. "Bet Sam's little friends are sad you left."

"I'm sure Sam will keep them busy." I grin at her.

"He always does."

"I wasn't interested in any of them," I tell her.

"Really? They were beautiful and young," she states.

"They aren't what I want." The anger on her face dissipates.

"Were you jealous?" she asks.

"Extremely." I smirk as I shove my hands into my pockets. "Were you?"

Issy mulls over my question for a while before a smile forms on her face. "Extremely."

"Fuck, Issy. I want to reach out and touch you, but I can't." I keep my hands in my pockets.

"Shall we get out of here?" she says.

"Yes."

And with that, we disappear out of the club.

24

PIERRE

My phone rings and I reluctantly grab it, when I look down at the screen, I see it's Harper. What the hell is she calling me for so early in the morning? Issy is naked and snuggling in my arms, she groans at the early morning wake-up call.

"Harper, it's fucking early," I grumble as I pick up the phone.

This gets Issy's attention. She rolls over, grabs her phone, and stares at it before she starts cursing. Oh no. What the hell is going on?

"I know. But massive news has just dropped. There are images of Bill and Kitty in Capri together. And Bill is very handsy," Harper explains.

Issy opens her phone and shows me the images. They were taken with a telescopic lens, and it's of Bill and Kitty at dinner together, and his hand is under the table and up her skirt. There is no denying what is going on. She is laughing and having a great time unaware that her life is about to blow up.

"Holy shit."

"Everyone knows that the man Kitty was cheating on you with was Bill Reeves. They just outed themselves, which means all those Devils fans who roasted you in the media, and those former teammates who stopped talking to you, they will now understand why you left," Harper says. This is great, but all I can think about is poor Michelle and her family.

"Thanks for the heads up, Harper."

"You're going to have to be ready, this is huge, and now the media knows you are in New York they are going to try to find you," she warns me.

"I assumed I was living on borrowed time. I better go, my phone is going off," I tell her as I hang up.

"Are you okay? You seem a little freaked out," Issy asks me.

"I don't know how I feel," I tell her.

"Come on, let's go downstairs and grab some breakfast. You think better on a full stomach." She grins. That is true.

Frankston jumps up from where he was sleeping and rushes out of the bedroom. That was strange as we both get up and follow him. Moments later, the buzzer to Issy's apartment goes off, but Frankston is there angrily growling at the door, his hackles are up.

"Check the security cameras," I tell Issy, who quickly opens the app, and when we see the media throng congregated outside Issy's apartment, my stomach sinks. Our little bubble has just blown up. "Close the blinds," I yell at Issy, who clicks onto another app and hits a button that closes all the blinds in her home, throwing the home into darkness. I put my hands on top of Issy's shoulders. "I'm so sorry I brought this to your front door."

"This isn't your fault," she reassures me.

"How did they find me?" I ask her.

"Someone noticed and tipped them off." How is she being so calm? "Look, how about I go get dressed and speak to them.

They are trespassing, walking up the stairs. Maybe I can get them to move on."

"They're vultures, Issy."

"You eat, and I'll talk to them. Maybe we can get Harper to come up with a statement regarding the matter," Issy reassures me before she walks over, wraps her arms around my neck, and kisses me slowly.

Moments later she is dressed in a killer suit looking like a badass as she walks toward the door. I grab Frankston and hold him by the collar, he isn't happy about her answering the door. "It's okay, boy, she's got this," I reassure him.

She steps outside and I hear the shutters start and people screaming questions at Issy.

"I can't answer your questions if you are talking over each other," she says sternly. "Look, I understand you are here after witnessing some photos online. Now I have no idea if the photos that have been published are real, and I think until they are proven, my client will not be making any statements."

"Is it true that you and Pierre used to date?" a reporter asks Issy.

She laughs. "We did as teens, but we are nothing but friends now. As you know, the St. Pierre boys are close to my family. My dear father being both boys' first agent. Pierre and I are friends and when he needed somewhere to stay after what happened at his wedding, I said yes without hesitation. Pierre has asked for this time to heal, and I hope that you will all respect that. This is my home. My sanctuary, and coming and knocking on my door will be considered trespassing after this point. I respect that you have a story to write, and this does appear to be salacious, but Pierre will not be giving any more statements on the matter. You can contact Pierre's media team which is represented by The Rose Agency if you wish, but please do not come to my home or my office for comments."

Everyone starts shouting, but she closes the door and comes

back inside. I let Frankston go, and he rushes over to her, she gives him a big cuddle. "You were such a good security doggy this morning."

"Thanks for doing that. Do you think it will work?"

"Not a chance. I did warn them. I'll give my security company a call and get some people to man the stoop," she explains.

I walk over and wrap her in my arms. "I'm sorry."

"Don't be. This isn't your problem," she says, kissing me.

⁂

AFTER THE MEDIA ruined our morning, Issy and I went back to bed and had a nice destress session which included many orgasms until my phone started ringing again. This time when I look over, I see it's Michelle Reeves calling me.

"Shit, it's Michelle," I tell Issy.

"Answer it," she tells me.

"Hey, Michelle," I say, putting the phone on speaker.

"Why didn't you tell me? You knew they were fucking each other, and you didn't tell me." She swears down the line at me.

"I'm sorry, I couldn't. He made me sign a contract," I tell her.

"He did what?" she screams. Hope that wasn't breaking any clauses, shit.

"How long have they been messing around for?" she asks me.

"I don't know, she wouldn't tell me."

"That fucking asshole. Does he seriously think that tramp is with him because of love?" She hisses. "You saw them at your wedding. What were they doing?"

"They were together in the garden," I explain to her.

"Fucking?"

"Yes."

"Fucking bastard," she curses. "I'm sorry, I don't mean to yell at you, it's just ..."

"Sounds like you were blindsided," I tell her.

"Finding out the same time as everyone else, yes, that's pretty blindsided," she says angrily.

"I wanted to tell you, Michelle, but I couldn't. Not sure if now that it's out in the open if I'm allowed to say something or not," I tell her.

"Don't you worry about that, sweetheart. That man will not do anything to you. I can't believe they were screwing each other during your rehearsal party. I am so sorry, Pierre, he did that to you. That must have been devastating to find out," she says.

"Honestly, Michelle, I was relieved. I should never have gone ahead with the wedding, but I felt trapped and was a coward and went along with it."

"Oh, sweetheart, I had no idea."

"I was only with Kitty for a couple of years, you were with Bill for decades. I'm sorry for you," I tell her.

"You're sweet, my love, but this isn't the first time this man has cheated on me. But it is the first time he has been busted so publicly. Luckily, after the first time I caught him cheating, I got a post-nup that said I would get fifty-fifty of everything if he was ever caught in public cheating on me. He kept his affairs hidden for forty-plus years until her. He's lost his damn mind." I'm stunned silent. "None of the kids knew about our arrangement but they do now, and they are the ones pushing for me to divorce him. And I think I might. He can have his little plaything. Let's be serious, she is only after the money."

"He knows that. He gloated to me about it on the phone."

"I bet he did. I'm sorry we had to lose you from the team, but I understand now why you left. Hope New York is going to treat you better."

"I think it will," I tell her as I reach out and link my hand with Issy's.

"That's good. You are a good guy, Pierre, and I wish you nothing but happiness. You deserve it. I hope one day you can fall in love again, and that little tramp hasn't scared you for life because she is not worth it. Take it from this old woman who is now taking her own advice. There is someone out there who will love you right, and I hope one day I get to meet her," Michelle says.

I lay a kiss on Issy's hand. "I'll let you know when it happens."

"Good luck next season and don't be a stranger," she says before hanging up.

"Wow. That wasn't at all where I thought the conversation was going. It started off rough, and then once she sort of got her anger out, she mellowed. I really feel for her. All those years married to that cheater," Issy says, shaking her head.

"Maybe one day I'd like to introduce you to her. I think the two of you will get on well." I smirk. Issy frowns before shaking off whatever she was thinking.

⸎

IT HAS BEEN the week from hell. Every single day Issy leaves for work, she is accosted by the media. They even follow me around Central Park when I go jogging with Sam and Felix. I can see the stress of the situation is getting to Issy, and she doesn't deserve this.

"How was work?" I ask as Issy walks in, looking exhausted.

"How are they still standing outside a week later? Do they not have anything better to do?" she grumbles. I hold open my arms for her, and she walks into them and hugs me.

I kiss the top of her head. "Sit down, have some wine, while I plate dinner." She does as I asked and sits down and pours us both a glass of wine. Dinner tonight is chili herb salmon and salad. I'm not sure how Issy is going to take my news, but I know it's for the best. "Hey, um, I have something to tell you." Issy stills and I can see the concern on her face. "I found an apartment."

"Oh," Issy says, sounding surprised.

"I got the keys to it today."

"Oh," she says again, putting her fork down.

"I've disrupted your life for long enough and it's not fair." I reach out and grab her hand, my thumb running along the back of her hand. "This is your home, your sanctuary, and those vultures outside have destroyed it, all because of me."

"This isn't your fault, but I understand. It's probably for the best," she says quietly.

"I don't want to stop what we have going on," I tell her. Issy pulls her hand from mine.

"Those were the rules," she says, not looking at me.

"Fuck those rules. Things have changed between us, Issy. I know you feel it too. We deserve a second chance at happiness together."

Issy looks up at me, and I just know the words that are about to fall from her lips I'm not going to like. "We agreed. This was only until you found a place. You found a place, so this is over. We go back to being friends."

"Issy. No. Come on. Don't be so fucking stubborn. I know you have feelings for me, and I get it, you're scared but please, give me a chance. I want a chance," I beg of her.

"I can't," she says, looking up at me with those chocolate-colored eyes.

"You can, you just won't."

"Don't you put this on to me. You promised me. You said it was casual. You agreed no feelings were to be involved." Tears stream down her face.

"I lied."

Issy gasps on a sob as she rushes from the table and up to her room. I was a fucking fool for thinking I could get Issy to fall in love with me again. To give us a second chance. I thought I showed her that I had changed, that I wasn't the same guy I was all those years ago. But she doesn't want to see it. She is never going to see it.

And that hurts.

25

ISABELLE

I haven't seen Pierre since he moved out a week ago. As soon as the media saw him moving out, they left my home and followed him to his new one. From what I hear, it's a high-rise building with tight security who are not keen on the media camping out, and they eventually moved on. It sucks coming home to an empty home, no slobbery kisses greeting me at the door, no half-chewed shoes, no home-cooked dinner waiting for me and most certainly, no orgasms. I'm miserable. But I know in time that feeling will pass. Hopefully.

This weekend we are heading to The Hamptons to hang out with the gang, and it's going to be the first time seeing Pierre, and I'm dreading it. He's probably been having the time of his life at The Paradise Club now that he's free of me. Urgh. Why does that hurt me to even think about it? *Because you have feelings for him.* We're friends, I have friendship feelings for him nothing more.

I arrive at the heliport and run into Harper, Felix, and Meadow in the terminal.

"Hey, are you okay? You don't look crash hot," Harper asks as she hugs me.

"Might be coming down with something," I tell her.

"Or are you missing someone?" she whispers in my ear. I give her a filthy side-eye which makes her smirk. "I'm so looking forward to this weekend. We are going to have so much fun," Harper says.

"Just like we used to in high school," I say, trying to crack a joke.

"Is this the same place where we used to go during the summer?" Pierre's deep voice surprises me, making me jump. I turn around and I hate how fucking gorgeous he is dressed in shorts that mold against his tight ass, a tee that clings to every muscle in his body, and he's unshaven. How does that make him better looking? It's not fair.

"That's right. We had some great summers there." Harper laughs.

I can't look at him, those hazel eyes have been haunting me every night, so I concentrate on Frankston, who strains on the lead his owner his holding until he lets go and Frankston launches himself at me and barrels me over. I'm covered in slobbery kisses as I hug him.

"Hey, boy, yeah, I've missed you too. My shoes haven't, but I have," I tell him. I've packed his favorite cookies in my bag to give him this weekend. Felix greets his brother as do Harper and Meadow.

"Hey, Issy," he grunts before securing Frankston back onto his lead. I give him an awkward wave, which he doesn't see as he turns his back to me. Rude.

Thankfully, a steward tells us our helicopter is ready, and we head out onto the tarmac, which freaks poor Frankston out with all the loud sounds. Pierre picks him up and carries him like a big floofy baby to the helicopter. We jump in and do up our seat belts. I sit across from Pierre so that Frankston can snuggle between us on the floor. Our legs touch and tingles slide over my body, but Pierre quickly moves his legs away from me so there's no way they can ever touch again. My stomach sinks, Pierre hates me. This is going to be a great weekend.

Frankston hated the trip. He howled the entire way even with me and Pierre trying to soothe him. It was a long forty minutes. When we arrive at the Southampton heliport, two cars await us. Harper, Felix, and Meadow jump into the first car. Bitches. Leaving me with Pierre and Frankston in the second. We jump into the car, and there is nothing but silence between the two of us.

"How's the new apartment going?" I ask, trying to break the awkward silence.

"Great," Pierre says, staring out the window.

Right. Okay. Noted, you don't want to talk to me this weekend. I'll stop trying. Luckily, it's only a five-minute drive but it felt like hours. We pull in behind the other car, and I shoot Harper daggers which she pretends not to see. Bitch.

Camryn Starr, event designer to the stars, and Nate Lewis, the owner of The Paradise Club, have just gotten back together after some time apart and are there to greet us as are Sam and Kimberly, who happens to be Camryn's business partner.

"Are you okay?" Sam says, giving me a hug.

"Peachy," I answer sarcastically.

"Tense flight up, was it?" he asks.

"Frankston howled the entire way, so yeah," I say as Sam shows me to my room. "Was that the only thing?" he pushes. What is he getting at? Does he know about Pierre and me?

"What else could it be?" I ask him.

Sam rolls his eyes as he opens the door to my room. He walks in and places my suitcase on the rack for me.

"That man out there misses the hell out of you. He just wants to love you, Issy. Why won't you let him?" Sam says.

I still. "I don't know what you're talking about."

Sam glares at me. "Issy, I've known you most of my life, you can talk to me."

"I have nothing to talk about," I tell him while internally freaking out.

"You're so stubborn. I love Pierre. He is great. I want to see you happy, and you two were even though you were hiding it. Don't worry, I'll be having the same discussion with Harper about Felix. The fact she is letting him move out and in with Pierre is ridiculous. She's just as stubborn as you are," he says, giving me a talking to.

"And what are you doing about Kimberly?"

"We aren't talking about me," Sam states.

"You're asking me to take a risk with my heart, and yet you won't do the same," I argue with him.

"I get your point, but this is about you guys. If you don't want to take my advice, then so be it. I'm just saying he is miserable without you. And I think you should give him a chance, a proper chance because I truly believe you two would be happy. That's all I'm going to say on the issue that I know nothing about. Just to be clear, it's just from my observations," he adds.

"I appreciate you wanting to look out for me, but sometimes things are the way they are because it's for the best."

Sam shakes his head. "You are going to regret this one day when Pierre is married to someone else because he will eventually move on, and this time, he won't marry someone like Kitty. He will marry someone who is amazing, and you are going to watch them together and realize you made the biggest mistake of your life letting him go for a second time," he says before disappearing out the door.

I'm shocked. I sit down on the edge of the bed and burst out crying.

Fuck.

26

PIERRE

Dinner was great, and we are all now sitting around the fire pit drinking wine. Nate Lewis, Sam's friend and owner of The Paradise Club, is a great guy. When the boys were alone earlier, he was explaining how he got Camryn back after what happened between them. He didn't go into too much detail, but from what he did say, it was horrible what they went through. He explained how he sought therapy which helped him move through what happened between them. Nate knew that he needed to be patient, just because he was in love with Camryn and ready for forever, didn't mean she was on the same timeline. She had to sort through her own demons before she was ready to accept forever with him. His words resonated with me. Especially seeing how happy the two of them look together now after the hell they have been through. I wonder if Issy and I could ever look that happy. *You did. You were.* But she won't take the risk to find out. I could make her so freakin happy.

"Issy seems to be having fun," Sam mentions as I look over through the fire to the sand dunes to where Kimberly and Issy are dancing and giggling to the music.

"It's the wine," I mumble.

"Same with Kim." He chuckles. I take a sip of my beer and watch my brother get up and whisper something to Harper as they link hands and walk off along the beach. "We might be brothers in law soon, if my sister will allow him in."

"I don't know why he is moving in when he's so happy with her."

"They got together because of Harper's ex. Felix was trying to protect her and in the process this "fake dating" thing they thought they were doing turned into something more. I know Harper told him that it was until her ex got the message and left her alone, and that once the season started they would go back to being friends, but the genie is out of the bottle, and those two are in love. I know my sister and she's scared. She doesn't have the best track record when it comes to dating," Sam explains.

"She never did in high school or college either," I add.

"Exactly, so I think your brother showing her what it's like to be truly loved scares her. I want my sister to be happy, and your brother makes her happy. But I'm not going to meddle in their relationship, they both need to figure it out." I nod in agreement as I take a sip of my beer. "Now I'm going to meddle with yours. How are things with Issy?"

"Just perfect," I answer sarcastically.

"She's a stubborn one." Sam chuckles.

"Don't I know it." I sigh. "I've been miserable without her. Even Frankston was depressed for a couple of days. But what can I do? She's not willing to put the past aside and try again."

"It sucks, man. I feel for ya," he says, clapping me on my back. "All I can say is, be patient. Nate waited almost six months to be with Cam again. He's been miserable this entire time, but look at him now, he would tell you it was all worth it."

"The difference is, Cam wanted to come back. Issy disappeared fifteen years ago. I know she can go and never come back. The only reason I had a chance again is that I was forced onto her. She never wanted me," I explain.

"Look, I think you and Issy should be together. But also, don't forget, a month ago you were marrying someone else. Yes, you and Issy have come a long way in such a short time, but don't you think she is worried that she's the rebound even though you know Kitty was," Sam states.

"Kitty was a mistake in so many ways. I just don't know anymore, Sam. I'm sick of her using the past as an excuse. I'll be patient, but I won't wait forever. It's not fair to keep punishing me," I tell him.

"I understand."

FELIX COMES BACK from the beach and doesn't look happy. "Goodnight, team, I'm going to head to bed. Too many beers for this guy." He grins, but I can see the smile is forced. When I look over to Harper, she looks devastated and is huddled with Meadow in the corner. What happened? Sam and Nate tease my brother, who takes it on the chin and waves us goodnight.

"I think we might need to get those two girls to bed too," Sam says, elbowing me in the side as I look over to where Issy and Kimberly are rolling around in the garden laughing. They have progressively been getting worse with each bottle of wine they have consumed. Cam and Nate are in their own bubble, kissing and cuddling, and have no idea what's going on around them.

"Yeah, shall we go grab them?" I ask.

Sam nods. "We're going to call it a night. I think everyone has had too much sun," he tells Camryn and Nate before looking over at Kimberly and Issy.

"Make sure they get to bed okay." Cam winks at us. Nate

picks her up in his arms, making her squeal as they head upstairs.

Sam and I walk over to where Issy and Kimberly are on the grass giggling and talking incoherently, but they both seem to understand each other.

"Ladies, think it might be time for bed," Sam says, looking at them. Both flip us off before bursting into fits of laughter. Next thing I know, Sam is scooping Kimberly up and starts walking off with her, singing something about coconuts.

Issy's smile falls when she sees me. "Don't you fucking touch me," she warns through slurred words.

"I think you've had enough to drink. It's time for bed," I tell her.

"You don't tell me what to do." She points at me as she tries to stand up, but she falls right back over again. "The moon is spinning." She giggles. I've never seen Issy this drunk before. I do the same as Sam and scoop Issy up in my arms and head inside. "You're so strong," she says, her face nuzzling into my neck, her lips touching my skin as she talks which makes it hard to carry her when I'm sporting a semi. Then she licks me neck. "I miss licking you," she says.

"Issy," I growl because she's so drunk she has no idea what she is doing to me. I take the stairs two at a time and walk into her bedroom. I place her down on her bed, but she won't let go of my neck. "Issy, you have to let go of me."

"I don't want to," she grumbles.

"But it's bedtime, you need to go to bed." I extricate myself from her koala grip. She stays sitting up, those chocolate-colored eyes look up at me, and I see nothing but hurt and pain behind them.

"I miss you. My home isn't the same now." she sighs. Does she realize what she's saying? "No home-cooked meals when I get home. I'm so hungry. Nothing I cook tastes the same." She's been cooking. "I liked coming home and being slobber

attacked as soon as I entered my door by that golden floof ball."
She giggles. "I liked coming home and talking to someone
about my day. It's so quiet now. So empty. I don't like my home
anymore. You ruined it." She huffs. Living in my new apartment
isn't a walk in the park either. "You ruined me." Issy pouts as
she finally looks up at me, teary-eyed. "You were supposed to
stay in the box." The box? I frown. She starts making gestures
of a box. "Nice and safe in a box. But no, you couldn't do that.
You had to come into my life again and mess it all up. Confuse
me. Make me feel things for you again." I still at that comment.
Feel things? Does she have feelings for me? Why does this
make me happy. "You're supposed to be in the box," she
mumbles again.

"What box?" I ask her.

"The do not open one. But I opened it and now I can't close
it again." She sighs, wiping the tears from her eyes.

I take a seat beside her on the bed. "Would it be so bad to
love me again?"

Issy looks up at me, her lip wobbles with emotion. "I never
stopped and that's what scares me."

Oh. Wow. Wasn't expecting that. I reach out and start
wiping away her tears. "I feel the same. I miss you, Issy. My life
doesn't feel the same without you in it."

"I want to give you a chance, Saint." I love it when she
uses my nickname. "But my heart won't let me," she says with
a shrug. "I don't know what to do. I'm very confused. I
thought drinking that wine would help me make sense of all
this," she says, swirling her hands around her head, "but
nothing makes sense anymore." I can see the war that is
going on inside her regarding her feelings toward me, and I
hate that loving me comes with such conflict. "I know you're
going to find someone else one day. Someone who can love
you like I can't. You deserve to be loved, Saint. I want you to
be happy. I'm not sure if it's with me." Oh. "I'm tired." Issy

moans as she lies down in bed. I pull the covers back and tuck her in, and she snuggles into the duvet. I press a kiss to her temple.

"I'll wait," I reassure her.

Issy reaches out stilling me, her eyes are still closed so I'm not sure if she is asleep or not. "I don't deserve it." And with that she passes out.

I DIDN'T SLEEP at all last night. After putting Issy to bed, my mind kept running over the very drunk conversation we had. In one breathe she told me she loves me and in the next she said we can't be together because she couldn't love me. It's giving me whiplash just like today has with her. She ignored me all day, I'm not sure if she is embarrassed or not.

"How did things go last night?" Sam asks, catching me out by the pool, throwing the ball to Frankston.

"Not great. She's ignored me all day."

"Did something happen?" he asks.

"Just drunken words," I tell him.

"Seems like those drunken words may have stung," he asks, sitting back on his sun lounger.

"She kept saying last night that I wouldn't stay in the box. That now she's opened the box she doesn't know what to do. What the hell does that mean?" I ask him.

"I'm no expert, but sounds like in her mind she put you in a box. Probably a do not touch box, it was how she was able to avoid you all these years." That makes sense. "But you're back in her life now, she opened the box, and now she's fallen for you again she can't stick you back on the do not touch shelf in her mind and she doesn't know what to do with you."

"She did confess last night that she has feelings for me. But she doesn't think she's the right person for me," I explain.

"See. You're off the shelf and she is pushing you away because she is so scared of getting hurt again," Sam says.

"I would never hurt her again."

"You know that. I know that. Deep down she knows that. Fear does crazy things to people. If Issy told you today that she's all in, what would you do?"

"Jump the next flight to Vegas and lock her down."

Sam bursts out laughing. "The thing is you would. Look, Issy is here," Sam says, holding his hand at his chest. "And you are here." He moves his hand over his head. "You're going to have to meet in the middle," he says, moving his hands to the middle, "if you want things to work out." He's not wrong. "Issy is in her head. Women tend to overthink things and come up with a million and one scenarios in their minds. Their brains are scary places. She's going to need to work through some steps to be on the same page and they may not be in a logical order either."

"Are you telling me I'm just going to have to go with the flow."

"Yes. Which might be a new concept to you, but if you want the girl you're going to have to wait. Remember Nate. He is not a patient man in anything else other than Camryn. If he wants something he goes out and gets it. That situation with that attitude wouldn't work and would push her away. Look, he was miserable but you're about to head into training camp you can be miserable there. Give her the time."

"We're talking about Issy though. I gave her time last time and she took fifteen years."

"You make a solid point there. Well, I don't know then. You're screwed." He chuckles.

Gee thanks for the chat, man.

27

ISABELLE

Miss Alessi,
This arrived for you.
Rosa.

Opening the bag, I peer inside and it's a foil box. I'm so confused but there is a note on top of it.

Issy,
Now you don't have to be hungry.
PSP

When I open the foil lid, I see a home-cooked meal inside. Did Pierre make me dinner? Tonight, it was chicken and rice casserole. Pulling out the meal, I follow the instructions and heat it up in the microwave. This was so sweet that it gave me butterflies. I'm going to have to thank him because, honestly, I couldn't look at another takeaway menu.

Issy: I got your parcel. Thank you so much.

Pierre: Not a problem. I made too much and thought you'd enjoy it. You said that you haven't been eating much since I left.

Issy: That is true. Well, thank you. That was so kind of you.

Pierre: Anytime.

I pull out my meal from the microwave, take my glass of wine, sit down in front of the television, and turn on the sports channel. Something we would do most nights, and now it's just me. Alone. Which sucks.

"ISSY THERE WAS A DELIVERY, it's on your desk waiting for you," Anna my assistant says as I walk into the office. I wasn't expecting anything. Then I see the lunch bag on my desk.

Issy,
I know you have been skipping breakfast.
Don't.
It's important.
PSP

I reach in and find a yogurt with granola and a fruit cup.

Issy: You sent me breakfast. Thank you.

Pierre: Because I knew you hadn't been eating it.

Issy: You don't have to look after me.

Pierre: I know. Have a great day at work.

FOR THE LAST couple of weeks, every single night after work there is a home-cooked meal waiting for me, and I look forward to coming home and grabbing them. It's one of the sweetest things a man has done for me. And every morning, a lunch bag is waiting for me on my desk with breakfast. Of course, I text him when I get home and then again in the morning after I get my breakfast, it would be rude not to. Slowly over the course of the past couple of weeks, the text conversations have been getting longer until we are chatting until late most nights. We both sit down with a glass of wine and watch the sports channel, and text each other about what we are watching.

I think I'm falling for him.

Today the boys headed off to training camp for three weeks, and Pierre informed me he wouldn't have time to cook me meals every night like he has been, so he batch-cooked three weeks of dinners and breakfasts and sent them over for me to pull from the freezer. I couldn't believe he did that for me. He also said that he would try to text me while he is gone, but I know how hard the guys work during training camp. He is going to be exhausted, and I don't want him to stay up talking to me. I told him I'll speak to him again when he's back, which seemed to settle him. He's become part of my daily routine again. And I like it. I look forward to it. I need these three weeks to work out my feelings toward Pierre. I don't want to lead him on. He's doing everything right, and he doesn't have to. I hate the thought that I'm making this man jump through hoops for me, but my feelings are my feelings. But I need to sort them out soon.

It's girls' night and we are all heading to Harper's place to help cheer her up, and little do they know they are cheering me up, too.

I let myself in, we all have keys to each other's homes. When I arrive, everyone is in the living room with glasses of champagne and nibbles. Harper, Kimberly, Meadow, and Camryn.

"Issy, you made it," Harper slurs. Looks like someone has started the party early. I lean over and give her a kiss, but then she starts crying.

"Oh, babe, I'm sorry," I say, hugging her tightly.

"We were so close to being sisters." She sniffs. I don't know about that.

"She's been like this all afternoon," Camryn whispers.

"I'm sick of talking about Felix and me, I want to know what's going on with you and Pierre," Harper asks.

I still. Every woman's eyes are on me.

"Issy and Pierre?" Camryn questions.

"They used to date when they were teens until she caught him cheating," Meadow explains.

"No." Camryn gasps.

"They were each other's first," Harper adds tearily.

"Didn't you two date for a couple of years?" Kimberly asks.

"Three years. High school and college. He used to live with us," I explain to the group. If they want me to answer questions, I'm going to need a drink.

"Here," Meadow says, handing me a glass of champagne.

"I had no idea you two were childhood sweethearts. I didn't think you knew each other at The Hamptons," Camryn states. That was on purpose.

"They haven't seen each other in fifteen years until I forced Issy to babysit him," Harper adds.

Camryn is surprised. "Okay. Can we back this story up? I have so many questions." She looks over at me.

"Basically, we were dating in college. Harper didn't trust him as she had heard around campus that he was cheating. She forced me to go to a party at his frat house, and I walked in on him getting a blow job from Missy Jenkins."

"She was such a bitch. I heard that she's getting divorced, her husband caught her screwing her boss who happened to be her best friend's husband," Harper mumbles. No way. Guess she hasn't grown up since college.

"Then what happened?" Camryn asks.

"I fled to Europe and ended up in London for the next ten years, running the European division of our company," I tell her.

"And you never saw Pierre again?" Camryn asks.

"On and off, but no. I tried to make sure that I wouldn't run into him. He flew to London that summer we broke up, looking for me, but couldn't find me. My dad kicked him out of the house and stopped inviting him to family dinners. I had no idea any of this had happened till he told me at his funeral," I explain.

"Which was the next time she saw him," Harper adds.

"I'm sorry about your dad," Camryn says.

"Thanks," I say, taking her condolences. "I never told any of you what happened at the wake. It's why I freaked out so much when you showed up on my doorstep with Pierre." I look over at Harper.

"Issy!" She gasps.

"What happened?" Kimberly asks.

"He kissed me."

The room erupts. "He was still engaged to Kitty then," Meadow adds.

"I know. I was so angry with him. For making me the other woman," I explain to them.

"How did it happen?" Harper asks.

"We started arguing. I was so annoyed to see him in my childhood bedroom. Suddenly all these memories of the two of us hit me. I was already an emotional wreck. Then he hugged me. I broke down and he comforted me."

"Bet he did," Harper says, wiggling her brows. I give her a filthy look which makes her giggle.

"Next thing I know he is kissing me."

"Was it good?" Meadow asks.

"Yes, for one blissful moment until I remembered he was engaged, and I lost it. He made me think he hadn't changed. He cheated on me, and now he's cheating on his fiancée."

"Totally understandable," Kimberly adds.

"I can't believe you never told me," Harper says, sounding hurt.

"I was mortified. I couldn't believe I let him kiss me. I wanted to forget it ever happened."

"Until I showed up on your doorstep with a runaway groom." Harper gasps. I nod. "And I told you it would be a great idea. Thinking that you would just magically iron out your differences, but you were struggling. I'm so sorry, Issy."

"Not your fault. You were right, though. I needed to talk through what happened all those years ago because it changed me, and not for the better when it came to relationships. There was a lot of anger that I had against him, and it wasn't healthy to hold on to it, especially after all these years," I explain to the group.

"And what about now?" Meadow asks.

"Confusion," I answer honestly.

"Because you guys reconnected?" Kimberly asks. I nod. The girls squeal.

"He asked me to take a chance on him. I kind of turned him down." My friends gasp. "All because I'm scared. What if he breaks my heart again?"

"Every relationship is a leap of faith, Issy. Do you miss him since he's moved out?" Camryn asks.

"Yes. He used to cook for me every night and give me foot rubs while we watched sport together," I confess.

"Girl." Meadow looks at me as if I've lost my mind.

"I know when I say it out loud, he sounds perfect. In The Hamptons, I drunkenly told him I've been hungry since he left."

"I bet you have," Harper teases which makes me laugh.

"He's been sending me home-cooked dinners every day to my home and delivering breakfast to the office after his morning runs." The girls ooh and ahh over that. "We've been texting every night since, and now I don't know how I feel."

"Do you have feelings for him?" Meadow asks.

"Yes," I answer honestly.

"Is it love?" Kimberly pushes.

"Maybe," I confess.

"Would you be jealous if he started dating someone else?" Harper asks. "Because I think I would die seeing Felix with someone else. It would rip my heart out."

"I think I would feel the same," I tell her. Harper gives me a knowing, sad smile telling me she gets it.

"But you're just fearful he could cheat on you again?" Camryn asks.

"Yes."

"And that's your only worry?" Camryn questions.

"Yes."

"Has he done anything that would make you feel like he would cheat again? Like checked out girls. Gotten a girl's number?" Camryn continues to ask.

"He was not in the least interested in those four girls that Sam brought over when we were at the club," Kimberly adds.

That's true, he looked uncomfortable. "But was that because I was there?" My friends all look at me as if that question is ridiculous. "I'm overthinking this."

"We like to overthink things." Harper chuckles. Hope this is helping her.

"Do you want a second chance with Pierre? Can you see a future with him now that he is permanently in New York?" Kimberly asks me.

"Yes." Covering my face, I hang my head in shame.

"Hey, this is good," Kimberly says, wrapping her arm around me.

"Don't you think this is all too soon? It's only been a couple of months since he left Kitty."

"She was screwing that old guy, and by the sounds of it they were over way before the wedding," Harper advises.

"What do I do, guys?" I ask them.

"Drink more champagne," Harper says.

Sounds like a good idea.

"HEY, did you want to catch up with Eve and me for lunch today?" Violetta asks.

My sister never invites me to lunch. "Sure," I answer.

"Great, meet you at The Antipodean at 1:30 p.m.," she tells me before hanging up.

I head down to the local Australian bar around the corner from my office and see my sisters sitting in a booth, but the closer I get to it, I see that someone else is with them.

"Collette?" I ask, arriving at the table.

"Surprise." She smiles and gets out of her seat to hug me.

"What are you doing here?" I ask her.

"I just had an interview with The Mavericks for a job in their marketing and PR department." She grins.

"No way. How did it go?"

"I got it." She squeals.

"We are here to celebrate," Vi says.

"This is fantastic. Congratulations! I can't believe you will be living in New York. Have you found somewhere to stay?" I ask her.

"I'm moving in with my brothers which should be interesting. I haven't lived with them since I was a kid because they were both gone as teens." She chuckles.

"Vi is going to be so excited having you close by." Violetta and Collette are the same age and became close once Felix moved in, they have maintained that friendship ever since.

"I'm so glad she is back in a real city. We need a shopping day," Vi says.

"Issy said I could give her a makeover so we're in," Eve adds.

"Is this true?" Vi asks, sounding hurt.

"Yes."

"But I've been wanting to give you a makeover for ages," Vi whines.

"She got in first," I tell her.

"You can give me one, Vi," Collette says. This makes my sister smile widely.

We catch up on what Collette and her family have been doing since the wedding, and how she and her mom spent the past month traveling through Italy. She's been back home finishing up her contract at the South Dakota Devils while packing up her life. She had resigned anyway, but she didn't want to leave her colleagues in the lurch because the owner was a dick. When the news broke about Bill and Kitty's affair, she said the team was very upset, and it made everything clear why Pierre left. She told us how most of the players asked for transfers, and the only way the players wouldn't start leaving was if Bill resigned as CEO of the team, which he did when the board unanimously voted against him and voted for Michelle to be the new CEO. Apparently, they are in court over it, but it looks like Michelle is going to be the new CEO of the South Dakota Devils. Which is wild. *Hope Kitty was worth it, Bill.*

Now I find myself being pulled from shop to shop by my sisters, begging me to try on things like I'm their little dress-up doll. Not everything is hideous that they put me in but most of the clothes aren't me. I bought some things they each love me in, even if I don't, to make them happy and so they will never put me through this again.

"Last place," Vi says as she brings us to a lingerie store. "As a new single woman in the city, you need some sexy underwear," she tells Collette. "You need some, too. Maybe it might help you land a man," Vi tells me. Gee, thanks. Eve tries to hide her laughter, but I shoot daggers at her instead. "Can you please try this on?" Vi asks, waving a chili pepper red lace one-piece, with a sheer robe and fluffy heels at me. "It's simple and sexy. You need something because whatever it is you are doing is not working."

"I look like I'm some 1950s woman about to murder her husband." I stare at the outfit.

"At least you would have had a husband," Vi quips. I roll my eyes and head into the change room. This is ridiculous. I look silly. I sashay out of the changing room and do a twirl.

"Are you happy now?" I say to the girls, but stop dead in my tracks. "Pierre! Felix!" I scream, not expecting them here. Felix quickly looks away, but his brother doesn't do the same. He looks exhausted, but still so handsome. Those hazel eyes run up and down my exposed body, giving me goosebumps.

"Looking good, Issy," he says, giving me a wink.

"Turn around," I scream at him, which makes him laugh before I disappear into the change room. My cheeks are burning bright. Of all the people who could possibly be standing in this lingerie shop, I never thought it would be him. What the hell is he doing here? Is he back from training camp? I'm mortified. I quickly get changed and come out again.

"I'm so sorry, Issy. My brothers wanted to catch up. They just got back from training camp, and were ducking in to let us know they were here and would wait for us next door. Then you came out and ...”

“I'm sorry, but that is kind of iconic you walk out just as they arrive.” Vi laughs.

“It's all good. I'm going to leave you guys. I've embarrassed myself enough for one day.” I give the girls a wave and head outside.

“Issy, wait up,” Pierre calls out to me. I stop, turn around, and look up at him. “I'm sorry about that.”

“No, you're not.”

He chuckles. “No, I'm not. You looked fucking hot.” He bites his bottom lip.

“You're back from camp,” I say.

“Yeah, today. I wanted to catch up with Lettie to celebrate her new job. Can you believe it, all three of us at The Mavericks.” He grins, running his hands through his hair.

“We just celebrated it earlier. Vi is so happy for her to be back in the city,” I say.

“And what about you?” he asks.

“It's great to see Collette again,” I answer.

He smiles. “I meant me being back in the city.”

Oh. “It's good to see you, too.”

He seems shocked at my answer. “You mean that.”

“I do.” It's the truth. I didn't realize how much I've missed him until now. My stomach is doing that fluttery thing.

“Fuck, I've missed you,” he curses.

“Me too.” Again, he's surprised at my candidness, and so am I. “Did you want to come over to my place for dinner tomorrow night?” I ask him.

“Yes,” he answers without hesitation, which makes me smile.

“See you around seven?”

“I'll be there.”

“See you then,” I tell him as I walk away.

28

PIERRE

I 'm freaking out. I've bought Issy a bouquet of flowers, a bottle of champagne, some homemade cooked meals for her, and a present. Not sure if she is cooking, but I don't care, the fact that she is even inviting me over for dinner is good. All through training camp, I couldn't stop thinking about her, and I know my brother was the same over Harper. Walking into that lingerie shop to meet up with Collette who starts next week at the club, and seeing Issy strut out looking like a wet dream was not what I was expecting. I went back in after she left and bought the exact outfit she was wearing and have brought it here tonight with me. She could either hate it or model it for me later if the night goes well.

> Issy: Hey, just come right on in, my hands are busy. You know the code.

> Pierre: Just arrived now.

I walk up the stairs, punch in the code, and enter her home. The house smells amazing the further I walk in, but as soon as I turn the corner, I notice the kitchen is empty.

"Hey, Issy, I'm here," I call out to her.

"I'll be right down," she calls from upstairs. I place the bottle of champagne down, as well as the flowers and her presents. I go in search of a vase while I wait for her to come down. The dining room table has been set and there are candles, she's gone to some effort for dinner tonight. Please mean that this is a good sign of where tonight is heading. I find a vase and put the bouquet in it, move it to the table, and place it beside the flowers that are already in the middle of the table.

"Hey," she calls out.

When I look up, I almost have a heart attack. There she is standing in one of my college hockey jerseys. I've lost the ability to speak. My heart is thundering in my chest. I just stare at how beautiful she looks. Flashes of her in a Mavericks jersey with my name on the back and a baby in her arms wearing the same thing flash through my mind. I want forever with her. She is my everything. Issy has always been it for me, and it's taken me fifteen years to grow the balls to finally do something about it.

"I love you." The words tumble out of my mouth.

"I love you too, Saint." She grins, and the next thing she is launching herself into my arms and kissing me. Thank fuck. I kiss her back feverishly. I pick her up, my hands cupping her ass as I place her on the kitchen counter, her legs wrapped around my hips. "I want us to have a second chance," she tells me, cupping my face. I kiss her desperately because this is all I have ever wanted.

"I'm sorry it's taken me so long to get you back," I tell her as my hands run down her sides, taking in my old jersey. "I can't believe you still have it."

"I couldn't bear to get rid of it," she confesses.

"I will never make you regret giving me another chance, Issy. I'm done. This is it. You and me. I want forever with you."

"Me too. I'm sorry I locked you out of my life for so long."

I cup her face. "This is the last time you and I apologize to each other about the past. Deal?"

"Deal." She grins as I kiss her.

"We look to the future now. You and me."

"And Frankston," she adds.

"And Frankston," I say, kissing her softly as she wraps her arms around my back. "I got a present for you, but I think I kind of like what you're wearing now."

"You did?" She grins.

"I bought the lingerie I saw you in yesterday. The whole set," I tell her.

"No way." She giggles.

I nod as I lean in and whisper in her ear, "But I would rather see you bent over the sofa so I can see my name on your back while I fuck you."

Issy groans.

TONIGHT, my brother and I are playing with The Mavericks. It's an exhibition game, but it's against Felix's old team, and he is going to have to play against his ex-best friend and teammates who slept with his ex. I think shit is going to go down tonight, but I've got my brother's back.

"Get your head in the game, man. Those assholes from LA are in the next changing room and deserve some fucking revenge," I tell my brother as I slam my hand against his helmet. He needs to focus. I know he sent Harper his jersey to wear tonight. If she comes to the game, then she says yes to getting back together, but if she doesn't come then I don't even want to think about it. Issy messaged assuring me Harper would be there, that she's wearing my brother's jersey. I may have bought Issy a couple of new ones to wear while I fuck her. New kink unlocked. Issy in my jersey bent over the sofa while I fuck her. My name on her back makes me fucking come so fast. *Also makes me want to change her name permanently to mine.* Just can't wait till she has my name for real. My brother suggested I should wait and propose next year because it's probably not good luck ditching one wedding with one woman while preparing to marry another in the same year. And I would have to agree. I just want reassurance that she is mine, I'm still worried that all this happiness could vanish.

"We have your back," Emmett Black, the Captain of the team, says as he walks past, so do a couple of the other guys.

"Envision annihilating them," I tell my brother. "Felix," I knock our helmets together, "nothing matters more than beating those assholes. You hear me."

"Yes."

"Good, now let's get out there and fuck their shit up," I say, firing him up. I want to show The Mavericks fans what I am made of.

We walk out of the locker room and wait in the tunnel until we get called out. This is the moment the adrenaline kicks in. You can hear the crowd going crazy. The music is pumping. The boys are all hyping each other up. One by one, they call our names out, and the crowd goes wild.

"Welcome to The Mavericks, Felix St. Pierre." The announcer calls out my brother's name, and I watch him launch himself out on the ice as the crowd goes wild. Some of the other guys jostle me, jeering me up for my turn.

"Keep that Mavericks welcome coming for Pierre St. Pierre," the announcer says, and I skate out to the stadium going crazy. I take a moment to look around and wave at everyone, appreciating their support before skating out to warm up with the other guys.

"She's not here," Felix says as he stretches.

"She might be running late or grabbing a drink," I reassure him. His eyes move and watch his old teammates skate around.

Stephen looks over and sends daggers my brother's way. There's no way these two aren't fighting tonight.

"Head in the game. Forget everything else. We beat those fuckers. Show them they can't mess with the St. Pierre brothers. Yeah."

"Yeah." My brother smiles, and I can see him finally focus.

We skate around our fans' areas and sign pucks and shirts for fans, but I am starting to worry as the minutes on the clock for the warmup count down and our girls aren't here. I see our sister and skate over to her.

"Where are the girls?" I ask her.

"Don't tell Felix but shits gone down," she says.

"Is Issy okay?"

"Yes. She's fine. She's with Mom up in the family suites. She didn't want to come down and distract you. But Harper isn't, and we need Felix's head in the game," she warns me.

Shit.

"Hey, Lettie," Felix says, skating over and joining me.

"Hey. You guys look good out there together. Can I get a picture?" she says, changing the subject. We pose for photos for her which has Felix smiling.

"Do you know if Harper is coming?" he asks her.

"She should be. There's an accident, so traffic is crazy," she reassures him. This relaxes him, and he gives her a thumbs up before skating away. "Smash them," she says.

"I'll do my best."

LA has been playing dirty all night. I can see them chirping away at Felix every second they can, and he is trying to ignore them, but he's failing. They are relentless. I body check a couple of players into the wall, which is satisfying as does the rest of our teammates. Who knew this would be the team bonding session we needed?

Felix joins me on the bench and squirts his face with water

to cool down. "Would you stop letting them get into your head," I tell him as I watch him make simple mistakes.

"Fuck you, I've got this under control," he yells at me.

"I don't think you do. You're missing simple passes."

"I know, okay. But I've got this." He slams his stick into the wall a couple of times.

"You better," I warn him as we head back out on the ice again.

I hear one of the guys say something about nudes, and my brother sees red.

He scores. Hell yes. Everyone goes wild. I skate over to congratulate him.

"In your face," he screams at his old teammates.

"Like your woman's tits are in everyone's faces." Stephen chuckles.

That's low.

"What the fuck did you say?" Felix asks as she pushes him.

"Oh no, you don't know." Stephen bursts out laughing. My brother pushes him again. The refs' whistles blow, and I call out to my brother, but before I know it, he's taking off his helmet, throwing his gloves down, and launching himself at his ex-best friend. One in all in. And the rest of our team starts in on the other team. I am pummelling this guy, and the next thing I know, the entire stadium goes quiet. I pull away from the guy and turn to see Felix on the ground, not moving.

Fuck.

I skate over to him.

"Felix. Brother," I scream at him. He's knocked out cold, he doesn't move, and everything in me breaks. I launch myself at Stephen. "You fucking bastard. What have you done?" I scream at him. My teammates pull me away as the ref puts me in the penalty box for the rest of the game for misconduct. "Motherfucker, I'm going to kill you," I scream as my team pulls me from the ice.

"We've got him. He's going to be okay," Emmett reassures me.

"He cracked his head on the ice. That isn't good."

"He is going to get the best medical treatment, okay? Trust me. But you getting yourself into any more trouble is not going to help him." He's right. I move into the penalty box and slam my stick against the walls, letting my anger and frustration out. The fans boo Stephen as he's sent to the other penalty box, he's been kicked out for the rest of the game too. As the medical team comes and stretchers Felix away, the entire stadium stands up and cheers for him.

I pray he is going to be okay.

29

ISABELLE

"Issy, my love. It's been too long," Pierre's mother, Claire, says, greeting me warmly. I'm not wearing Pierre's jersey as we are not ready yet to go public with our relationship.

"It's lovely to see you, too. You must be excited to see your boys play today."

"I couldn't be prouder of them." She smiles before linking her arm with mine. "Thank you for making my son happy again," she whispers. I'm shocked. I didn't realize Pierre had told his mother. I mean, our friends know as do my sisters, so of course it would stand to reason that he would have told her. "I always hoped the two of you would get back together after all these years." Again, I'm surprised she knows about us dating before too. Before I get a chance to say anything my phone goes off.

"Please excuse me," I say, picking up the call from Sam.

"Hey, I thought you guys would be here by now, the game's about to start," I ask.

"Issy. Things have gone to shit. Has no one told you what's going on?" I can hear the panic in his voice.

"No. Sorry, I've been in meetings," I tell him.

"Josh released AI nudes of Harper today."

Shit.

"Is she okay?" I ask.

"No. But she's not coming to the stadium. The media attention would be too huge and she can't face all those people knowing they might have seen fake photos of her naked."

"I don't understand how he can do this to her." My stomach turns.

"Jackson is looking into it. Don't worry, I am going to make him pay," he says angrily. "Harper wants you to reassure Felix that she'll see him after the game. That she's wearing his jersey. But she doesn't want him to know, otherwise, he will be off his game."

"I'll take care of it. Look after her," I tell him before hanging up. I've got to find Collette.

THE GAME HAS STARTED, and Collette is back in the suite with my sisters, who have joined to watch the game. They are all aware of what is going on, and Collette reassured me that Felix thinks she is coming but she's stuck in traffic so that he doesn't have to stress. The game is a physical one, and a lot of abuse is being hurled at Felix by his ex-teammates. Then it becomes an all-in brawl between Felix and Stephen, and we watch on in horror as Felix goes down in a sickening fall and doesn't come back up again. Felix's family starts freaking out and The Mavericks try to reassure them that everything is okay. The stillness that takes over the stadium just shows how bad it really is. Next thing we know, Pierre attacks Stephen and starts fighting him. His teammates pull him away while he continues to hurl abuse at Stephen, who is also being taken away. He's sent off for the rest of the game for misconduct, same with Stephen. I hate seeing Pierre look so fucking help-less as he smashes the walls of the penalty box with his stick. Marcus, who happens to be in the box, too, talks to the team and we all rush off to the hospital to wait for Felix. I hate leaving Pierre there, but his mother is very upset. Collette said she would stay behind and wait for Pierre. My sisters, Claire, and Marcus all head to the hospital. I text Sam to let him know which one Felix is going to so Harper can come up and see him.

Harper and the gang arrive, and she looks distraught. Claire is with Felix as only family can go in and be with him.

"Issy, is he okay?" Harper cries.

"They've rushed him in for some tests. They believe it's a bad concussion, but they want to make sure there's no bleed-ing." I tell her what I know.

"This is my fault, I distracted him." She sobs.

"It was always going to be a heated game between Felix and his old team, especially after everything."

"My shit today probably added to it."

"It's going to be okay," I try to reassure her.

It's a long time before another doctor comes to speak with us.

"Is there a Harper here?" he asks the waiting room.

Harper stands up. "That's me."

"He's asking for you." The doctor smiles, and I see the relief on her face.

"Is he okay?" she asks.

"Mr. St. Pierre has a severe concussion. He's going to be out for two weeks to recover," the doctor advises.

That's not good.

"Can I go see him?" she asks the doctor.

"Yes, just one at a time for the moment. He's in Room 2105," he states. I give her the thumbs up, letting her know everything is going to be okay. She follows the doctor, and moments later,

Claire comes back still looking pale but lights up when Pierre rushes in.

"How is he? Is everything okay?" He looks frantic.

He sees his mother crying and rushes over to give her a hug "He's fine, he's going to be okay." She sinks into his arms, the relief on his face as he looks over his mother's shoulders to me is palpable. He releases his mother and walks over to me. He cups my face and kisses me.

"I fucking love you," he declares.

"I love you, too." My hand grazes the bruising on his face from the fights on the ice.

"I was so scared for him. That fall was bad." I can see the anguish on his face.

"He's going to be fine. He's out for two weeks, but of course, the team doctor is going to have to clear him. It was a bad concussion, and they are going to want to observe him. I think they won't play him until the season starts, they don't want to risk it."

"I agree. He's going to hate that."

"I'm sure Harper will help him recover quicker." Pierre pulls a face, but at least he is smiling. "I don't want to hide us, Issy. I wanted you by my side today in the crowd where I could see you."

"Don't you think it's too soon?"

He shakes his head. "I don't care what anyone thinks. I care about you and me."

He's right. "Okay. Probably a good time to go public while everyone's distracted."

"Is Harper going to be okay? Collette filled me in on what happened. I can't believe her ex did that to her."

"Harper's strong, especially now she has Felix by her side."

"Guess that means Harper is going to become my sister-in-law," he says, scrunching up his face.

"Yep."

"Lucky I love you." He grins as he kisses me again.

EPILOGUE
PIERRE

The Mavericks made the Snow Classic this New Year's Eve as the most wins, and we got home advantage, it means we have to cut our winter break short to play in it. Harper, Felix, Sam, and Kimberly have flown back in from Christmas at Harper and Sam's cabin in Aspen where Nate proposed to Camryn on Christmas day. But they couldn't wait, so Sam got ordained online and married them in the middle of a blizzard. I was surprised it was Nate and Camryn getting engaged because I thought for sure my baby brother would have proposed.

We spent Christmas in Quebec with my mom, and Issy invited her sisters to join us. She didn't want to be apart from them as it was the first Christmas without their dad. She also thought it might be better to be out of New York for the holidays due to the memories, which is understandable. Mom was very happy to host the girls, as well as Collette and Joelle, who flew over from London. There was a lot of screaming going on, but they were all happy so that was the most important thing. There was a hell of a lot more screaming when Issy opened her Christmas present, and it was a key to our new home in

Connecticut. Felix delivered the same present to Harper for Christmas, too. We asked Sam to help us both find a perfect home for our girls, seeing as he knows them so well, and Collette gave the homes a female check over to see if the girls would like them.

We are on the same street. The perfect place to bring up our kids together. We found out later that both Sam and Nate bought houses in the next street over so that we could all be close to one another, our gang has become a little co-dependent. It's nice seeing Collette and Issy's sisters become close. I know she misses Joelle, but that is all about to change now that Joelle has got a job at The Mavericks as the team's new physiotherapist. As much as she loved her life in London, she missed all of us, and who can blame her? Our gang is a load of fun. Collette and Joelle live in the apartment that Felix and I were renting, which we ended up buying when the owners wanted to sell. So, the St. Pierre family has taken over The Mavericks and New York.

Tonight, we won the Snow Classic, and we are headed to The Mavericks New Year's Eve party hosted at one of the Rose hotels. I asked everyone to stay back after the game, friends, family, and teammates. Camryn and Kimberly have turned the outdoor rink into a winter wonderland while everyone else has been keeping Issy busy. Felix is going to ask Issy to come to the rink to look for my lost glove, which I left in one of the boxes to get her out here. All the lights are off, and it's filled with nothing but candles along the red carpet out into the middle of the rink.

I see the moment Issy walks out dressed in the most gorgeous red evening dress and notices me standing in the middle of the rink surrounded by candles. She gasps and tears start to fall down her cheeks, she looks so fricken beautiful. My heart is thundering out of my chest and my hands are shaking as I watch her walk toward me. When she is halfway down the red carpet, I fall to one knee, which makes her start sobbing.

"Hey," I say, staring up at her.

"Hey, what are you doing?" she asks back.

"I've loved you already for a lifetime. And I was wondering if you would let me love you for another. Isabelle Sofia Alessi, will you marry me?"

"Yes. Yes. A million times yes." She cries as fireworks launch into the sky.

I slide the three-carat diamond ring onto her finger, which fits perfectly. Then I stand up and kiss her.

"I love you, baby," I tell her.

"I love you, too," she says, still crying.

We watch the fireworks shoot off into the sky as the snow starts to fall, and we hear the screams from our families as they all rush toward us.

The End

Audio coming soon stay tuned.

ACKNOWLEDGMENTS

Thanks for finishing this book.
Really hope you enjoyed it.
Why not check out my other books.
Have a fantastic day !

Don't forget to leave a review.
xoxo

ABOUT THE AUTHOR

JA Low lives on the Gold Coast in Australia. When she's not writing steamy scenes and admiring hot surfers, she's tending to her husband and two sons and running after her chickens while dreaming up the next epic romance.

Come follow her

Facebook: www.facebook.com/jalowbooks
TikTok: https://geni.us/vrpoMqH
Instagram: www.instagram.com/jalowbooks
Pinterest: www.pinterest.com/jalowbooks
Website: www.jalowbooks.com
Goodreads: https://www.goodreads.com/author/show/14918059.
J_A_Low
BookBub: https://www.bookbub.com/authors/ja-low
Amazon Author Page: https://www.amazon.com/stores/JA-Low/
author/B01BW9LU0G

Thanks for finishing this book.
Really hope you enjoyed it.
Why not check out my other books.
Have a fantastic day!

Don't forget to leave a review.

xoxo

INTERCONNECTING SERIES

Reading order for interconnected characters.

Paradise Club Series

Paradise - Book 1 - Camryn & Nate's story.

Lost in Paradise - Book 2

Paradise Found - Book 3

Craving Paradise - Book 4

Connected to The Paradise Club

The Art of Love Series

Arrogant Artist - Book 1

Arrogant Playboy - Book 2

ALSO BY JA LOW

Connected to The Paradise Club

The Dirty Texas Box Set

Five full length novels and Five Novellas included in the set.

One band. Five dirty talking rock stars and the women that bring them to their knees.

Wyld & Dirty

A workplace romance with your celebrity hall pass.

Dirty Promises

A best friend to lover's romance with the one man who's off limits.

Bound & Dirty

An opposites attract romance with family loyalty tested to its limits.

Dirty Trouble

A brother's best friend romance with a twist.

Broken & Dirty

A friend's with benefits romance that takes a wild ride.

One little taste can't hurt; can it?

If you like your rock stars dirty talking, alpha's with hearts of gold this series is for you.

Interconnected with Dirty Texas

Under the Spanish Sun

Hotshot Chef Book 1 - Sebastien's story.

The Lost Boys Series

Frayed Strings - Book 1

ALSO BY JA LOW

Bratva Jewels

Book 1 - Sapphire

Book 2 - Diamond

Book 3 - Emerald

Connected to The Bratva Jewels

Italian Nights Series

The Sexy Stranger - Book 1

The Sexy Billionaire - Book 2

The Sexy Enemy - Book 3

This series is out on audio - Grab book 1 here.

ALSO BY JA LOW

Playboys of New York

Off Limits - Book 1

Strictly Forbidden - Book 2

The Merger - Book 3

Taking Control - Book 4

Without Warning - Book 5

This series is now on Audio - Start book 1 here.

Spin off series to Playboys of New York

The Hartford Brothers Series

Book 1 - Tempting the Billionaire

Book 2 - Playing the Player

Book 3 - Seducing the Doctor

Printed in Dunstable, United Kingdom